THE VERGLAS FILE

WARWICK WOODHOUSE

THE VERGLAS FILE

MEMOIRS

Cirencester

Published by Memoirs

MEMOIRS
PUBLISHING

25 Market Place, Cirencester, Gloucestershire, GL7 2NX
info@memoirsbooks.co.uk www.memoirspublishing.com

Author's Note

With the exception of the identified historical characters, historical references to
the Spear of Longinus, Wewelsburg castle and the Amber Room and place names,
all other characters and events are wholly fictitious and any similarity to persons
dead or alive is purely coincidental.

ISBN 978-1-909020-97-9

For my two girls

Ranks of the Waffen SS used in the story, with British and American equivalents

Waffen SS	British Army	American Army
SS Obergruppenführer	Lieutenant-General	Lieutenant-General
SS Gruppenführer	Major-General	Major General
SS Standartenführer	Colonel	Colonel
SS Obersturmbannführer	Lieutenant-Colonel	Lieutenant-Colonel
SS Sturmbannführer	Major	Major
SS Hauptsturmbannführer	Captain	Captain
SS Obersturmführer	Lieutenant	First Lieutenant
SS Hauptscharführer	Warrant Officer 2nd Class	1st and Master Sergeant
SS Scharführer	Staff-Sergeant	Staff-Sergeant

Verglas: Black ice

12 October 1938

Hofburg Museum, Vienna

It was unusual for the time of the year to see flurries of snow sweep across the frontage of the museum. A black Mercedes followed by two military trucks entered the Michaelerplatz and pulled up outside the main entrance of the museum. Dusk was approaching and the Vienna skyline looked grey and unwelcoming.

The silence of the museum was interrupted by the sound of boots on the marble floor as twelve black-uniformed SS troopers, led by SS Obersturmbannführer Kautenberg and a Dr Strausser, entered the Hofburg.

There was purpose in their step; they knew exactly where they were going. A man approached from a side room, a short man wearing a double-breasted brown suit not dissimilar to the suit worn by Dr Strausser, except that this man was not wearing a Nazi Party gold and enamel badge on his lapel.

'I am Doctor Alfred Hesse, the curator of the museum. May I ask what you are doing here? The museum is about to close!'

Hesse despised that Hitler fellow and his thugs. The SS, in his opinion, were the lowest of the low, the dregs of humanity, and the tone of his voice reflected his disdain.

'I know who you are, Doctor Hesse' said Kautenberg, not breaking his stride or slowing his pace. Strausser thrust a sheet of paper into Doctor Hesse's hand. 'This is authorisation from the Reichskanzler Adolf Hitler, for the removal into protective custody of the Heilige Lance. Ensure the cabinet is unlocked immediately.'

The curator stopped and read the letter he had been given.

'You can't do this... ' he began, but he was talking to no one as the SS group was already forty feet away from him and entering the room where the Heilige Lance was displayed.

Hesse scurried after the group, caught up with Kautenberg and grabbed his arm. 'You have no authority to remove the lance.' He never finished his sentence. Kautenberg slapped him across the face, knocking him to the floor. Hesse tasted the saltiness of the blood from his split lip.

'You have your orders, so carry them out. Now open the display case, Doctor Hesse.' Kautenberg looked into the case housing the lance. The lance, or rather the lance head, was about 18 inches long, of blackened iron, with gold and silver wiring adorning the shaft. It was nothing special as a piece of art, yet it had enormous significance in the western world.

The Heilige Lance also went by the name of the Spear of Longinus or the Spear of Destiny. Adolf Hitler was fascinated by it and was familiar with the legend surrounding it; it was one of the most important Christian relics of the Passion of Jesus Christ. Legend had it that the Spear was used by a Roman soldier, Gaius Cassius, later called Longinus, to pierce the side of Christ as he hung on the cross. Bathed in the blood of Christ, the Spear was believed to have acquired tremendous mystical power. The first sign of that power was the purported healing of Gaius Cassius's failing eyesight with blood from the wound.

It was said that any leader who possessed the Spear would become invincible. Charlemagne and Frederic of Barbarossa were undefeated in battle, until they let the Spear fall from their hands. A legend arose that whoever claimed the Spear would hold the destiny of the world in his hands for good or evil.

Doctor Hesse unlocked the cabinet and Dr Strausser, now wearing white gloves, removed the spearhead and carefully placed it in a velvet-lined mahogany box held by one of the SS troopers.

Kautenberg turned to the dumbfounded Hesse, who knew better than to protest further. He had heard the rumours of people who had opposed the Nazis and had never been seen or heard of again. 'Your cooperation has been noted, Doctor Hesse, and will be included in my report' he said. Hesse went quite pale at the thought that his name would appear in a report held by the SS.

The SS group left the museum as quickly as they had entered; they had been there for less than fifteen minutes. They walked down the front entrance stairs and climbed into the Mercedes and the two trucks. SS Scharführer Eberle, Kautenberg's personal driver, carefully placed the mahogany box on the back seat between Kautenberg and Strausser. Thirty minutes later, as dusk settled over the city, they had left Vienna and were heading towards Nuremberg.

The group travelled throughout the night, arriving in Nuremberg just after midnight, where they went straight to the church of St Katherine and were met by more SS. The package was taken to the crypt within the church, where it was secured and a guard force put in place. Kautenberg and Strausser left the church with their escort, their task completed.

Hitler had instructed Heinrich Himmler to recover the Spear from the museum and take it to Nuremberg. But unbeknown to Hitler, Himmler was as fascinated by the Spear of Destiny as he was.

Prinz Albrecht Straße, Berlin, Reich Main Security Office (RSHA)

SS Sturmbannführer Helmut Kautenberg lit another cigarette as he read the file in front of him. It was 7 am and he had been at his desk since six.

He looked up as his orderly entered and placed a mug of coffee on the desk. Helmut was always early into the office. He found that he was at his most productive before the hustle and bustle of the normal working day.

'Thank you, Priem' he said. He sipped his coffee and walked across to the window. It was just getting light outside and there was snow on the ground. He hated Berlin in the winter, so bleak and grey. He returned to his desk and continued reading the file.

Helmut was on the personal staff of Heinrich Himmler, the Reichsführer SS, and at 22 was the youngest Sturmbannführer in the SS. Helmut had no specific job description. He reported directly to the Reichsführer on a range of Special Projects, which seemed to be mainly information gathering and the compilation of reports for Himmler.

Helmut had been one of the earliest recruits of the fledgling SS and in particular Adolf Hitler's personal bodyguard, as part of the Leibstandarte SS Adolf Hitler. The Leibstandarte was an élite force that epitomised the purity of the Aryan race, and in its early years it was principally used on ceremonial duties. When war came, it became a formidable and much-feared fighting force, noted for its courage and ruthlessness.

Helmut had been attracted to the Nazis and, in particular, Hitler's vision for a new Germany, a Germany that would once again be a dominant player on the world stage. His father had been an infantry officer who had fought in the First World War and had been heartbroken by Germany's defeat and the subsequent humiliation by the Allies which had caused so much suffering to his people. He had been a Junker, a member of the landed nobility of Prussia and Eastern Germany. He was a man of honour, fiercely proud of his regiment and country and totally loyal to the Kaiser. He had imbued these qualities into Helmut but, with the demilitarisation of Germany, there seemed to be no future for his son.

Helmut's father became increasingly embittered, and his hatred for the allies, particularly the French, knew no bounds. He could never understand why the British were allies with the French when for so long they had been friends with Germany. He had once said to Helmut, 'Weren't the Prussians allies of the English when they defeated the French at Waterloo?'

Helmut's mother had died following complications during his birth. As an only child he had been brought up in a privileged environment, with his staunchly disciplinarian father overseeing his development.

Helmut had had to watch helplessly as his father's health slowly deteriorated affected by the humiliation of his beloved country. When he died at the age of forty, heartbroken, it had been devastating for Helmut. But Helmut inherited the estate and large tracts of land in Saxony, and much to his surprise a considerable quantity of gold bullion which his father had placed in a Swiss bank. It had been put there, in his father's words, 'to keep it away from the bastard French.'

Helmut need never have worked again, but his sense of honour and the desire to serve his country were soon to be realised. When Hitler came to power and promised a new dawn for Germany, Helmut wanted to be part of it. So it was that Helmut joined the Leibstandarte SS as a trooper. The SS motto 'Loyalty is my honour' sat comfortably with his own personal values.

His talent and fervour soon came to the attention of his commanding officer and also that of the Reichsführer, and it was on Himmler's personal recommendation that Helmut was sent to the SS Junker-Schule at Bad Tolz in Bavaria and from which, having been top of his class, he was commissioned and returned to his regiment as an SS Obersturmführer.

Helmut was classically Aryan, tall, blonde and with the physique of an athlete; the archetypal SS officer. The Reichsführer maintained his interest in his young protégé and it was not long before Helmut was promoted and invited to join Himmler's personal staff. Himmler's faith in Helmut was well founded. He carried out his duties diligently and efficiently and further promotion came quickly.

The telephone rang. It was SS Standartenführer Wilhelm Schmeichel, Himmler's Personal Staff Officer.

'Helmut, it's Wilhelm, good morning.'

'Good morning sir.'

'The Reichsführer and I are at Wewelsburg and he would like to see you at the Schloss as quickly as you can get here. A car should be waiting for you at the front entrance.'

Helmut looked out of the window and saw a Mercedes parked by the entrance.

'The car is here sir, I will leave immediately.' He looked at his watch; it was 7.15 am. 'I should be with you by 1700 hours.'

Wewelsburg Castle was not built by the Nazi régime; its history started several centuries before the National Socialists came to power in 1933. In its current form, the castle was built between 1603 and 1609 as a secondary residence for Fürstbischof Theodor von Fürstenberg, the prince-bishop of Paderborn, whose primary residence was the castle at Neuhaus. A castle had existed on the site since the 9th century. For much of the 19th century the castle had remained unused, with the exception of an apartment for the local Catholic vicar. This continued until 1925, when it was clear that some action was required before it fell into ruin.

It was Johann Hartenstein, Himmler's personal architect, who saw the potential of Wewelsburg. He hoped to convert it into the SS Reich Leaders' School, Reichsführerschule SS, and so brought it to the attention of Himmler. Himmler visited the castle for the first time on 3 November 1933 and agreed with Hartenstein that Wewelsburg should become the site for SS training. The castle also straddled a number of ley lines. This impressed Himmler with his interest in the occult, and greatly influenced his decision to acquire the property.

The courses to be taught at the castle would cover mythology, prehistory and archaeology, topics that fitted Himmler's interests. The castle of Wewelsburg was to become of particular significance to Himmler with his interest in pagan Germany and obsession with the Holy Grail. Himmler's SS had been modelled on the Teutonic knights, supposedly the custodians of the Grail, and Himmler had even despatched SS teams in search of the Grail as well as the Ark of the Covenant.

In 1934, Himmler signed a 100-Mark, 100-year lease with

the district of Paderborn to renovate the castle and convert it into the Reichsführerschule SS.

Himmler believed that Wewelsburg would become the New Jerusalem and the centre of Germany; he even called it the 'Centre of the World.'

Helmut made good time and arrived at Wewelsburg just after 4.30. It was dark, but he could see the castle silhouetted in the cloudless evening sky. He was taken immediately to the crypt, where the Reichsführer was deep in conversation with Hartenstein. Helmut came to attention and saluted.

'Heil Hitler, Reichsführer.'

Himmler turned around. 'Ah, Kautenberg, you have made good time. Hartenstein, would you please excuse us.'

Hartenstein left the crypt and Himmler beckoned Helmut over to him.

'When I'm dead this is where my body will be interred, here in my Grail castle. This will become my SS Reich Academy and from this will rise an even greater SS than we have already achieved. We will conquer the world, Helmut. It is my destiny, your destiny.' Himmler paused. 'Did you know that I am the incarnation of Heinrich I, the founder and first king of the medieval German state? I am the natural and foreseen ruler of the greater Germany.'

'No Reichsführer I didn't know.' Helmut had never seen the Reichsführer so energised. There was an almost manic look in his eyes. It would be many years before Helmut would realise the truth behind the SS and Himmler's vision.

Himmler shivered. 'Come, it's getting cold, let's retire to my office.'

They ascended from the crypt in silence and entered a room just off the great hall. Helmut noted that one of the walls was covered by a large tapestry depicting a medieval scene with knights in full armour. There was a very small photograph of Hitler on the wall, but it was overshadowed by a painting also depicting medieval knights.

Himmler directed Helmut to take a seat. Helmut was desperate for a drink and a cigarette, but he knew the Reichsführer neither smoked nor drank alcohol.

'You are to cease all your current work and take on a new project for me' said Himmler. He withdrew a file from the desk drawer. 'It will be the most important project of your life. You are one of the few men I trust to carry out this sacred mission; you will report to me and me alone. The mission must be executed with the utmost secrecy. We will soon be at war with Europe and so what I am directing you to do may take many months, perhaps even years, but you must succeed. The future of our thousand-year Reich depends on it.'

Helmut felt his pulse racing. 'It will be an honour to serve you, Reichsführer.'

'Good.' Himmler passed the file over to Helmut, who noticed it had the code name VERGLAS written on the cover. 'In here you will find a list of artefacts, treasures, which you will appropriate and bring here, to Wewelsburg. You will have unlimited authority granted by both myself and our Führer. You will also have a dedicated force of SS at your exclusive disposal, and you will be billeted with them here at Wewelsburg.'

Himmler pressed a button on his desk, and shortly after the door opened and a man dressed in a brown suit entered the room.

'SS Sturmbannführer Kautenberg, this is Dr Strausser' said Himmler. 'He will work as your deputy and will smooth all the administrative elements of the mission.' Helmut stood to attention and clicked his heels. 'Herr Doctor.'

Strausser had been a member of the SS from the beginning. An academic at Heidelberg University, he had come to Himmler's attention because of the Doctor's expertise in German mythology and in particular the Teutonic knights.

They could not have been a more mismatched pair. Strausser was short, balding and overweight. He wore steel-rimmed spectacles, not dissimilar to those worn by the Reichsführer. Helmut thought Strausser looked a typical petty bureaucrat.

Himmler must have sensed Helmut's thoughts. 'Dr Strausser is crucial to the mission' he snapped. 'He is an expert on the artefacts we seek and he will be invaluable in advising you how best to preserve and protect them. I will expect you to have your team operational and ready to deploy in one month. You will stay here at Wewelsburg and will not return to Berlin. Arrangements have been made to have your uniforms and possessions transferred here. Gentlemen, our meeting is at an end. Wilhelm is waiting to dine with you.'

Himmler rose from his desk and approached Helmut. 'One more thing, I expect my officers to be correctly dressed at all times.' Helmut wondered what was wrong. 'I expect my Obersturmbannführers to wear the correct rank.' Himmler was smiling as he said it.

Helmut was somewhat taken aback by the promotion as well as the Reichsführer's humour. He was not known for it.

He turned and saluted. 'Thank you Reichsführer. Heil Hitler!'

St Katherine's Church, Nuremberg

It was 11 pm and a miserable night in Nuremberg, which was coated in a fine layer of snow. The temperature was below freezing. An unmarked Mercedes came to a halt outside the church. Two SS Sturmbannführers, both in uniform and wearing long trench coats with collars upturned to ward off the icy wind, climbed out of the car.

Heinrich Kluge and Otto Branalt entered the church and presented their credentials to the guards, who took them to the duty SS Scharführer. They handed the Scharführer a letter informing him that they were conducting a snap inspection of the vault personally authorised by Heinrich Himmler. Scharführer Mittel read the letter, noting that it was signed by the Reichsführer. He placed the letter of authority on his desk and directed the officers to the vault where the Spear was housed. As they left the office, Mittel failed to notice Kluge pick up the letter and place it in his pocket.

The Scharführer opened the vault door, which was guarded by two SS troopers, and the two officers entered the vault, closing the door behind them. Branalt undid his trench coat, removed a leather bag from a specially-made pocket inside his coat and placed it on a chair by the mahogany case. He withdrew a replica of the Spear from the bag, while Kluge removed the original Spear and placed it in the leather bag.

Branalt then placed the replica in the box, closed it and returned the bag to the pocket inside his trench coat. They left the room. Branalt approached Mittel.

'Everything is in order,' he said. 'I congratulate you Scharführer, this will be noted in my report. Good night. Heil Hitler!' He made the Nazi salute and he and Kluge left the church.

At 8 am the following day the SS Hauptsturmführer of the guard detachment at St Katherine's carried out his regular changing of the guard. It was the usual unexciting routine, although the Guard Commander believed it a great honour to carry out a duty at the express instructions of his Führer. He was met by the Scharführer.

'Good morning Mittel. Anything to report?'

Mittel gave the expected negative response. 'All in order sir, and the snap inspection of the package went well.'

'What snap inspection? Why wasn't I informed?'

'It was late sir, about 11 pm. Two Sturmbannführers arrived with orders to carry out an inspection. Their documents were all in order, even signed by Reichsführer Himmler himself. They were here less than ten minutes, and I didn't want to bother you. Is there a problem sir?'

'Open the vault, quickly man, quickly!' The Haupststurmführer left the office at the run, closely followed by Mittel. The door was unlocked by the Scharführer and the Haupststurmführer entered the vault alone. Only he and two other officers of the guard knew what was in the case. The Scharführer knew that he and his men were guarding what they all called the 'package' but they had no idea what it was.

The Haupststurmführer opened the case. He emitted an audible sigh of relief when he saw that the Spear was still in its place. He left the vault and the door was relocked. He returned to the office with Mittel.

'All is well. Where is the letter of authority they showed you last night?'

'It was here on the desk sir, but I presume one of the Sturmbannführers must have taken it with him.'

'Who were these officers? What were their names? What unit were they from?'

'I don't remember Sir. They were Sturmbannführers, and the written order, well it was signed by the Reichsführer,' Mittel stammered nervously.

The Haupststurmführer was under strict orders that no one was to be permitted to enter the vault other than himself, his fellow guard officers, or someone authorised personally by the Führer himself.

'Nothing happened, do you hear me Scharführer Mittel? The package is safe. Nothing happened. Let me see the log'.

The Haupststurmführer was perspiring in the chill air and very worried. Any breach of regulations would be seen as a gross dereliction of duty, and as the detachment commander, the consequences for him did not bear thinking about.

Luckily Mittel had used a new page to record the visit. The Haupststurmführer took out a small switchblade and carefully removed the page, placing it in his pocket.

'Nothing happened. There was no visit. Do you understand, Mittel? There was no visit!'

Mittel wasn't about to rock the boat. 'Nothing has occurred sir, there was no visit.'

It had started to snow again as Branalt and Kluge drove through the night cursing both the atrocious weather and the temperamental heater in the car. Dawn was breaking as they drove through Paderborn and out towards a castle on a hill outside the town.

Branalt and Kluge had brought the Spear of Destiny to Wewelsburg.

Tsarskoye Selo, Russia

The convoy moved at speed down the magnificent tree-lined drive of Catherine the Great's summer place at Tsarskoye Selo, 16 miles to the south of St Petersburg. Its baroque splendour had lost a little of its magnificence in the grey, early morning rain, but it was still a beautiful building.

The architecture was of no interest to the men in the convoy and their leader, SS Obersturmbannführer Helmut Kautenberg, or to Dr Strausser. With the same clear purpose and focus they had displayed on that day in Vienna in 1938, they strode up the steps of the palace, accompanied by twelve SS troopers. The convoy included a further fifty SS troopers, who remained in their vehicles.

As soon as the Russians had retreated and the area had been occupied, an SS advance guard had taken up residence. This was very much to the annoyance of the regional commander, but even he was not going to go up against Himmler.

Kautenberg was met by an SS Sturmbannführer. 'Good morning sir. If you will follow me, everything is ready for you.'

The Sturmbannführer led the group through the main entrance and turned right towards a set of tall double doors in the east wing of the palace. He opened the doors and led them into a darkened room, where portable lighting had been set up. The lights were turned on and the light reflected off the walls like a thousand golden suns as the Amber Room came alive with radiance. Even Kautenberg was overcome briefly by the room's beauty. The room was some eleven feet square and comprised a number of panels made from amber and gold, in all over a thousand pounds in weight.

It was in 1716 that the King of Prussia had presented the Amber Room, a masterpiece of baroque art, to the Russian Tsar Peter the Great. Catherine the Great later commissioned a new generation of craftsmen to embellish the room and had it moved from the Winter Palace in St Petersburg to her new summer residence just outside the city in Tsarskoye Selo. 'When the work was finished in 1770, the room was dazzling' wrote art historians of the period. 'It was illuminated by 565 candles whose light was reflected in the warm gold surface of the amber and sparkled in the mirrors, gilt and mosaics.'

As the group looked at the room their silence was interrupted by the distant sound of artillery fire. Kautenberg turned to the SS detachment commander.

'Sturmbannführer, let's get on with it. I want the room dismantled and packaged by nightfall and I do not want a single item damaged. Dr Strausser will supervise the work. I hold you personally responsible for its integrity.'

Dusk was falling as the last of the twenty-seven crates needed to transport the room was loaded on to the trucks. Kautenberg shook hands with the Sturmbannführer, saluted, and left the building. With SS motorcycle riders clearing the route ahead, the convoy moved at speed. They stopped overnight in Riga, and continued the next day. When the convoy entered the castle of Königsberg it was dark -it had taken the convoy nearly 24 hours to reach East Prussia. The crates were unloaded and placed in the castle cellars, and an SS guard force was put in place.

It was nearly midnight when Himmler's aide informed him that 'Package Amber' had been recovered and was safely stored at Königsberg. Himmler knew that his trust in Helmut had been well placed.

Königsberg

Things had not been going well for Germany since 1944. The allies had invaded Normandy, British and American bomber aircraft were hitting Berlin and the Soviets were advancing on all fronts. The Third Reich was collapsing.

It was late at night when Branalt and Kluge, both now promoted to the rank of SS Standartenführer, arrived at Königsberg castle. They were now accompanied by an SS convoy. While one team of men removed from the castle the twenty-seven crates containing the Amber Room and loaded them on to the lorries, a team of SS Engineers set about the task of placing explosive charges throughout the castle, and in particular those parts of the keep which were over the cellars where the Amber Room had been stored. They were to be clear of Königsberg by 0500 hours and were on a tight schedule.

There were two reasons for this; the charges were set to explode at 0510 hours and an Allied air raid was expected between 0500 hours and 0515 hours, so the convoy needed to be well clear of Königsberg by the time of the raid. The Allied bombers had already left their East Anglian bases and were en route to Germany. German intelligence knew the target was to be Königsberg. The air raid would be used as cover for the destruction of the castle, and of course the Amber Room.

By the time the first bombs began falling at 0509 hours

Branalt and Kluge's convoy had cleared Königsberg. The castle was almost totally destroyed when the keep collapsed, burying the cellars where the Amber Room had been stored.

Plön

Following Hitler's suicide in April 1945, Heinrich Himmler, the Reichsführer SS, C in C of the Reserve Army, Reichsminister of the Interior and Chief of Police, was dismissed by Grand Admiral Doenitz, the new head of the German state. Admiral Doenitz despised and distrusted Himmler and would have nothing to do with him.

Himmler knew that the Allies would soon be looking for him, so he needed to escape from Germany. His aides had already contacted the Odessa, a secret organisation set up by the Nazis to protect senior members of the party and to facilitate escape from Germany.

Taking a few escorts, medical advisers and his ADCs, Himmler headed south to his home in Bavaria. Himmler had false papers disguising him as ex-Sergeant Heinrich Hitzinger of a Special Armoured Company, attached to the Secret Field Police, demobilised on 3 May 1945. Himmler had shaved off his moustache, removed his pince-nez glasses and placed an eye patch over his left eye. He wore civilian clothes.

The group crossed the Elbe estuary by boat and then mixed with the great mass of German troops of all services who were hemmed into the peninsula formed by the North Sea Coast and the rivers Elbe and Ems. They moved by easy stages in a southerly direction and on the 18 May reached

Bremervörde, a small town on the river Oste. Four days later Himmler and two of his escorts, an SS Obersturmbannführer and an SS Sturmbannführer, walked through Bremervörde and crossed the bridge over the Oste, which at the time was guarded by British troops of the 51st Highland Division. A checkpoint had been established on the bridge and was manned by men from the 45 Field Security Section.

The Obersturmbannführer and Sturmbannführer walked ahead of Himmler. Their upright military bearing gave them away. Himmler looked insignificant; he was wearing an odd selection of civilian garments over which he had a blue raincoat. He would probably have passed unnoticed if the Sturmbannführer had not kept looking back at his master. An alert British soldier noticed this strange behaviour, and a patrol arrested all three of them. They were brought into the checkpoint building.

The fact that all of them had documents identifying them as attached to the Secret Field Police beggared belief as membership of the Secret Field Police was, for the Allies, an automatic arrest category. Himmler's true identity, however, was not discovered until a few days later, when having arrived at an internment camp he asked for an interview with the Camp Commandant, Major Thomas Sylvester, and told him who he was. An Intelligence Officer bearing a specimen of Himmler's signature was sent by HQ 2nd Army, which was located nearby, and checked against the prisoner's signature; identification was complete.

The removal of Himmler's clothing and two body searches failed to reveal anything untoward. At 9.45 pm Colonel Michael Murphy, Chief of Intelligence at HQ 2nd British Army arrived to take personal charge of the prisoner.

He immediately arranged for a medical search of Himmler to be carried out at Lüneburg and at 10.45 pm a doctor, having searched the prisoner thoroughly, inspected Himmler's mouth, where he noticed a small blue object sticking out of the gingival sulcus, an area between a tooth and the surrounding gum tissue. He slipped his finger into the prisoner's mouth to sweep out what he had seen, but Himmler clamped his teeth down on the doctor's fingers. They struggled and Himmler wrenched his head away, crushing the glass capsule between his teeth. In under five minutes the cyanide had done its deadly work.

An autopsy was carried out on Himmler's body, and following formal identification by Allied staff officers, he was buried on 25 May 1945 in an unmarked grave outside Lüneburg.

It was 04.30 hours on the next day. Dawn was breaking and in the hollows of the heathland there was ground mist. A small truck approached the place where Himmler had been buried. The vehicle stopped and SS Standartenführer Branalt and a small team of SS soldiers dismounted. They were all dressed in civilian labourers clothes, and they carried an empty black funeral casket and a dead body wrapped in hessian.

It took them less than an hour to exhume Himmler's body and place it in the casket. The body wrapped in the hessian was unceremoniously dumped into the coffin, placed in the grave and buried.

Himmler's body was replaced by the body of a Jewish banker. Himmler would have appreciated the irony.

The old man winced, the pain had got worse and the pills were becoming less effective against the cancer. He knew he was dying and now they had found him, having thought that he was dead, he was reviewing his life and the events of over seventy years ago.

He could have walked away from his past. The secret lost forever. What could they do; torture him. What was pain?

He had always been an arrogant and selfish man and, although the protector of the file, his ego demanded that instead of passing quietly he would lead them a merry dance and perhaps someone else could benefit from the wealth of the secret; something good coming from evil.

He smiled. Perhaps it was time for a treasure hunt. He swallowed another pill. Time was running out.

2010

Brown's Hotel, Mayfair, London

Jack Cunningham was seated in The Donovan Bar named after the late and great photojournalist, Terence Donovan. He was drinking his first martini made with Bombay Sapphire gin straight up with three olives. Jack was relaxing after a frustrating day having had to deal with his accountant and his editor. They had both been asking things of him which, frankly, he couldn't be bothered with; at least, not today.

Jack very rarely drank more than two martinis in a row. The third was always an under-the-table job although he was not averse to following them with a bottle of red wine and, maybe, a single malt later in the evening. Ted, the head barman, always made Jack's martinis for him. They were invariably huge, probably reflecting Ted's time when he had worked as a bartender in Dallas.

Jack stood just under six foot two and weighed in at around 190 pounds. He was a freelance journalist who had built his reputation with some gritty and intelligent feature articles on the Balkan conflict. Editors were aware that he was always meticulous in his research and, no matter how controversial his views, it was always backed up with irrefutable evidence. If Jack pitched an idea to a features editor it was invariably taken up.

He had started life as an officer in the British armed services and had served in the RAF Regiment, the RAF's army. He had also served with 14 Intelligence Company, a Special Forces unit that had been formed to carry out covert surveillance operations in Northern Ireland. Jack had distinguished himself in Ireland and had been Mentioned in Dispatches. The Operators, as they were known, considered themselves SAS but with brains. They worked closely with the SAS and many of their operations were erroneously reported in the press as SAS missions, which suited the more secretive nature of 14 Int.

Following three tours in Bosnia Jack had quit the Regiment at the age of 28, as an Acting Squadron Leader. It had been frustrating for him to have left the intensity of 14 Int's operations. He no longer believed that he was doing real soldiering but that he had just become a bystander looking on as disparate groups, who had previously lived together happily for years, were now slaughtering each other. He had never understood it. It was worse than the stupidity of Northern Ireland, where he had spent so much time.

Having left the Balkans Jack was perversely drawn back to the region. He returned as a freelance journalist and managed to have his work accepted by the *Daily Telegraph*. He had always thought it ironic that as a soldier he hated the place and everything it represented, yet felt compelled to return to it. 'It's my war and I miss it so', became his catchphrase. But after a time the horror of it all took its toll. Too much alcohol and some dabbling in recreational drugs to blank out the nightmares had brought him close to a mental and physical breakdown.

A fellow journalist, Emma Swift, who worked for the *Independent* on the current affairs desk, became his angel of mercy. Emma was now in her early forties and an only child like Jack. She was tall and willowy and exuded sex appeal. She also had a wicked sense of humour. Her shock of closely cropped flame-coloured hair and forthright views made her attractive to many men but scared the life out of others. If you behaved like an idiot she would most likely tell you to your face, always following up with the most outrageous laugh. Most of the men hid their shortcomings by suggesting that she was a lesbian or as mad as a box of frogs but it didn't stop her being invited to every party worth going to. Like Jack, she was a highly accomplished and respected journalist and had won a number of prestigious awards.

Emma and Jack had met at one these parties and immediately hit it off, perhaps because they were both rebels in their own way. Jack had been slightly the worse for wear from cocaine and vodka and had looked like shit. Whatever the attraction between them, they had become the closest of friends, though never lovers; perhaps she saw him as a challenge. They had now known each other some ten years, during which time he had dropped the drugs. Although he was probably still drinking too much, he was in control of himself and had regained his fitness. Whilst they had both had several short term affairs, neither of them had married, and they always returned to each other.

For many who knew them, Jack and Emma's relationship was a strange one. Here were two attractive and intelligent people with an obvious affection for each other who had remained just friends. Sadly, and possibly because of Jack's typically British male restraint, he had never told Emma he loved her. She teased him often about his 'bloody stiff upper lip' and accused him of being so stiff that he must have starched his underwear.

He and Emma had an unwritten agreement that each

would retain their independence and agreed that they would always be there for each other. Close friends called them brother and sister and Jack would often act as her walker, she, as his partner, when he needed a woman to be with him. Jack never realised that his love for Emma was reciprocated.

Emma was instrumental in putting him back on course and for introducing him to her editor, Mike Whittle, who commissioned him to do a number of feature articles on corruption in the London business district, the Square Mile. This work took him away from the war stuff and the nightmares and enabled him to channel his investigative skills into new areas.

He was now 45, slightly smug and contented, financially secure, but not wealthy. He had a regular income and was able to support a lifestyle that enabling him to have a large apartment located just behind Harrods and to drink martinis regularly at Donovan's. His hair, previously jet black was going grey at the temples and he had begun to joke with Ted that his pubic hair had also turned grey.

Jack had an addictive personality. The words 'self restraint' didn't fit with his hedonistic lifestyle. His doctor had told him many times that he wouldn't make old bones if he didn't control himself, but Jack didn't want to be ninety with arthritis, fed through a tube and impotent.

He was having a short break from writing before starting work on a series of features about 60s rock bands. As he sipped his martini, he reflected that life was pretty good.

'Evening, my darling shithead,' Emma chirped as she sank languorously into the armchair opposite him. She draped her long legs over the arm of the chair. As usual, she was tastefully dressed, today in jeans and a Prada top complemented by a pair of Tods loafers.

'Piss off, flame head,' Jack said smiling, as they gave each other a peck on the cheek. Jack lingered briefly. He adored her understated elegance. She always smelled fresh and fragrant, with a hint of Chanel No 19.

'Ted darling, one of your lovely Cosmos please,' she said. Jack never understood why she always said this to Ted. In all the years they had been coming to Donovans, she only drank Cosmopolitans. Without pausing she said to Jack, 'Well, what is your tiny brain working on at present? Something meaty, I hope? The features world is so boring these days, it's all too predictable. I hear some hack is writing yet another series on sixties pop culture for the Times.'

She knew, of course, that he was the hack in question. He laughed. 'All right Em, I know it isn't exactly challenging stuff, but it pays well.'

'You've got too complacent, you old fart.' Emma sipped her Cosmo. They had always exchanged this banter which, for those who didn't know them, was often misunderstood. Emma took another sip of her Cosmo and turned to Ted. 'As always Ted, you excel yourself. Thank you.'

She looked at Jack pensively and said, 'Jack, seriously, you seem to have lost your edge. You can do something better than sixties rock bands. Your work is still very good, but it has all become a little pedestrian. I know this stuff pays well, but what was the point of you profiling Torquay? What a load of bullshit! You haven't written something with a real edge for ages.'

'You're right Em, perhaps I need to get off my fat arse. I don't think I'm hungry enough; life has become a bit too comfortable. Ted, same again please.'

'Look, talking of hunger, I'm having dinner later this

evening with an old friend of my father's. I've told you about him before. You know Daddy was in the army during the war. He was a Captain in intelligence seconded to the US army and he captured a German officer and they subsequently became friends. After the war had finished, Daddy tracked him down. He lives in Paderborn. He has been part of my life ever since. Since Daddy died, Heinrich has been like a surrogate father to me and we always have dinner whenever he's in town. Join us. I think you'd really get on.'

'I don't know Em, I wouldn't wish to intrude.'

'Oh you're such a stupid sod, you're family anyway, and it's about time you met Uncle Heinrich. I've booked a table at La Trompette.'

Jack knew the restaurant well and needed little persuasion. They finished their cocktails, agreed the time they would meet and went back to their apartments to change.

When Jack arrived at La Trompette he had to wait half an hour before Emma appeared with a man Jack was introduced to as Uncle Heinrich. Apologising profusely for her lateness, Emma made up for it by being on sparkling form and that evening La Trompette lived up to its reputation. She had been right. Perhaps because they were both ex-soldiers, Heinrich and Jack hit it off immediately.

Heinrich must have been in his nineties and was a tall upright man. He still had a full head of hair and looked fighting fit but Jack noted that his left hand had some crookedness, perhaps caused by arthritis. He spoke excellent English and had a ready wit. It was obvious that he adored Emma and having never married she was the closest that he had to a daughter.

Their conversation was animated, ably assisted by a couple

of bottles of Puligny Montrachet. The evening passed quickly, suddenly it was after midnight and they were the last guests in the restaurant. Heinrich generously paid the bill. Jack saw Heinrich and Emma to their cab having declined a lift with them.

Heinrich shook Jack's hand. 'I have enjoyed our meeting, Jack.' He paused; Jack noticed a hint of sadness momentarily in his eyes. 'I think, Jack, that we will meet again, and soon.'

Although Jack could have asked the restaurant to order him a cab, he chose to walk to Chiswick High Street to hail one. He was thinking that the meeting with Heinrich was perhaps not by chance.

It was after 1am by the time Jack got back to his apartment. Emma had left a message on his answering machine. Her speech was slightly slurred. 'Jack love, great evening. Meet me tomorrow at the George on Smith Street, say at 12.30. Call me only if you can't make it.'

The George was not one of Jack's favourite pubs but he arrived bang on 12.30. His military training for punctuality had remained with him and he would get seriously pissed off at the lack of punctuality by others. It was the only thing he and Emma usually rowed about, that and, 'I'm ready, just got to swap handbags', which usually took a further 20 minutes. Like most men, he wondered how women could ever find anything in their handbags. He had been amused by an article by the journalist Jeremy Clarkson in which he had written that the reason no one had found Osama Bin Laden was that he was probably hiding in a woman's handbag.

The George was a Victorian pub unspoilt by modernisation and full of character. This also meant that everything was brown in colour, the loos were cramped, smelly and filthy and the wine was almost undrinkable. The landlord was also a miserable git. Jack had not been there since the smoking ban, but he noticed that the ceiling was still that nasty yellow smoke-stained colour.

Emma, unusually, was already there; there was a first time for everything. She had chosen one of the few booths which lined the back wall. The booths were a bit cramped but Jack had found them useful when he wanted to have a private conversation.

As he approached the booth, Heinrich, who had been hidden by the high back of the booth, rose and proffered his hand. 'Jack, good to see you again, what may I get you to drink?'

Jack wondered why he wasn't surprised to see Heinrich. 'A glass of château plonk, red, a large one please' he said. As Heinrich went off to the bar Jack leaned over and kissed Emma.

'What's this all about, Em? Last night and today were no accidents. Heinrich is checking me out.'

'I have no idea what it's about Jack. Heinrich hasn't told me anything although I suspect we're about to find out. He seems quite agitated.'

Heinrich returned with Jack's wine and sat across from him and next to Emma.

'You're an intelligent man Jack so you've probably guessed that this is not a chance meeting,' he said. 'It is not that I don't wish to have a drink with you so soon after our first meeting, though I must say under different circumstances I would have been delighted to meet again at a social level. Let me cut to the chase.' Heinrich had never lived in Britain, so Jack was surprised by his use of an English colloquialism. 'Emma said that I could trust you. I have researched your work as a journalist. I'm impressed.'

'I appreciate that' Jack smiled, 'Em is a great judge of character.'

Heinrich turned to Emma. 'I'm sorry, Emma, that I have not spoken with you earlier but a lot has happened over the last three weeks. I have not been well for some time. The doctors tell me that I may be dead next month or in the next six months. I have a cancer that is inoperable. One month or six makes no difference; I am not for this earth much longer, but at 94 I've had a good run.'

Emma was shaken by the news. She snuggled closer to Heinrich and slipped her arm through his and squeezed his hand. 'Heinrich! Why didn't you tell me sooner?'

'I am sorry Emma but, since learning of my potential demise, I thought initially it would be better to keep it from you. However, recent circumstances have changed all this. There are things I must do, must tell.' He leaned closer to them.

'It was 1945. The war was close to the end when I was captured by your father near Düsseldorf. I was dressed as a colonel on the staff of Army Group A. By this stage in the war the Allies had air supremacy and, as we were driving near Dortmund, my staff car was caught in the open by one of your fighter aircraft and my driver and aide were killed. When your father found me I was trapped by the overturned vehicle. I had taken shrapnel in my arm, and though my wound was not too serious I had lost a lot of blood.

'Your father tended my wound and staunched the flow of blood and, with his men, he released me from the car. I can't explain it, but there was an immediate natural empathy

32

between the two of us. I felt I was in the presence of a good man, an honourable man. He took me to a field hospital in Dortmund and my arm was saved; you will have noted Jack that I do not have a great deal of dexterity in my left hand.

'While I was in hospital I learned that the war was over and that Hitler was dead. It was maybe a day later that your father sought me out. He had been appointed to lead a number of teams to interrogate all prisoners and to establish their true identities. You will appreciate that some of my fellow countrymen had committed a number of atrocities and, by this time the concentration camps were being liberated, so everyone was looking for war criminals and in particular members of the SS.

'Over the next few weeks your father visited me regularly and brought me small things, cheese, some ham, even whisky. He was a very kind man and we subsequently became good friends.

'When I was discharged from the hospital I was sent to an internment camp for officers and it was there that your father was in charge of my interrogation. I initially thought that his friendship had been a front, a means to get to know me prior to formal interrogation. He would have had every reason to be suspicious. I was not Colonel Heinrich Walke; that man had been killed on the Eastern Front the previous year. Nor was I a member of the staff of Army Group A. I was, I am, SS Gruppenführer Helmut Kautenberg, a member of the SS and Head of Special Projects for Reichsführer Himmler. I reported to him directly and to no one else.' He paused to let Jack and Emma to absorb the information.

'You were a Nazi, SS?' said Emma, taking a very large gulp of her wine and almost choking on it. 'Did Daddy know?'

'I don't think he ever knew. The strange thing was that my

33

interrogation was handled personally by your father but in no depth. I suspect that he knew something was not right and chose not to delve too deeply. I think my answers to his questions were not very convincing. He probably saved my life but to his dying day he never asked me about my past and I never told him anything. It was an almost unspoken agreement between us.'

'I don't know about you but I need another drink' Emma interjected.

'I need a pee' said Jack, 'I'll get the drinks.'

Jack headed for the loo, which took him around the horseshoe-shaped bar and through a door into what had formerly been called the snug. As he looked back at Emma and Helmut he noticed a man by the bar reading a newspaper. Yet he could see that he was not really reading it as he kept glancing over the top of the newspaper looking towards their booth.

On returning from the loo Jack deliberately stood close to the man as he ordered more wine. He guessed the man was in his mid thirties. He was of medium build and wore blue jeans with a short black leather jacket, reeking of cheap aftershave.

Jack returned to the booth and Heinrich continued.

'Our friendship remained strong until your father passed away. I saw him every time I came to London and we wrote regularly to each other.' He turned to Emma and squeezed her arm. 'I don't think James was ever the same after your mother died. It was as if a part of him had also died. As you know, he had married late in life and she was his real soul mate; he loved her deeply. They were like swans.'

He paused and then returned to his story. 'I had become a senior member of the SS and was also a member of the Nazi party from its early beginnings. I never took part in any atrocities, nor was I involved in the Final Solution, although I knew all about the Wannsee conference.'

'What was the Wannsee conference?' Emma asked.

'It was a meeting of senior officials of the Nazi régime, held in a suburb of Berlin suburb, Wannsee, on 20 January 1942. The purpose of the conference was to inform the administrative leaders of the departments responsible for various policies relating to Jews that Heydrich had been appointed as the chief executor of the 'Final solution to the Jewish question' and to obtain their full support. I knew almost everything going on as I was part of Himmler's inner circle. I suppose I am guilty by my tacit approval of everything we did in Hitler's and Himmler's names.'

He paused for a few moments, a sadness in his eyes. 'I was appointed personally by Himmler to head his Special Projects Group. It was to do with Himmler's obsession with mysticism and, in particular, the creation of the SS as the supreme master race. The whole of the SS, the Order of the Death's Head, was based on the order of the Teutonic Knights who were thought to have been the custodians of the Holy Grail. My role was to obtain artefacts that Himmler believed were part of the myth of the Knights. Hitler was similarly interested in mysticism, but he had no real idea how much more obsessed Himmler was. Himmler had already decided that there was no place for Hitler in his vision for the future. But it had been Hitler who had instructed Himmler to remove the Spear of Longinus from Vienna to Nuremburg.'

'The spear of what?' Emma and Jack both interjected.

Helmut explained the story of the Spear of Longinus. 'Himmler instructed me to replace the original with a replica;

Hitler never knew about the substitution. It's all about Wewelsburg and the future of the SS. I had teams searching for the Holy Grail and the Ark of the Covenant but we never found them. I stole the Amber Room from the Soviets. I was the only individual other than Himmler who knew the whole plan; we even spirited away Himmler's dead body. I know where the file detailing the location of these and other treasures is hidden. The file also details the location of a large quantity of Nazi gold which people have been looking for fruitlessly in numerous lakes in Austria and Germany.

'To the Nazis, it's not so much about the value of the objects in money terms but their symbolism to the SS. They represent the foundation for a future Fourth Reich. Out of the ashes of the SS emerged an organisation which called itself Totenkopf which means Death's Head. It's a very secretive and powerful force which was set up to perpetuate the legacy of the SS. The Totenkopf thought I had died and the file was lost forever. I don't know how but they must have discovered my true identity. I was telephoned by a member of the organisation, a man called Wunsche who used my real name. I immediately hung up. I knew I was in danger and decided that I had to leave Paderborn and London was the obvious place for me to go. I have been in London for these past five days. Two days ago I recognised, on the street, a man I had seen on several occasions in Paderborn outside my apartment building. This is why we are having this meeting; I suspect I have little time before they find me.

He removed an envelope from his jacket and passed it under the table to Emma. 'The contents of this envelope are for you and will enable you to follow a course until you find the file and the treasure....' Helmut's words trailed off as he looked at the bar. There was sudden panic in his eyes.

'There's a man at the bar. It's the same man I recognised from Paderborn. They have found me. I must go. It's too late; they know. I have placed you both in great danger. Please forgive me.'

He stood up, kissed Emma and shook Jack's hand. He went out of the pub by the door nearest the booth and, as he left, Jack saw the man with the newspaper follow him out into the street. Jack moved swiftly towards the door in pursuit but in his hurry he bumped into another customer carrying a beer which was spilled down Jack's front.

The man apologised profusely. 'It's my entire fault,' he said. 'I am so sorry. I must pay for your cleaning.'
Jack tried to get to the door but the man was in his way. 'No it's fine; I bumped into you,' Jack said. 'Let me get you another beer.'

'No no, it was my fault. Give me your address and I will send you the money for the cleaning. Even better let me give you some money now.'

The man got out a £20 note which he tried to give Jack. Jack brushed past him to the door and stepped out into the side street. There was no sign of Heinrich nor of the man who had followed him out.

He ran into the main street, which was thronging with the normal lunchtime crowd. Jack returned to the pub. The man who had spilt the beer had gone. Clearly, it had all been a ploy to stop Jack following Heinrich.

He sat down opposite Emma.

'What was all that about and why was Heinrich so agitated?' Emma asked. 'Why did he suddenly leave, and what is this Wewelstein place?'

37

'Wewelsburg' said Jack. 'Did you notice those men?'

'What men? I only saw the man you bumped into. You're soaked. You smell like an old brewery.' Emma tugged at his sodden shirt.

'Emma, I don't know what's going on but there were two men, one at the bar who was watching us and the one I bumped into. I am convinced he deliberately slowed me down so I couldn't follow Helmut.'

'Jack, I'm scared. Do you think they were after Helmut; I hope he's safe? Maybe something in the envelope will give us a clue as to what is happening.' Emma went to remove it from her handbag but Jack placed his hand on hers. 'I think we should go somewhere else, just in case we're still being watched,' he murmured.

They got up and walked out into the street and down to the road junction, where Jack stopped and looked back to see if anyone else had left the pub behind them. He scanned the area ahead of them but they were alone.

They walked a couple of blocks and entered a Starbucks. While Jack went off to get them some coffee Emma found a table and opened the envelope. It contained a single sheet of paper and what looked like a door key.

Jack returned with their coffee. 'What is it?'

Emma showed the paper to him. It had an address and a black and white symbol printed on it. 'That's Helmut's address in Paderborn' she said. 'The key looks like a door key. I presume it's for his apartment. I have no idea what the symbol means. As for Verglas, your guess is as good as mine. Jack, it's a real revelation to learn this about Heinrich after all these years. Not even my father knew.'

'Verglas may be a code name,' said Jack. 'The military always give code names to things to hide their identities.' He turned the paper in his hands and held it up to the light.

Emma glanced at her watch. 'Look Jack, I have to go, I'm already late for a meeting with my editor and he'll kill me if I'm not on time. He's always telling me off when I'm late. Call me later.'

'OK. In the meantime I'm going to do a little research on the Amber Room and Wewelsburg. Go carefully, Em.' He pecked her on the cheek and watched her leave.

Jack returned to his apartment and began 'Googling' Totenkopf, Wewelsburg and the Amber Room.

It was evening when he rang Emma. 'You know Em, I'd forgotten just what a bunch of sadists and mass murderers this SS lot were and Himmler was as mad as a hatter. I could find no mention of Totenkopf but there's quite a lot on the Spear and the Amber Room. Wewelsburg has been rebuilt, it's just outside Paderborn. It's a fascinating mystery and would make a great feature article, perhaps a Pulitzer in it, and the thought of all that Nazi gold!'

'You mercenary bastard!' Emma laughed. ' On a more sober note, I've been totally unable to find out if Helmut is still in London and I can't call him because he's never owned a mobile phone. If he has returned to Paderborn it's too early to call him at his apartment. I'll keep trying him tomorrow. I think that if we're to learn any more the answer will be somewhere in Heinrich's apartment. I suggest we go to Germany as soon as we can. I'll try and arrange a trip if you're game for it.'

'Of course, I'm game! Let me know when you can go.'

Paderborn, 14 Horst Strasse

Helmut was strapped with duck tape to a heavy wooden chair. On leaving the George pub he had been bundled expertly by three men into the back of a windowless Ford Transit van which had been parked in the side street. He vaguely remembered a hood had been placed over his head and the prick of a needle in his forearm. The rest was darkness.

He was awake now in his own apartment and his body ached all over. He noticed there were four men with him. Two were expertly searching the apartment; he noted they all wore gloves. Sitting opposite him in the shadows was another man whose features he couldn't quite make out.

'Hello Helmut,' said the man. His voice was soft, almost conciliatory, like a parent gently chastising a child. The man moved closer to Helmut revealing his features.

'My name is Franz Wunsche. Do you recall our brief telephone conversation of a week ago? I did not have the opportunity to properly introduce myself. I am the grandson of General Hans Wunsche who you will remember.'

Hans Wunsche had been an SS General and a favourite of Hitler. He had been an unsubtle man, almost brutish, and noted for his beer drinking and foul language. To the end he was very much a sergeant-SS Sturmscharführer-type; an unsophisticated non-officer class. What was never in question was Hans' courage, and he ended the war as one of the most highly-decorated generals. After the war the War Crimes Commission had tried to have him indicted for the massacre of American troops during the Ardennes offensive, but it was never proved. He had died of a heart attack in the 1960s.

His grandson looked very like him. He had primitive features and was of medium height with thick pudgy fingers and a protruding lower lip.

Franz Wunsche was an avid Nazi and a member of the Totenkopf. He liked to think of himself as a gentleman, but in truth he was a sociopath, a coward and a bully. Helmut despised men like Wunsche.

'What do you want from me?' Helmut knew it was all about the Verglas file.

'Helmut, you know who I am, and you know what the Totenkopf is. You should be proud of us. You and I are all part of the SS family protected and perpetuated by the Odessa which has become Totenkopf."

The Odessa had been an organisation which had facilitated the escape of many of the SS from Germany via an underground network set up in 1937. Even before the war the SS hierarchy knew they might have need of an escape route. They had also made financial provision for the future by redirecting millions in Reichsmarks, gold and precious stones, all stolen from Jews, to a series of Swiss banks. Very few of these SS men were now alive but the organisation continued, run by the sons and daughters of these people and their progeny in turn. Totenkopf had infiltrated all levels of German business, government and the security services and was waiting for the time when the Fourth Reich could be born.

Franz Wunsche was the Head of Operations for Totenkopf, reporting to a 'board' of nameless individuals whose true identity he had never known. While he spoke with them regularly over the telephone, he had never met any of them.

The best security for any illegal organisation was to form it into independent cells, so that if one cell was penetrated the larger organisation could not be compromised. Totenkopf was structured in this way.

'Very well Helmut, let me make it very clear to you. You know exactly what we want so I want you to be in no doubt as to our intentions and capabilities. We can do this in one of two ways; firstly, we know you are terminally ill and so, you can give us the location of the Verglas file and your final days will be lived out in total comfort with the best medical help one can buy, and your natural death will be peaceful and painless. Or - I think you can guess the alternative. It will be painful, not only for you, but also for Miss Swift. I can assure you that before you die you will personally witness the slow and extremely painful destruction of Miss Swift. So you see it's a very simple choice and such a simple decision. We only want the file Helmut, it can't mean anything to you.'

Helmut remained silent for at least a minute and then sighed. 'You are right, I am a stupid old man. I'm dying and I have no need of Verglas. I will tell you anything you want, but you must swear on our SS oath that no harm will befall Emma.'

'Did you tell her anything?'

'She knows nothing, I always see her when I am in London. Her father and I were old friends.'

'And who was the man with you?'

'He is a journalist, an old friend of Emma's. I met him for the first time the night before.'

'Very well Helmut, I swear that she will be safe. I knew you would see sense. Shall we call the incident a minor aberration? Untie him.' He directed one of his men. 'A brandy perhaps?' Wunsche turned towards a decanter on Helmut's desk.

Helmut suddenly seemed racked with pain. He had not taken any of his medication for 24 hours. 'I need my medication,' he groaned. 'It is in the left hand drawer of my desk. The bottle with the pink capsules, two of them.'

'Of course, fetch him his medication.' Wunsche instructed another man. The search of the apartment continued. The second man placed the capsules in Helmut's mouth and gave him a sip of water.

'There, Helmut, we're not barbarians. We don't want to hurt you. Just tell us where the file is located.'

Helmut's body suddenly went into convulsions. Spittle ran down his jaw line. He was smiling.

'Untie him quickly!' hissed Wunsche. 'You stupid old man, you will pay for this!' One of the men untied Helmut and tried to remove the capsules from his mouth. But by the time he had been untied, he was already dead.

Wunsche smelled the odour of bitter almonds on Helmut's breath.

'Damn, the old man took cyanide.'

Wunsche calmly went to the phone on the desk. 'Clean the old man up, strip him, put him in his nightshirt and place him in his bed.' Any subsequent autopsy would reveal that Helmut had died in his sleep of a heart attack.

He turned to the other men. 'I take it you have found nothing?' Their silence said it all. He picked up the phone and dialled a Duisburg number, which unknown to Wunsche was automatically rerouted to a Münich address. A man's voice answered.

'Emmerich, it's Wunsche. Kautenberg is dead. He took his own life he had a cyanide capsule. The man that was with Swift is another journalist.'

Emmerich, not, of course, his real name was one of the leaders of Totenkopf. 'This is unfortunate' he said. 'Very well, track the man and Swift down. I am convinced Kautenberg must have told them something, he was with them too long for it just to have been small talk. I don't like journalists; they are too inquisitive. Find out more about the man and, under no circumstances, are they to come to harm at this stage. We must know what they are up to. We have to recover the Verglas file.'

Government Communications Headquarters (GCHQ), Cheltenham, England

James Coleridge was a middle-ranking analyst responsible primarily for keyword monitoring. His department had been created out of the highly effective work that had been done by the Americans at Fort Meade, Headquarters of the National Security Agency (NSA). The NSA had developed a highly sophisticated technology that enabled them to monitor key words used in electronic communications. Every time a relevant keyword was picked up, for example, 'nuclear weapon', the second most powerful supercomputer in the USA would identify who was using the words and their location. This was then passed to the FBI, who would investigate whether there were any sinister connotations or it was just innocent usage.

This part of the NSA's work had been replicated by GCHQ, the British equivalent, and Coleridge was in charge of this keywording work. He was good at what he did and his department was respected but he was not considered to be a high flyer worthy of promotion. At the age of forty-eight he was likely to stay in the department until his compulsory retirement at fifty-five.

Coleridge had an inflated opinion of his abilities, bolstered by his wife's even more inflated opinion, and he made no effort to hide this or his disdain for peers and seniors whom he thought less talented. He had always had a chip on his shoulder because he perceived his lack of a public school education and Oxbridge background as a major impediment to his advancement. GCHQ could ill afford to have these prejudices - it was just that Coleridge was not senior management material. In fact he was not management material at all but his masters recognised his contribution as a technician. James Coleridge was the original grey man.

Coleridge's disaffection made him the perfect target for recruitment by the FSB, the Russian intelligence service, and in particular the department which was interested in the Amber Room. He had arranged for the words 'Amber Room' to be incorporated into his keyword database.

A full-scale reconstruction of the Amber Room had been commissioned by the German government in the 1980s and, in 1997, they presented it to President Valen. But the original Amber Room was valued at more than $150 million - the Russians had never stopped looking for it.

The Russians paid Coleridge a generous monthly retainer which very adequately supplemented his meagre Civil Service salary and he was happy to report to his handler the details of any searches on the internet or telephone communication that referred to the Amber Room. He had been doing this now for some five years but the words had come up less then a dozen times.

He didn't see any harm in what he was doing. In his opinion his actions posed no threat to Britain's national security so they were not traitorous and, anyway, he needed the money because they didn't pay him enough. This self-delusion confirmed what his superiors already thought about him - that he was indeed unfit for further promotion.

One of Coleridge's junior analysts popped into his office. 'The Amber Room has come up 'Googled' from a computer in central London. The details are all here,' he said. He handed Coleridge a piece of paper and left the room wondering, as he always did, what was so special about 'Amber Room' and why Coleridge insisted on being told every time the words came up. He assumed it was a codeword. Why should it bother him? Everything was on a need-to-know basis, and he didn't need to know.

Coleridge placed the paper in his jacket pocket. On his way home he stopped at a public phone box and called a London number.

'Hi Roly, it's James, I'm coming to London on Thursday. Fancy an early evening drink, say 6.30, the usual place?' There was a short pause before Roly replied 'OK, I'll see you then.'

'Great, see you then, love to Mary.' Roly was Coleridge's Russian handler and 'love to Mary' was his authentication code.

Coleridge travelled to London every second Thursday to attend a routine intelligence co-ordination meeting at the Ministry of Defence in Whitehall. Following his meeting he met Roly (Major Uri Greschkov of the FSB) at their usual watering hole, the Tattershall Castle, a converted ferry, now pub, moored on the Embankment near Charing Cross. Lots of the MOD staff drank there, the Navy lads having nicknamed it the Admiral Belgrano after the Argentinian warship torpedoed by a British submarine in the Falklands war. They shook hands and ordered their drinks, Roly footing the bill as usual. Anyone observing them would think that they were chums sharing a bottle of wine after work in a place crowded with similar people.

They made small talk and Coleridge handed over the slip of paper that the junior analyst had given him. Roly pocketed the paper. They finished their wine and shook hands. Coleridge returned to Paddington to catch his train to Gloucester and Roly went to a safe house in Chelsea. For those working in the Russian Embassy, Roly was a junior cultural attaché although most guessed that he was linked in some way to intelligence but no one would dare broach any question about Roly to his face. Not even the ambassador knew that Roly was a member of an obscure department within the FSB.

On reaching the safe house in Smith Street, Roly sent a signal to Moscow station for the attention of a Colonel Vladimir Organov.

Amber Room
Subject. Jack Cunningham, British freelance journalist. Google accessed at 170021SEP10Z. Subject also surfed a number of related sites for 75 minutes. Also Googled Spear of Longinus and Wewelsburg Castle. Cunningham is a respected features journalist and ex-soldier. Recommend we do not ignore this. Cunningham lives at 14A Kensington Mews, London, SW1 6HE. Telephone. 02073334562. Cell 07713480932. Request further instructions. Uri.

FSB Headquarters, Lubyanka Square, Moscow

Colonel Vladimir Organov ladled a fourth teaspoonful of sugar into his tea and buttered some dark rye bread. He opened a side drawer in his desk and pulled out a jar of Marmite and spread some of the dark paste on to the bread. Organov had developed a taste for Marmite some fifteen years before when he had worked at the Embassy in London. Anyone from his department who visited London was always tasked with bringing a few jars back for him.

Organov liked the British and their quirky habits and customs fascinated him; only the British could play such a ridiculous game as cricket. He spoke excellent English without any hint of an accent and could easily be mistaken for British himself.

He picked up a report that had been given to him that morning from the London Station. 'Station' was the name given to any intelligence section in a Russian embassy.

Vladimir Organov was a member of the FSB, which stood for the Federal Security Service of the Russian Federation *(Federalnaya sluzhba bezopasnosti Rossiyskoy Federaciyi)* and was the main domestic security service of the Russian Federation, the primary successor agency of the KGB. Officially the FSB was responsible for internal and border security, counter-terrorism, counter-intelligence and surveillance.

Colonel Organov was head of the Cultural Projects

Department, based in the former KGB headquarters on Lubyanka Square. The department's name was a cover for operations whose sole purpose was the tracking down and recovery, by whatever means, of art and artefacts stolen from the former Soviet Union. The department had been set up by President Valen in the days when he had been head of the KGB, and it continued to report to him directly, even circumventing the normal chain of command within the FSB.

Organov had taken command of the department some 19 years after its creation in 1980. Although he had the rank of Colonel, the normal rank for the head of such a department, he was in fact a full General but it would have looked very suspicious having such a senior rank in charge of a mere cultural department. He had an almost unlimited budget and, although the number of staff based in the Lubyanka was relatively small, some fifteen members, he had command of some 1500 agents located around the world, all operating as discrete and independent teams. Not even the respective Russian embassies in the countries where they were located knew of their existence.

Organov also had the highest of security clearances and enjoyed full access to all Russian intelligence monitoring capabilities.

All this power belied his almost paternal appearance; he was like someone's uncle. In his late fifties, he had a small pot belly, the result of his penchant for German beer and was slightly bald with his remaining hair close cut. His large frame and height, over six feet gave him an intimidating physical presence. He had dark brown eyes, which his wife called his fawn eyes. He was, in fact, an extremely good-natured man with a great sense of the ridiculous and a dry wit. He was passionate about the Goons and '*Monty Python's Flying Circus*' and loved the famous parrot sketch, much to the frustration of his long-suffering wife. She had never found any of this remotely amusing but still had to sit through interminable screenings of the shows at home, with Vladimir laughing so much that tears ran down his face.

Colonel Organov had a formidable intelligence and an ability to evaluate situations rapidly and to act decisively. He was also ruthless, and would tolerate no obstruction by anyone in achieving his department's mission.

Organov had earned his stripes as a member of the Directorate of the KGB responsible for counter terrorist operations and had built a fearsome reputation for his ruthlessness. In 1987 Hezbollah had kidnapped a member of the Russian staff from their embassy in Beirut. Organov had taken a team to the Lebanon, tracked down the son of one of the Hezbollah leaders and decapitated him. He sent the head to the young man's father in a basket, with instructions for the release of the Russian. Within hours the Russian was released and returned to the embassy, unharmed. No Russian hostage was ever taken again in the Lebanon. Organov was personally thanked by the President for the success of the mission and his future was assured.

Organov scanned the report again. Interesting. London had discovered that a journalist, a Jack Cunningham, was carrying out rather a lot of research on the internet into the Amber Room.

Despite the Germans having given the Russians a replica of the room, President Valen had decided that every effort was to be made to find the original. When Hitler had invaded the Soviet Union in 1941, his troops overran Tsarskoye Selo, dismantled the panels of the Amber Room, packed them up and shipped them to Königsberg (today's Kaliningrad). In January 1945, after air raids and a savage ground assault on the city, details of what had happened to the room were lost.

After the war, a German official on Himmler's staff had said the crates were in a castle that had burned down in an air raid. In the ruins of Königsberg castle a Soviet investigator had found a charred fragment of amber from the room. But others thought the Amber Room had been on board a submarine that had sunk in the Baltic Sea, or had been hidden in an abandoned mine in Thuringia. Over the years serious historians of the subject had little hope that the room would ever be found.

Reality caught up with the fantasy when in 1997 a group of German art detectives, including a former Stasi agent, the old East German secret police, heard talk that someone was offering a piece of the Amber Room for sale. Police raided the office of a lawyer in Bremen who was trying to sell the work for a client, the grandson of a German officer who had accompanied the wartime convoy to Königsberg. No one knew where the piece had come from, so the mystery was reborn.

The President's personal interest in the Amber Room was the reason Organov's department monitored the internet and London Station kept an eye on the last-known surviving member of the original convoy that had taken the Amber Room to Königsberg, SS Hauptscharführer Wolfgang Eberle, who lived in London. He had moved there some forty years earlier.

Organov leaned over to his intercom. 'Ivan, can you come in here please?'

Major Ivan Terpinski, in reality a full Colonel, entered the room. 'Vladimir, why do you insist in eating that brown muck?'

He pointed to the jar of Marmite. Terpinski and Organov had been close friends for years. Ivan was ten years younger than Organov but was one of the few who the General truly trusted. In private they had a totally informal relationship - however they slipped easily into formality in the presence of others. Ivan had been Vladimir's second-in-command on the Lebanon operation. Their understanding and mutual respect for each other made them a formidable partnership.

'I'm a weak man, Ivan,' Organov smiled as he handed Ivan the report. Ivan sat down.

'Tea?' Organov handed the Major a glass of the Black Caravan tea so loved by Russians. He waited a few moments to give Ivan the opportunity to absorb the import of the signal report.

'Ivan, I want you to drop everything you are doing and give it to Olga. Alert Team Bravo, step up surveillance on Eberle and put a team on Cunningham. It may be nothing, but Cunningham doesn't sound a crank. I want the full surveillance, including computer and telephone taps. We might just get lucky. If Cunningham is serious he might get to Kautenberg's driver Eberle, who must now be well into his eighties and might feel like telling a journalist something before he dies. We'll monitor Cunningham's progress; perhaps even feed him information about Eberle. Make sure you fully brief Uri.'

Paderborn, Germany

Jack and Emma caught a flight to Düsseldorf and hired a car. They were soon clear of the airport and en route to Paderborn some 130 kilometres away.

'How did you persuade Mike Whittle to give you time off, Em?'

Emma smiled. 'I used my feminine charms on him.'

'What, Mike Whittle? He's only interested if there is a story. He probably doesn't even know you're a woman.'

'I told him I was on to a really explosive story about Nazis and hidden gold. He was almost salivating by the time I had finished.'

'That's more like it, a sensational story always gets Mike's juices going.'

'How much further?'

'I reckon we've got maybe an hour to go.'

Emma adjusted her seat and closed her eyes. 'I'm going to have a nap.'

They arrived in Paderborn slightly ahead of schedule and checked into the Landhotel Waldwinkel, a pleasant four-star hotel near the centre of the town and within walking distance of Helmut's apartment. Emma telephoned the apartment again as she had been doing over the last few days but there was still no reply. They agreed that it was too late to visit that evening and decided to leave it until the following morning. They had dinner in a nearby Gasthof and discussed the events of the past 48 hours.

'What do you think has happened to Heinrich? I wish I

knew why he left so suddenly?'

'I think he was scared, Em. I think one of the men in the pub had been following him. What I don't understand is why he hasn't been in touch with you since.'

'I think it's really strange. He may have been a Nazi but he's still Heinrich and I love and care for him. I do hope nothing dreadful has happened to him.'

Jack sipped his wine. 'What I don't understand is all this cloak-and-dagger stuff; the slip of paper. It's pretty obvious he wanted us to come to Paderborn but why such a convoluted way of telling us? We're still none the wiser.'

'I think he was trying to protect us. He knew he was being followed otherwise he would have been more open when he slipped me the envelope. I wonder if this Totenkopf organisation is part of it.'

They finished their meal and returned to the hotel. Outside Emma's room Jack kissed her on the cheek and turned to go to his room. 'Let's hope tomorrow gives us a few answers. Sleep tight Em.'

'And don't let the bedbugs bite, sweetie.' Emma squeezed his hand, opened the door and entered her room.

In his room Jack stayed up for a few more hours reading about Wewelsburg and studying various other articles he had printed from the web.

For Himmler, Wewelsburg was not so much the location where the Grail was hidden but where his 'Grail Order the SS' and its sacred treasures would be brought, and from which the magical power of the Nazi régime would ultimately radiate.

Germany and the SS of 1933 were vastly different from what they became by 1940. At the time, the SS and Himmler were subordinate to the Chief of Staff of the SA, but on 20

July, 1934, following the murder of the top SA leaders in the Night of the Long Knives, Hitler issued a decree stating that the SS would become an independent organisation within the National Socialist Party. This increase in status was reflected in a rise in membership, from 280 members in January 1929 to over 52,000 by 1933. It was now clear that the SS which had originally been created to guard Hitler was now becoming something much more powerful.

The new religion of the Nazi régime was often referred to as the 'Irminen belief', though specific details about what it contained and which ceremonies were performed at the castle remain unknown. The Irminen belief was largely the brainchild of Karl Maria Wiligut. Wiligut, who was often labelled Himmler's Rasputin, claimed that the site of Wewelsburg was important, referring to an old Westphalian legend, the Battle at the Birch Tree which stated that an army from the East (Russia) would be beaten by an army of the West (Germany).

The main part of the castle was not only for housing some of the SS leaders or for social functions but for gathering a vast library, linked with a series of study rooms, some of which carried names such as 'Gral' (Grail), 'König Artus' (King Arthur), 'Arier' (Aryan), 'Runen' (runes), and 'Deutscher Orden' (Teutonic Order).

All SS officers carried a *Totenkopfringe*, the Death's Head ring, and Wewelsburg was to be the place for preserving the rings of those SS officers who had fallen in battle. The officers had to make provision that in accordance with their oath, and upon their death, their rings would be returned to Wewelsburg. When American soldiers arrived at the castle in April 1945, they found hundreds of SS Death's Head Rings. Many took them back to the USA as souvenirs.

The design of the castle and the estate around it was in the shape of a spear underlining the belief that the site would become the location where the Spear of Destiny would be held.

The labour force created to realise Himmler's dream was taken from the concentration camp at Sachenshausen. All of the 3,900 prisoners who had worked at Wewelsburg were executed when the work on the castle had been completed; there were to be no witnesses to Himmler's Grail Castle and its secrets.

In 1944, when the project was 'temporarily' stopped, the estate was incomplete but the castle was finished. The North Tower marked the veritable centre of the SS world, starting in the crypt, which had been redesigned as a circular vault, in which twelve seats were placed – references to King Arthur and the Twelve Knights of the Round Table. The SS was divided into twelve main departments (SS-Hauptämter), hence each seat was for one of the twelve leaders of these departments.

In the centre of the ceiling was a swastika which symbolised the creative, active life force. The vault, which some have labelled the 'Himmler Crypt', was to be the place where Himmler would be interred after his death. It is known that Himmler believed he was the reincarnation of Heinrich I, the founder and first king of the medieval German state, who was apparently the king to whom the vault was going to be dedicated. It was Himmler's belief that Heinrich I protected Germany from invaders from the East. The urns of dead SS leaders would have been placed on pedestals in the vault. Finally, the never-finished upper floors were meant to be used as a meeting hall for the entire corps of the SS Gruppenführer. The top of the tower was to be completed by a huge dome with a structure containing lanterns to illuminate the interior, but this was never built.

On Good Friday 1945, 30 March, when the Nazi régime was about to fall, Himmler ordered SS Sturmbannführer Heinz Macher to come to his headquarters in Brenzlau. He ordered Macher to destroy Wewelsburg. Macher arrived in Paderborn around 10 am on Easter Saturday, and, by 1 pm, the team, mounted in three Jeeps, was at the castle and starting to place explosives. Macher found he had insufficient explosives, so his team had to resort to using anti-tank mines, with which they managed only to destroy the southeast tower.

It was then decided to burn the castle down. Once the fire was under way, Macher left the area, reporting to Himmler in person on the Easter Sunday afternoon. When, on the following day the US Third Infantry Division seized the grounds, they found it completed gutted by fire, with only the outside walls remaining.

After breakfast the next morning, Jack and Emma walked to Helmut's apartment, which was only a short distance from the hotel. Paderborn was a pleasant enough city, clean and with some fine architecture. Helmut's apartment was on the first floor of an 18th century town house in the old part of the city.

Jack inserted the key Helmut had placed in the envelope and opened the front door. They found themselves in a hallway which had two single doors and a set of double doors leading off it. They entered through the doors into a large room which had polished wooden floors covered in rugs. The ceiling was high, with tall windows looking out on to the street. It was tastefully and elegantly furnished, with some fine paintings on the walls two sofas on either side of an ornate fireplace. One wall was totally dominated by a series of shelves full of books, with a library ladder positioned to the left of them. By the windows was a large desk. Leading off from the room was a small but well-appointed kitchen. It was very quiet and there was no sign of Helmut.

Emma noticed a jar of instant coffee on the worktop. 'Why don't you have a look at the rest of the apartment while I make some coffee?' she said.

Jack went back into the hall and through the first of the single doors, which led into a small bedroom with an en suite bathroom. It looked as though it was a guest bedroom. He then went through the other door into a darkened room. He walked over to the window, drew the curtains and turned around.

Helmut was in the bed lying on his back, with his eyes closed as if in sleep. It didn't take long for Jack to ascertain that he was dead.

He drew the sheet over Helmut's head and went back into the drawing room just as Emma entered, carrying two mugs of coffee. He took them off her. 'Em, I think you had better sit down.'

'What is it?'

Jack placed the coffee mugs on the table.

'Helmut is dead. He's here in his bed. It looks as though he died in his sleep.'

'Oh my God!' Emma looked straight ahead and then started to cry, 'Poor, poor Helmut.'

Jack noticed a decanter on the side table. He sniffed it; brandy. He picked up two glasses and poured two large measures for each of them. He gave one to Emma and took a large slug from the other.

Emma sipped her brandy trying to collect her thoughts. 'We should call the police.'

'I don't think that would be wise. How would we explain

our presence? I know he was your... uncle, but, with what has been going on, I think we had better get out of here; perhaps call the police from a public phone. Come on let's drink up, wash the coffee cups and glasses, and get out of here.'

As Jack stood up he accidentally nudged the coffee table, spilling coffee across the glass surface. He managed to rescue a pile of books before the liquid got to them.

'That was a close one.' He went to put the books on another table and then noticed that the spine of one of the books bore the symbol that had been on the paper Helmut had given them. 'Em, look at this; it can't just be a coincidence.'

'What?' She muttered as she wiped up the spilt coffee, 'God you're a clumsy bugger.'

'It's the symbol.' Jack handed her the book and the piece of paper that Helmut had given them. She opened the book, and noted was set in German Gothic script and had been printed in Münich in 1938.

She flicked through the pages and shook it. Nothing fell out, and there were no indications of anything of importance or unusual.

'It is certainly the symbol' she said. 'Maybe there is something in the text. This is going to take ages and my German may not be up to it.' She gave the book back to Jack. 'I'll wash up and then let's get out of here.' Jack thought her composure was amazing, as if she was in denial. He knew she had been terribly fond of Uncle Heinrich but perhaps not of Helmut the Nazi.

They left the apartment, ensuring that no one saw them leave, and headed back to the centre of town where they found a café and ordered coffee. At Emma's suggestion they decided to get clear of the area as soon as possible and not call the police. Jack agreed. It would raise more questions than answers, and the last thing they wanted was any involvement with the German police.

Emma started to read the book, leaving Jack to his thoughts. Jack was mulling over Helmut's illness and wondering whether there was anything more sinister about his death.

'It's a history of the Teutonic Knights,' said Emma. 'Wasn't that the basis for the SS? Isn't it linked to Wewelsburg?'

'That could be interesting.'

'It's not far from here. Have we got time to visit it today?'

Jack looked at his watch; two o'clock. 'I reckon we have the time.'

Jack suddenly stopped.

'What's the matter?' asked Emma.

'Damn,' Jack replied. 'I covered Helmut's head with the bed sheet. Anyone who finds him in that state, particularly the police, will think it very fishy. I'd better go back to the apartment. I'll meet you back at the hotel.'

He paid the bill and they left the café. Jack returned to the apartment, where he placed the sheet back in its original position. He had failed to notice a young man in his early thirties who had been seated in the café near the door, and who had then followed Jack back to the apartment. The same man had also been in their hotel lobby when he and Emma had left that morning, and had followed them to Helmut's place.

Jack wiped down the door handles as much as he could but he was sure they must have left fingerprints. He rejoined Emma and they collected the car. They drove out of the car park just as a silver coloured Audi A6 picked up the man who had been trailing Jack. The car followed them on the thirty-minute drive to Wewelsburg.

The castle came into view; it was nothing spectacular as far as castle architecture was concerned, but in its elevated position it dominated the skyline. Its principal feature was its single north tower. The rest of the castle was a partial ruin, and there was evidence of some restoration work in progress.

They parked the car and walked to the main gateway. The castle was not normally open to the public, but the concierge had told them that there was a caretaker present during normal working hours. It was just their luck that a note on the door of the castle explained that the caretaker was away and would not be back for a further six days.

They checked the main door, which was securely locked. There was no obvious other entrance, and the high windows prevented them looking inside.

'Well that buggers that up' said Jack. It had now started to rain and Emma was feeling the cold. She shivered. 'Let's go back to the hotel. I've had enough excitement for one day.'

They got into the car and drove back to Paderborn, followed by the silver Audi.

'Well that was a waste of time, Em. I drag you out to Germany to find Heinrich dead, or whatever his bloody name is. Sorry, that was very insensitive of me.' Jack squeezed her hand.

'That's OK. It's just so strange to find out that you really know nothing about a person you have known most of your life. You drag me to this shitty ruin, it's raining, Paderborn is a gastronomic desert and you haven't even tried to shag me. What a disaster!' She started laughing.

'Come on Em, you know I only shag pretty women.'

'You bigoted bastard!' She hit him in the chest with the book.

A tiny waxed package fell out of the spine of the book and lodged between Jack's legs. He grinned. 'Get that for me?'

'Get it yourself, you dirty old man.'

He retrieved the package and handed it to her. It was now overcast and getting dark, so she turned on the internal light. The package was about two inches in length and just narrower than the spine of the book. She undid the wrapping.

Inside was a small, modern brass key and a piece of paper on which was typed an address in Nuremberg. Dellbach Bochman AG, 22-24 Barbier Gasse. There were also two sets of numbers, A347829Z and B287166Z, and a name.

'What is it, Em?'

'I don't know. It looks like a business address, as it ends in AG. I once wrote an article on German businesses and AG stands for Aktiengesellschaft which is used after the title of a German company to identify it as a public limited company. But what type of company Dellbach Bochman, is I have no idea. Then we have two numbers, a key, and a name, Doctor Heinz Gutterman. Let's check out the address when we get back to the hotel.'

They returned to the hotel just as darkness descended. They went to Jack's room and logged on to the internet. It didn't take long to establish that Dellbach Bochman AG was a private bank and that the key was probably for a safe deposit box and that the numbers could be for accounts.

'So what's the doctor link, Em?'

'I suspect he's part of the bank. He's probably not a medical doctor. It's common practice to use the title 'Doctor' in Germany if you have a university degree. I suppose it makes them feel important. As it's a private bank, I expect we'll have to make an appointment.'

Jack checked a route planner on his laptop establishing that the distance to Nuremberg was about 300 kilometres.

'I reckon it'll take us about four hours in all but at least most of it will be on autobahns. If we leave early tomorrow we could be in Nuremberg for lunch. So, who should call Gutterman, and how do we explain our interest?'

'Well, there's only one way to find out.' Emma picked up the phone and dialled the bank.

'Good afternoon, I'm British and I'm afraid that my German is not very good' she began. 'Would it be possible to speak with Dr Heinz Gutterman? My name is Emma Swift.' There was a pause and then a man's voice came on the line. He spoke English with virtually no accent.

'Miss Swift, Dr Gutterman speaking. I have been expecting your call. Is Mr Cunningham with you?'

Emma was taken aback; this was not at all what she expected. She put her hand over the mouthpiece and spoke to Jack.

'It's Gutterman and he was expecting my call and knows about you! Hello Dr Gutterman, Jack Cunningham is beside me.'

'I assume you wish to make an appointment to visit us. Where are you calling from?'

'We're in Paderborn.'

'Ah yes, Herr Walke's home town. How is Herr Walke?'

'He's fine, we've just left him. That's why I'm calling you, on his instructions. Could we visit tomorrow if it's at all possible, in the afternoon? We can drive to Nuremberg in the morning.'

'I can meet you at 4 pm. Would that be acceptable?'

'4 pm is fine. We'll meet you then. Goodbye Doctor.'

'Goodbye Miss Swift.'

Emma turned to Jack. 'The plot thickens. Everyone seems to know about us but I haven't a clue what this is all about.'

'Let's freshen up and grab a drink and a bite, preferably not based around sausages and red cabbage and head off early tomorrow' he replied. 'I'll go and see reception and meet you in the bar.'

Emma sighed and said, 'I don't know whether I am excited or fearful of all these events Jack but I'm so pleased you're with me'. She gave him a peck on the cheek and patted his bottom, 'Now get along. I won't be long but, if you're first down, order me a large G&T.'

The concierge recommended a restaurant nearby and Jack asked how long it would take to drive to Nuremberg. The concierge confirmed that it would take about four hours and suggested that, in order to avoid the rush hour that always caused problems near Kassel, they should leave at 7.30 am. He said he would arrange for coffee to be delivered to their respective rooms for 7.

Emma joined him in the bar. She had changed into a Diane Von Furstenberg dress which accentuated her slim figure. He thought she looked delectable, and wondered, not for the first time, why their relationship had stayed purely platonic.

'What do you think?' She did a little twirl.

'Ravishing, you minx.' Jack handed her a gin and tonic and after another round of drinks they walked arm in arm to the restaurant.

Shortly after they had left the hotel, a man approached the concierge.

'You have a guest who has just left the hotel. It's been years but I think I recognise him from my days on the *Times* newspaper. I think his name is Jack Cunningham. We were casual acquaintances.'

'Yes sir, Mr Cunningham is a guest. Would you like me to take a message for him as he's just gone out for dinner?'

'Thank you, that won't be necessary, I'll catch him tomorrow.'

'You'll have to be very early sir; Mr Cunningham is leaving at 7.30 am to drive to Nuremberg. Are you sure you don't wish to leave a message?'

'No that'll be fine, thank you.' The man left the hotel and climbed into his car; a silver Audi.

Jack and Emma each woke early. As promised by the concierge, coffee and pastries were delivered to their rooms on time. Jack thought that Germany might be the country of never-ending sausages and dumplings but they did make great coffee and pastries. Meeting in reception, the day concierge had just come on duty.

'Herr Cunningham, Fräulein Swift, I'm sorry I missed you when you returned last night; Albert had taken over. I do hope you enjoyed the restaurant.'

'Yes we did, very much so. Thank you for the recommendation, and thank you for breakfast this morning. Greatly appreciated.'

'I'm sorry you missed an acquaintance of yours from your days on the *Times*. He saw you yesterday but didn't get a chance to talk to you and I told him that you were leaving very early for Nuremberg.'

Jack was surprised and asked, 'Did he leave a name, a note?'

'No sir.'

'What did he look like?'

The concierge replied, 'He was in his thirties, tall, short dark hair, blue eyes and smartly dressed.'

'I wonder who that could be. I don't remember anyone like that. Did he say what he was here for?'

'No sir, but he may not be from this area. His dialect was Bavarian.'

'Many thanks...?'Jack asked

'Felix, sir.'

'Thank you Felix.' Jack slipped a €20 note into Felix's hand.

'Auf wiedersehen, Herr Cunningham, Fräulein Swift. Have a safe journey.'

The pair drove south on the A44 autobahn, Jack pondering as to who the stranger could have been.

'Em, I don't know any German journalists and certainly not anyone on the *Times*. Why would a stranger be interested in me, and how did he know my name? It's all very weird. I am beginning to think that we will need to keep our wits about us.'

They arrived in Nuremberg about midday and checked into the hotel Felix had booked for them. An excellent lunch in the hotel of smoked eel with a delicious bottle of Gewürztraminer raised their spirits. Jack spoke with the concierge who gave them a map and directions to Barbier Gasse which happened to be only a short walk from the hotel.

Before their meeting with Gutterman they decided to visit the church of St Katherine where the Spear of Longinus had been taken. There was only one crypt and they assumed this was where the Spear had been kept. But there was no reference to it anywhere, none of the staff they spoke to had ever heard of it. It was all rather disappointing but not surprising. No doubt it would remind people of things best forgotten.

They returned to the hotel and left at 3.45 pm to make their appointment with Dr Gutterman. They entered Barbier Gasse which was a cobbled street with 18th century buildings, all in a fine state of preservation. The street exuded an atmosphere of wealth.

They had no problem finding number 22-24 where they found the name Dellbach Bochman AG discreetly engraved on a perfectly-polished brass plaque.

Jack pressed a button on a panel which had a camera and microphone. He noticed that no fewer than four cameras were positioned overlooking the door and the street. He expected a reply, but there was just a buzzer sound and the door opened. They entered a vestibule opposite imposing double doors where there were more cameras.

The doors opened and a man entered the room. Jack noted that he was immaculately dressed in a grey suit and white shirt and was sporting a Hermés tie. He had beautifully polished classic Oxford brogues. He looked to be in his late forties and was tall with dark hair greying slightly at the edges. He approached them, smiled and offered his hand to Emma.

'Miss Swift, a pleasure, I am Heinz Gutterman.' He turned to Jack, 'Welcome Mr Cunningham. You are exactly on time; I admire people who are punctual. Don't you agree it's rude to be late?' His English was immaculate, with no hint of an accent.

'I agree absolutely,' said Jack, 'and may I compliment you on your excellent English.'

'Thank you Mr Cunningham, I spent four years at Harvard. Please come this way, Miss Swift.' He opened the doors and led them through to an elegantly-furnished room.

He stopped by a desk.

'I hope you will forgive the formality but may I see some identification please?' Jack was expecting this and gave him both his and Emma's passports.

'Thank you.' Gutterman looked closely at both passports and then returned them to Jack. 'All is in order. May I offer you some refreshment?' They both declined. Emma had been thinking a gin and tonic would go down well but then thought otherwise. Gutterman took them down a corridor which led into an antechamber which had an elevator to the front.

'Normally it is bank policy to permit only the key holder to enter the vault, but Herr Walke was most insistent that you both be granted access. Mr Cunningham, please enter the first of your account numbers, it begins with the letter A.'

Jack produced the paper from his pocket and entered the numbers on the console. A green light came on and the elevator doors slid open. The three of them entered, Gutterman pressed the single button on the lift panel and the elevator began to drop.

There was no indication as to how deep they were descending, but Jack reckoned the journey took at least ten seconds. The elevator stopped, the doors opened and they entered another antechamber. Here the walls were lined with steel and there was a single door, of considerable size and strength by the look of it. A console similar to the one located on the upper level was positioned to the left of the door.

'Please enter your second account number, Mr Cunningham.'

Jack entered the digits, a green light came on and the door slowly swung open. Gutterman led them into the vault and opened a cage-like door and they entered a room lined with hundreds of safe deposit boxes.

'I assume you have your key Mr Cunningham. What are the last two digits on the second set of numbers?'

'Of course.' Jack withdrew the small brass key from his pocket and looked at the piece of paper. 'The number is 66.' Gutterman had a similar key and inserted this into one of two key holes in box number 66. Jack then inserted his key in the lock and turned it. Gutterman then opened the door and withdrew the safe deposit box. He took the box to a side room, where there was a table and two chairs, and placed the box on the table. Without saying anything more he left the room, closing the door behind him.

Jack and Emma stood there for a moment looking at the box, saying nothing.

'Well, we'd better see what Uncle Helmut has got for us' said Jack. He lifted the lid and looked inside. There were two Iron Crosses. Jack noted that one appeared to have diamonds inset around the edge of the cross. There were a few more medals, a silver ring which had a death's head skull and SS runes engraved on it, and a Nazi party identity card. There were also two hefty wedges of US 100-dollar bills. Jack handed the money to Emma.

'We'll count these later, but there looks to be a tidy sum.'

The last object in the box was a large envelope in which lay an A4 beige-coloured file. It was slightly discoloured with age and had 'Geheimnis' printed on the top and bottom of both the back and front of the cover.

'Secret,' said Emma.

Also printed on the file was the Nazi eagle symbol, with SS runes below and the word 'Verglas' printed in red.

'So this is Verglas,' said Emma.

Jack opened the file. It was divided into four sections totalling about forty typewritten pages. With the exception of the top page, which looked relatively new, all the pages were discoloured with age.

The top page bore a list of names, each with another name beside each entry, an address and a telephone number. Helmut's name was at the top. Apart from his name and that of someone called 'Eberle/Smith', each of the other names had a line drawn through it and the word 'Tot' inserted at the end.'

'Tot means dead' interjected Emma.

'This fourth name, SS Scharführer Karl Eberle, is followed by 'Carl Smith'. I presume as it has the same layout as Helmut's entry, Smith must be his assumed name. He lives in London. I suppose he must be still alive.'

Emma's German was better than Jack's, but she agreed that they needed a fluent German speaker to help translate the file.

'I have a journo buddy on the Independent who is fluent in German,' said Jack. 'You've met him a few times, Martin Hunt? He would help. I think we need to get back to London pronto, first to get this translated, and secondly to visit this Eberle fellow. That's if he is still alive. We'd better leave first thing tomorrow.'

Jack opened the door and summoned Dr Gutterman, who entered the room carrying a brown leather attaché case. 'I thought you might need this, Mr Cunningham,' he said. He handed the case to Jack. 'Please keep it with the compliments of the bank.'

Gutterman turned so his back was facing them and Jack placed all the contents of the box in the case. He then handed the box to Gutterman, who replaced it in its recess and returned the key to Jack. Gutterman escorted them to the front entrance. He shook their hands and made his farewells, and they stepped out into the street.

It had started to rain as they walked across the slippery cobbles of the street and turned into the main road towards the hotel.

The man in the silver Audi got out and followed them while his driver rang a number in Duisburg. Wunsche answered.

'They have left the bank with a brown leather attaché case which they didn't have before,' the man reported. 'Hans is following them on foot. What do you want us to do?'

'Keep them under surveillance and I will call you back in one hour.'

Wunsche made a couple of phone calls. Exactly one hour after the original call he rang the Nuremberg man.

'I have dispatched an Alpha team to reinforce you,' came the response. He gave him a cell phone number. 'Arrange to rendezvous with them, and then I want you to lift Cunningham and Swift. I want them intact and unhurt. Take them to the house in Wurzburg, and make sure you get the attaché case. I'll meet you there. The team should be with you within the next two hours. Keep an eye on Cunningham and Swift and do nothing else until the Alpha team arrives.'

The driver parked the Audi and joined his companion. He had failed to notice a blue Saab parked nearby which had tailed them from Paderborn. They had no reason to suspect that anyone else was interested in them, least of all four Russian FSB agents.

The earliest flight Jack could book to London was at 11.35 the following day from Munich airport meaning a drive of some 170 kilometres. Jack rang Martin Hunt, who got very excited about what Jack told him and even offered to pick them up from the airport so he could get his hands on the file as quickly as possible.

Martin and Jack had been friends for ten years. They had first met at a press briefing in Bosnia where Martin was on assignment working for the Independent. They had hit it off immediately and had since become firm friends.

Martin was just over six feet tall and of medium build. He was slightly overweight and had a shock of blonde hair. He was the younger son of Sir Nigel Hunt, a successful city banker who had died the previous year. Martin had been to Winchester and had gained a first in English at Oxford. He was picked up by the *Independent* after winning the Young Journalist of the Year award during his time with the *Guardian* and was now a highly respected features journalist.

Jack met Emma in the hotel bar where they each had a glass of Sekt. Jack kept the attaché case close by. The concierge had recommended a restaurant in a village nearby, about 20 minutes' drive from Nuremberg. He had made a reservation in Jack's name for 8 pm, so they left the hotel at 7.30 pm.

The Audi men saw them leave and noted that Jack had the attaché case with him as he and Emma got into their car. They relayed this information to Wunsche.

Jack and Emma drove north out of the city. 25 minutes later they entered the little village of Engel where they had no problem finding the restaurant. Although, on the outside, it looked unprepossessing, the concierge had assured them that the restaurant was noted for the quality of the food and hospitality.

They were not disappointed by the welcome they received. If the food was as good as the menu offered they were going to be in for a special gastronomic evening.

Jack and Emma entered the restaurant just as the Audi pulled into a street across from it. The team leader called team

Alpha, relaying their current location. The Alpha leader told him that they were about 45 minutes away having been delayed by a tyre puncture on the autobahn.

The blue Saab was positioned about 100 metres behind the Audi and in the shadow of a nearby church. There were three male and one female FSB agents in the car. Two of them were cursing the fact that short of going into the restaurant there was nowhere for them to get food.

Team Alpha, travelling in a Mercedes estate, comprised four men, each armed with a Glock automatic pistol and a Hechler & Koch MP5K, the shorter version of the MP5. The MP5K was a weapon that was very easy to conceal and could be carried on a sling beneath the armpit. One of the men had his MP5K fitted in a specially-designed briefcase, which enabled firing via a trigger in the handle of the case.

Totenkopf had a number of discrete teams located throughout Europe which could be called upon to carry out all manner of operations for the organisation. The Audi team were from the Frankfurt area.

The FSB team saw the Mercedes arrive; there were now six Totenkopf personnel in the village. The FSB team leader called their control centre and briefed them on the situation, and Organov instructed them to protect the targets at all cost.

'I'm sure the Totenkopf men are not there for a dinner reservation. I suspect we don't have much time. Get Cunningham and the woman out of there now' he ordered.

Two of the FSB crew, a man and a woman, got out of the car. All the teams had at least one woman, which facilitated access to most places as a couple rarely raised any suspicion. To all intents and purposes the agents were a couple going into the restaurant to dine.

They entered the restaurant and spoke briefly to the owner

saying they were joining Herr Cunningham. Walking over to the booth where Jack and Emma were deep in conversation, the man sat down by Jack and the woman sat beside Emma, boxing them in. Before Jack could say anything the man spoke firmly in excellent English. 'There is no time to explain, your lives are in danger and we are here to escort you to safety. Trust us, we must leave now.'

'We're not going anywhere without an explanation,' Jack exclaimed.

'I haven't the time to explain anything now but this is all about what is in your briefcase. You must trust us, we have little time.' He called the waiter over, explained that they had to leave and gave him €300. 'This should cover the bill.'

The main door of the restaurant opened and a man from Team Alpha entered to reconnoitre the place. He was wearing a suit and carrying a briefcase. The FSB man recognised him immediately.

'Time to go,' he said, firmly grasping Emma's arm. The woman had placed her 9mm Browning Hi-Power pistol against Jack's ribs. 'Please come with us now, we mean you no harm, but we must move, now.'

As they rose from the table, the man with the briefcase spoke into his left-hand shirt cuff, which concealed a microphone. 'Target is with other people and about to leave, move now and cover the rear.'

Jack and Emma were dragged out of the booth and pushed towards the kitchen door just as the FSB man drew his Browning.

The MP5K has a rate of fire in the region of 900 rounds per minute. By the time the Browning's barrel was out of its holster the Totenkopf man had pressed the trigger on his briefcase. The FSB man was hit in the chest by five rounds. He died instantly, his body thrown back into the booth.

Pandemonium broke loose. One man in the next booth had been hit by the Heckler & Koch burst and was draped over a woman who was screaming over his bloodied body. The FSB woman fired a double tap, hitting the briefcase man in the chest and propelling him into a waiter carrying a tray of food.

By now Jack's military training quickly came into play and he had grabbed the dead man's pistol. Fortuitously the Browning had been standard issue to the British military and as a result he was very familiar with it.

The main door burst open and two more Totenkopf entered, each carrying an MP5K. Jack aimed and fired, hitting one of the men in the thigh and putting the other off his aim. Before they could recover and return fire, Jack, Emma and the FSB woman were through the exit and running through the busy kitchen.

Jack led the way with Emma staggering behind him and the FSB woman bringing up the rear, covering the kitchen entrance door. Jack found the rear entrance, grabbed Emma and propelled her towards the door, just as the second Totenkopf man burst through the kitchen door and opened fire. The FSB woman was too quick for him. She killed the man with two bullets to his chest.

Jack burst out through the door into a side street, Emma falling against him and sliding to the ground, clutching the briefcase with bloody fingers. A man appeared from the shadows, helped her up and bundled her into the rear of the blue Saab. Jack followed, the FSB woman landing on top of him. The car accelerated down the street.

Emma was leaning against Jack. Her breathing was shallow

and he could see that she was bleeding heavily. The FSB team leader gave Jack a towel to press against Emma's wound to staunch the bleeding. He cradled her in his arms. Two bullets had hit her.

'You're going to be all right my darling!' Jack said gently. She looked at him, eyes wide open in shock. 'You've never called me darling before, I'm just Em,' she murmured weakly. Her body convulsed as the pain in her side increased.

'It's not good Jack,' she said, her eyes closing. 'I must tell you now that I love you and I've always loved you.'

Jack wiped a dribble of blood from the side of her mouth. He knew she was bleeding internally. His voice quavered, 'I love you too. We've been fools.'

He kissed her on the lips and felt her body go limp. He could hardly believe what had happened. All the things he wanted to say to her and now it was too late. His eyes filled with tears.

The windscreen suddenly exploded as a hail of bullets hit the car from the shadows. The car veered to the right and smashed into a wooden telegraph pole. Jack hit his head against the car's bulkhead. He looked up, slightly dazed. The FSB driver and his partner were dead.

Jack checked Emma but he knew she had gone. He also knew that if he didn't get away quickly he would be finished too.

The FSB woman was now the sole survivor of the team. She had exited the car and positioned herself behind the open door, scanning the area in front of her over the open sights of her pistol.

Jack kissed Emma again. 'Goodbye my dearest love,' he whispered. He grabbed the briefcase, opened the other door and rolled clear of the car. Staying low, he crawled to the side of a nearby darkened alleyway just as the car burst into flames. He looked back and saw two armed men illuminated by the flames walk towards it.

Suddenly the car exploded, spraying flaming fuel and debris across the street. The FSB woman had been knocked unconscious by the explosion and Jack moved towards her, grabbing her collar and dragging her into the alley. Thank god he had not been seen. He knew he had to get out of the area but he couldn't immediately return to the car. They would be waiting for him.

The woman had regained consciousness; she was shaken, but soon regained her composure.

'You must get away, I'll cover you' she said. Jack tried to argue with her, to no avail. 'You must not let these men capture you. I will be all right. Hide until the coast is clear. The emergency services will soon be here.'

Jack could hear sirens in the distance. 'Make your escape, you should be able to use your car but wait until the coast is clear, now get out of here!' She turned away from him, checking the rounds she had left in her automatic pistol.

Jack ran down the alleyway. He knew he should not return to his hotel. Whoever these people were they must have followed him and Emma. Fortunately he had his passport with him. He needed to get to his car but took the advice of the unknown woman and thought it better to wait until it was all clear. Hopefully his attackers would think he had died in the car.

Finding an open shed, he slipped into it and sat in the corner in deep shadow. He could see the burning car through a small gap in the wooden panels of the shed. There came another eruption of gunfire, followed by silence.

Shortly afterwards the police and firemen arrived. He saw

one of the men who had shot at them get into a silver Audi and drive off. Where were the others?

He waited for 30 minutes, then, staying in the shadows, he moved towards his car. He kept watch for a further 20 minutes and when he thought it clear strolled over to the car and drove out of the village. He looked at his watch; 11.15.

He drove for about ten minutes, then pulled into a side road, turned on the car's interior light and dug a road map out of the glove box. It was then that he noticed his hands and clothes were covered in blood. He knew he couldn't go anywhere public in this state, and certainly not in daylight.

He decided to drive towards München and try to catch his flight to London. He would stop at dawn and clean himself up.

* * * * * * *

'You incompetent cretins!' shouted Wunsche to the men before him. 'What a fucking shambles, you were supposed to pick them up, not kill them!' He turned to face the leader of the Alpha team. 'Do you know if they are all dead and the briefcase destroyed?'

'We presume so.'

'You presume? Check, you fucking moron! I need to know if all the people are accounted for. Now do we know who these other people are?'

'There were a total of six, four men and two women, that includes Cunningham and Swift. They are all dead. They killed Helmut and Jan, and injured Kurt. We recovered Helmut's body and Kurt is with the doctor. We had no time to recover Jan's body but it's all clean.'

'No it isn't fucking clean!' screamed Wunsche. 'Until I

know the girl and Cunningham are dead or alive, it's not clean. I want you to find out how many bodies were in that car, and, if they are all dead, there should be four bodies. Check with our contacts in the Bundespolizei and also see if they have anything on the men and women you shot. Now get out of my sight!'

Christ, thought Wunsche, how am I going to explain this to Emmerich?

He rang Emmerich and briefed him on what had happened.

'I want to know if Cunningham and Swift were in the car and if they are dead, and I want the information by yesterday' Emmerich responded. 'This is most inconvenient, Franz. What with Kautenberg's death and now this. I do hope you are not going to make a habit of failure!' The unspoken threat was not lost on Wunsche. He knew only too well how ruthless the organisation could be.

'Of course, sir, I will not let you down.'

'I'm sure you won't, Franz, I'm sure you won't.' Emmerich rang off. Emmerich had never raised his voice; he didn't need to.

Jack knew that he had to get well clear of the area, so he drove for about an hour and then turned off the main road, switching off the car's lights. There was sufficient moonlight to enable him to see as he drove down a gravel track which gently descended until it ran parallel to a small, fast-flowing stream.

He stopped the car and went down to the water's edge. There he washed the blood off his hands and sponged down his clothing with his handkerchief. He climbed into the car and dozed fitfully until about 5.30 am.

Getting out of the car, he stretched his aching limbs, and looked at himself in the pale dawn light. He cleaned himself some more but he knew he wouldn't pass muster in a public place and certainly not in an airport. He needed at least to replace his white shirt which was a real mess. His jacket and trousers were black, which hid the bloodstains.

He realised that he had not eaten anything for nearly 18 hours; his stomach reminded him of this with gurgling sounds. He turned the car around and had a look at the road map that came with the hire car. He reckoned he was somewhere between Wolfsbuch and Winden. He needed to get to the A9 autobahn, which would take him to Münich with enough time to catch his 11.35 BA flight.

His best bet, he thought, would be to stop briefly at one of the many autobahn Rasthofs and get some food and a change of clothes. Because his flight was at 11.35 he had just about enough time do these things, drop the car off at the airport and get through security which he knew from past experience was particularly rigorous at the airport. It helped that he had an e-ticket and no luggage so he should be able to transit the airport quickly.

He suddenly wondered what he was going to do about his and Emma's rooms. He felt sick just thinking of Emma and how happy they had been the previous evening which finished in such a terrible and tragic way. He decided to ring the hotel in Paderborn. He got through easily and spoke with the concierge, who was only too happy to speak with the manager of the hotel in Nuremberg and arrange to keep the luggage in storage for him until his next visit, which Jack knew would probably be soon. He gave the concierge his credit card details to enable payment of the bill.

Leaving the track, he got back on the main road and headed south, joining the A9 near Denkendorf. After 30 kilometres he pulled into one of the many excellent rest facilities on the autobahn. He had plenty of fuel and so he went straight to the parking area. He turned the collar of his jacket up, fully buttoning it up before entering the service area. Going into the shop, he purchased a shaving kit, car upholstery cleaning kit and a black Harley Davidson T shirt, the most discreet of the clothes available.

Holding his collar to his neck he paid cash for the items; the checkout girl didn't give him a second look. He went to the toilets and into one of the cubicles where he stripped his shirt off and put on the T shirt. The bloody shirt was stuffed into the plastic shopping bag and into the nearby waste bin. He then had a quick shave and general tidy up. Leaving the toilets he went out and grabbed a large coffee and two cheese and ham rolls from a Schnell Imbiss. Thank goodness the Germans, unlike the British, took pride in the quality of the fast food they served at these rest centres.

Jack returned to the car and quickly demolished the food and coffee before cleaning the seat and dashboard of bloodstains. Fortunately the seat upholstery was vinyl and easy to clean.

Only then did he realise that he still had the Browning. He had parked the car close to some undergrowth which meant he was able to bend down with the car obscuring him from view and bury the pistol under a bush.

He pulled back out onto the A9 and headed south, joining the A92 at the Neufahn interchange. He was soon at Münich airport, where he went to the Hertz centre and returned the car before catching the shuttle bus to Terminal 1 to check in for his BA flight to Heathrow. He bought another coffee and rang Martin, telling him what time to meet him at the airport.

Martin was on time. After Jack had recounted Emma's death they continued the journey from the airport in silence. Martin took Jack to his apartment which was just off the Portobello Road. He made coffee as Jack showered and cleaned off the rest of the previous day's dirt.

Martin handed Jack a mug of black coffee with a slug of brandy in it, 'Get your head down Jacko, you look like shit, I'll get stuck into your file.'

Nuremberg, Bundespolizei HQ

Major Karl Junge was the head of the Bundespolizei for Nuremberg. He was 51 years old, married and had three teenage children. His career in the police had been unspectacular, but he was in the rank expected for his age. A number of his colleagues thought he was a bit of a pedant when it came to paperwork. He looked very much a bureaucrat and was not a very inspiring leader.

Junge was very conscious of his thinning hair, hiding his baldness with an obvious comb over. Strange that men who had combovers naively believed that no one noticed their baldness, failing to realise how ridiculous they looked with wisps of hair draped across the head.

Junge had a normal home life and was liked by his neighbours and friends. At work he was respected, but was thought by the younger firebrands to be a bit of a plodder.

What no one knew was that he was a member of the Totenkopf, and, being the original 'grey man', suited his cover perfectly.

It was just after one in the morning when he received a call from Wunsche.

Engel

Inspektor Klaus Schmidt, head of detectives, was surveying the carnage in the village. The fires had been put out and all the bodies had been recovered. There was a sickly smell of burned plastic mixed with charred flesh and petrol fumes. He turned to one of his detectives, Sergeant Willi Brunner.

'Christ Willi, what a bloody mess. It's more like downtown Baghdad than a sleepy village.'

Klaus Schmidt was considered an excellent detective. Although some of his techniques were thought unorthodox, sometimes verging on the illegal, he achieved results, so his superiors often ignored his ways of operating. Even his immediate boss, Karl Junge, recognised Schmidt's talents.

Schmidt's team of detectives adored him and, although, at thirty, he was younger than most of the people who worked under his command, they respected and admired his talents and leadership. He in turn respected his team which had achieved a reputation for excellence under his command. Klaus had a very easy manner and a great sense of humour. Standing at just over six feet tall with the build of an athlete, he had an imposing physical presence, helped by a very natural charm and good looks. He was also physically tough and had a black belt in karate.

Nuremberg had the usual amount of crime you would expect for a city with a population of just over 500,000, but over the last 12 months there had been a rapid increase in violent crime as Turkish and Bulgarian gangs had moved into the city and each had vied for supremacy. This was why Schmidt had been transferred from Hamburg, where he had successfully run an operation to limit organised gang activities. He had only been in Nuremberg for some 18 months but had already been successful with his task force, although there had been two attempts to kill him. His methods were hurting the gangs.

'Boss, the gangs have had a real go here.' Willi lifted the cover off three of the bodies, which were badly burned. Klaus caught the stench of the burned flesh. The smell was sickly sweet.

'It doesn't feel right Willi. Why here? This is way outside their normal operating areas. What's been recovered so far?'

'There were three bodies in the car they're very badly burned but it looks like we have two men and one woman so we'll probably need dental and DNA checks. There is another woman over there; she was shot at least four times. There's another body in the kitchen also with gunshot wounds, and one in the main restaurant. There are also two other bodies which the owner identified as guests who just got caught up in the crossfire.'

'Anything else from the restaurant staff?'

'Yup, according to the owner.' Willi looked at his notebook. 'He said a man and woman had just arrived and were then joined by another couple, and then one man followed by two others entered and all hell broke loose. A waitress said she saw the two couples leave through the kitchen and that one of the men was shot by the doorway.

'He said that, of the men who started the shooting, one was wounded, one was shot dead in the kitchen and another carried the wounded man away. There was also a dead man by the booth where a man and woman had been seated. We couldn't find any weapon with the dead man in the restaurant but he had two clips of Browning 9 mm ammo in his jacket. The dead guy in the kitchen had a Glock.'

'So we have three bodies in the car. Two men and one woman and another woman nearby. With the two men in the kitchen and the restaurant, we have six bodies excluding the civilians. What weapons have you recovered?'

'We found two MP5Ks in the boot of the car. The woman had a Glock. So did the men in the car. The other woman appeared unarmed.'

'Ok Willi, get Herman to check the hospitals. Who's going to be doing the autopsies?'

'It will be Julia, I suspect.' Julia Weisberg was the senior police pathologist, and very good at her job. She was also a great friend of Klaus.

Willi wandered off to speak to other members of the team and Klaus rang one of his informants.

'Wolfgang, its Klaus. There's been a major shoot out in Engel.'

'Where the fuck is that?'

'Listen you dipstick, you were born in the area so don't bullshit me. I need to know what the word is on the street. It looks gang related but I'm not sure. Call me back, and quickly.'

Klaus rang Julia. 'I'm sending you a pile of bodies. Segregate the two civilians, they're innocent bystanders and will be suitably tagged. I need to know as much as possible about the identities of the other bodies before anything else. Three are burned very badly. The others don't look Turkish or Slavic, that's one of the reasons I don't think it's gang-related. I know how they died, so focus on identifying them.' He rang off.

Willi came over. 'The guys have confirmed that the men in the kitchen and restaurant and the other woman had no ID and the labels from their clothes had been removed. They each had a small quantity of Euros on them. The woman didn't even have a handbag and both had shoulder holsters. Professionals.'

'Let's see what Julia can find on the other bodies. Better get them to her as quickly as possible. Oh, and make sure the civilians are tagged separately, I'm not interested in them.'

Klaus' cell phone rang.

'Klaus, it's Karl, what have you got?'

Klaus briefed his boss on what they had found.

'Sounds as though you have another gang-related killing. Perhaps they are at last doing us a favour and killing each other.'

'It may be that sir, but I'm not so sure, I have a hunch that it isn't. Julia should be able to throw some light on it.'

'Take my word for it Klaus, its gang-related. You and your hunches! Keep me posted on progress. There are a plenty of wealthy and influential people in the Engel area and they are very unhappy with what has happened. Too close to home. Some of them have already contacted the Bürgermeister, so we now have politics involved. Remember it's an election year.'

'Will do sir.' They rang off. Fucking politics, Klaus thought. They always want results, whether they are the right ones or not. He had experienced similar things on the politically expedient front when he had been based in Hamburg. He walked to his car.

FSB Headquarters

Ivan Terpinski informed Organov that there were three bodies in the burned-out car and a woman's body lying by the car. He confirmed that the dead woman by the car was FSB. Orlov had been killed in the restaurant and one of the bodies in the car was a woman. There was also another body in the kitchen, not one of their people.

'I think we can assume that the woman in the car is Emma Swift' said Terpinski. 'We know Jack Cunningham caught the 11.35 BA flight from München to London and he didn't go to his apartment so we must assume he's holed up somewhere else. I have the apartment under surveillance but at present, unless we get lucky and he surfaces, we have no way of finding him. That was one hell of a shootout at the restaurant. At least two of the Totenkopf team were killed along with two civilians. Our contacts at the Bundespolizei confirm that they're viewing this as gang related, a turf war, linked to criminal elements in the area. Fortuitously there is a drug war going on in the Nuremberg area'.

He paused. 'Who would have thought it?' He shrugged and gave his report to Organov who poured them some tea. He handed a cup to Terpinski and spoke.

'We need to find Cunningham as soon as possible' said Terpinski. 'It will only be a matter of time before Totenkopf find out he has escaped and I wouldn't be at all surprised if they already know and have people watching his apartment. I suspect Cunningham hasn't a clue what he has stumbled into. I want him alive. At present I am not sure what the Totenkopf's interest is in him. They either want him alive for something he has or knows, or they want him shut up. Brief London Station on their interest and get Team Kilo over from Paris to London. Put them in the Chelsea safe house and arrange the usual kit. I want them ready in the next 24 hours and to be able to react quickly when Cunningham reappears. And he will, Ivan, he will.'

London

Jack slept like the dead; he was emotionally and physically exhausted. When he awoke he took a scalding hot shower, noticing he had some minor cuts on his hands and a couple of hefty bruises on his left arm. He pondered the events of the last week and the loss of Emma. He leaned his head against the shower wall, a wave of emotion flooding his thoughts.

My darling Em, so much lost, and there was so much I wanted to tell you. What a fuckwit I have been.

An old South African friend, a woman, had once teased him for his very British stiff upper lip, accusing him of being emotionally constipated. He was certainly that.

He shaved and returned to the room, where Martin had left him some clothes. Luckily, Martin was bigger than Jack, but unfortunately he had no style. Jack had never seen so much brown clothing.

He went into the drawing room, where Martin had been working most of the night. There was a half-empty bottle of whisky on the table, surrounded by empty coffee cups.

Martin looked up. 'Hello, you old fart. You've been asleep for nearly fifteen hours but at least it's given me a chance to read the file. Coffee?' Martin proffered the pot and poured Jack a mug full, adding a shot of whisky.

'I know it's only 7 o'clock but it should set you up nicely. I don't know about you but I'm famished. There's a greasy spoon down the road that we can go to and I can bring you up to speed on the file. Oh yes, almost forgot, there is exactly $17,300 in cash, thought you'd like to know.'

Jack had forgotten that it must have been at least 24 hours since he had eaten anything of substance. He thought of Emma again.

'You know Martin, I really loved her. Wish I'd had the sense to tell her earlier.'

'I know that Jack. We all thought your relationship was deeper than just friendship. I should've kicked your arse into action but I didn't. The least you can do for Emma is to see this thing through. Now we need to eat. I'm ravenous and my body needs some carbs.'

He placed his hand on Jack's shoulder. 'We'll talk some more about Emma but later.' Martin stuffed the file and his copious notes into the leather case and headed for the door.

Martin's café was typical new Notting Hill, more upmarket than the traditional greasy spoon and priced accordingly. They found a corner table and ordered a full fry. Over a heart-stopping breakfast and rather too much coffee, Martin told Jack what he had found.

'This is explosive stuff Jack the sort of thing you read in a novel. The file is basically an operation order and it looks as though it's signed by Himmler. The operation has the codename Verglas. I've no idea why it was called that – translated it just means black ice.

'Anyway, the whole thing is about the tracking down and stealing of a range of artefacts from around Europe all listed in an appendix at the back of the file. I have no idea why, as the list doesn't seem to have a common theme. The man tasked to oversee the whole operation was...' - he turned to his notes - 'Gruppenführer Helmut Kautenberg; that's the equivalent of Major–General in our army, which probably explains the diamond-encrusted Iron Cross.'

'That was Em's surrogate father, her Uncle Heinrich. Remember I mentioned him?'

Martin continued. 'The page at the front of the file is much later than the other contents. It's a list of all the officers and NCOs and a civilian, a Doctor Strausser, who formed Kautenberg's team. Their ranks are all listed and other names are in parenthesis beside each entry. It looks as though these could be false names they were given at the end of the war. It's not really surprising as I suspect they wouldn't want their true identifies known, particularly as they're all SS. Apart from Kautenberg and a chap called Eberle, everyone else has the word 'tot' written by each name with a date, I presume this was when they died. If Eberle is still alive he is living in London, at an address in Putney to be precise.

'The list of items to be stolen is weird. Your Spear of

Longinus is there, plus the Amber Room and books and other relics which I have never heard of. There's also reference to a number of consignments but no mention as to what they are. Honestly, this really is straight out of an Indiana Jones movie. The file refers to an Appendix B which lists the location of the items in Appendix A, but it's missing.'

Jack took a gulp of coffee. 'Martin, this is incredible. I just can't believe it's true, but it must be judging by the amount of killing that's been going on. It must all be linked to the file. We're sitting on something pretty exciting but, of course, it's meaningless without Appendix B.

'Before the shooting started, a man and a woman were supposedly helping us get out of the restaurant to protect us. Then all hell broke loose and I haven't got a clue as to who they were.'

'Jack, I suggest we take this one step at a time. Look at the state you're in at the moment. I think you should stay at my apartment for a while. I'll go to your apartment and get whatever stuff you need, clothes, etc. Is there anything else you might want?'

'Get my laptop. There's a pile of recordable discs in the top left hand drawer of my desk.'

'OK', said Martin. 'I'll drop off your kit and then go to the office to photocopy the file and also scan it to two discs. I suggest, for security, that I keep the original file and one disc in the office.'

Jack went to Martin's apartment while Martin carried on to Jack's place. Martin was observed entering the apartment block by the FSB team and by two other men in a nondescript Ford Fiesta parked down the street; Totenkopf. Both teams noted him leaving the building 30 minutes later with a holdall, but thought nothing of it.

Martin dropped the holdall off with Jack and went over to the *Independent*, scanned the file and burned two discs. He thought the additional copies would be a useful precaution. He placed the original file and a disc in a folder marked 'Chelsea Flower Show 2005'. He had covered the show that year for the paper. He put the folder in his desk drawer between a number of other files.

It was about 3 pm when Martin returned from his office. He told Jack where he had hidden the original file and one of the discs.

'We had better hide the other disc.' Martin said. He took it and inserted it into the CD jewel case for Roxy Music's album *Avalon*.

'What now?' asked Martin, pouring them each a mug of tea.

Jack sipped his tea. 'I think we need to pursue this Eberle fellow. I can't believe Helmut would have gone to such great lengths to lead us to the file and leave out the most important part. It's as if he knew that someone would try and take it off us when we left the bank. I have to believe the file is the key. Eberle is the only one left alive and there must be a link to him. We're lucky that he lives in London, and Putney of all places, just down the road. Was there a telephone number for him in the file?'

Martin got out the disc and loaded it onto his laptop. 'I think there was… here it is.' He jotted down the full address and the telephone number, and Jack picked up the phone and dialled the number. A woman answered. Using the false name that Eberle had been given, Jack asked if he could speak to Mr Smith.

'Who's calling?' she asked.

'My name is Cunningham, Jack Cunningham. I'm a journalist.'

'I'm afraid my father is resting; may I ask what it is about?'

'I wonder if you could get him to call me on my cell phone.' He gave her the number. 'It's very important. Please mention to him the names Eberle and Kautenberg, he will understand. May I know your name?'

'Penny, Penny Smith.'

'Thank you Miss Smith.' He hung up the phone. He turned to Martin, 'Well that's that for the moment. We know he's there and that he has a daughter. We just have to hope he calls me back.

Pathology Unit, Nuremberg

Klaus entered the room. Julia was bent over the burnt corpses, taking photographs of the insides of the mouths. She looked up and waved to Klaus. She pulled her mask down, revealing a very attractive face when she smiled. Many thought she and Klaus were having an affair, but they were just great friends. Although both were unmarried, they were both in happy long-term relationships with other people. Perhaps in another time and place things might have been different.

Julia was in her late thirties and had previously been a lawyer specialising in family law but had given up a very promising career at 28 to become a forensic pathologist. Klaus never understood why she had left a highly-paid career to do something which was often gruesome and certainly not paid that well. But he was glad she had, as he thought her one of the most astute and professional pathologists he had ever worked with.

'When do you think you'll have something for me, Julia?'

'The dental checks could take quite a long time, say 36

hours. I've already sent off the DNA samples for analysis. We'll probably get those about the same time. I'll call you as soon as I have anything. The autopsies will also be completed in about the same timeframe. We may get interim reports before then.'

'Thanks Julia, I'll head over to the forensics lab to see what the guys have.'

Klaus left her and walked across the compound to the forensics lab. Willi was already there deep in discussion with two of the lab technicians. He saw Klaus and beckoned him over to one of the tables where there lay the scorched remains of two Glock pistols, the woman's Glock and the two MP5Ks.

'These are all the latest variants and every serial number has been expertly removed. The techies can get nothing from them, so we are sending the weapons over to Frankfurt University where they have more sophisticated scanning equipment.'

'What else do we have?'

'Four of the corpses having nothing on them, no ID, no cards, no jewellery, a few coins. With the unburned corpses, the man had 300 Euros and the woman 150. There were no labels on any of the clothing. The dead guy in the kitchen had a mike set-up which was pretty sophisticated and can't be bought over the counter. We've sent it to the comms boffins to ascertain where it came from. The cell phones in the car are all melted and we can get nothing there.'

He picked up a cell phone. 'Now this one is interesting. We found it on the other woman's body. It looks like an ordinary Nokia, except this little bugger has got some very clever technology inside. I wanted you to see it before I send it away. It's got what looks like two sim cards. All the data has been remotely wiped, including which network is being used. There is no way the gangs could get their hands on this sort of stuff.'

Willi took Klaus over to another table.

'The burned woman is a different matter. The parts of the clothing that aren't burned are of very good quality. The guys have already sent samples to a specialist textile lab. She did have a handbag which is pretty badly burned, and her plastic cards have fused together. Bertrand is working on that. He reckons he will have something in the next 24 hours. She seems to be the odd one out.

'What's interesting is that all the other corpses wore cheap wristwatches and she has a Rolex, so we're tracking down the serial number.'

'Well done Willi.' Klaus turned to the technicians. 'Good work guys, thank you.' Klaus knew that with that small acknowledgement of the technicians' efforts they would pull out all the stops to get the work done quickly. He left the lab and returned to his office.

Four hours later Klaus's informant rang him.

'It's Wolfgang. I've checked around and although everyone knows about the shooting it's not between or even done by the gangs. I really don't think anybody knows anything.'

Later that day the Bürgermeister made a press statement to the effect that the shootings in Engel were gang-related and were part of the drug turf wars between the gangs. His statement reassured the public that the Nuremberg police were on top of the situation, and this was followed by another statement by Junge supporting the Bürgermeister.

Klaus had seen the press conference on the TV in his office. What bullshit, he thought. He rang Junge.

'Sir, it's Klaus. What was that press statement all about? I am now pretty positive that this whole affair is not gang-related. My contacts tell me it has nothing to do with the Turks or the Bulgarians. We have found some very sophisticated kit which also indicates that this is not gang-related.'

'Klaus you are building this up too much. That big brain of yours has gone into overdrive. Now leave it be, let it go.'

'But sir, the weapons used were too sophisticated and too many things don't make sense. I will have full forensics within the next 48 hours and I am positive this will confirm my suspicions. I've had the weapons sent to Frankfurt University for more detailed analysis.'

'Klaus! This is clearly gang-related, so leave it alone. They are all scum; a few more dead will do no harm. Let's not waste any more of the taxpayer's money pursuing it. Just go home and leave it alone.'

Later that day Julia rang Klaus at his apartment.

'Klaus, it's Julia. I thought you should know that Junge has instructed that all the findings from the autopsies and the forensics are to be sent to him direct and with no further distribution, not even to you. He has never done that before why would he want this stuff?'

'I don't know Julia, but he is convinced that it is all gang-related and has instructed me to drop it all. This all stinks. Did anything unusual come out of your investigations?'

'Nothing really. They all died from gunshot wounds and I have sent the bullets to ballistics for matching. I haven't had the DNA analysis back yet. The dental records are a different matter. With the exception of our woman with the handbag the other bodies have all had new dental work and there's no way we can identify them, not even by the type of work. Our woman's dental work is different, we think it's British. The amalgam used in the fillings is unique to the UK.'

Shortly after that, Bertrand called Klaus and confirmed

that the serial number on the Rolex watch was from a batch exported to London and specifically to Selfridge's department store. He had asked a contact he had in the Met to see if he could track down who the watch was sold to.

36 Hours later

It had now been nearly 2 days since the shootout at Engel. Julia had just received an email from Frankfurt University with the detailed forensic report on the weapons. It confirmed what the forensic guys had originally thought. The serial numbers had been expertly removed and even the University's state-of-the-art technology could not produce any results.

She copied the report on to two discs, including her own autopsy and forensic results. One copy would go to Junge and she would give the other to Klaus. She then rang Klaus and arranged to meet at a café they frequented. Over coffee, she briefed Klaus.

'The guys have done a very good job on identifying one of the women. They recovered the remains of a press card, she's a British journalist and her name is Emma Swift. She's based in London.'

Klaus sipped his coffee. 'I'll get Willi onto it.'

Julia also told him about the serial numbers on the guns.

'That really confirms your view that this is not gang-related. To remove serial numbers leaving no residual evidence requires very sophisticated technology, and I mean very sophisticated. There is no way the gangs could get access to that type of kit. Do you think it's government related?'

'It could well be. It would certainly explain Junge's interest in suppressing the whole affair. But, if it is, who was shooting at whom and what's a British journalist doing there? Anything come in on the comms kit?'

'Sorry, yes. They've never seen such sophisticated kit, especially the cell phone. That's all they have at present. Their boss reckons it's the sort of stuff the security services would have access to and not necessarily our own.'

'Have you given Junge your report yet?'

'It was delivered to him late this afternoon.'

'Thank you Julia, I owe you.'

'You owe me nothing, but what are you going to do next?'

'I'm not sure. I will certainly have to be careful with Junge. I think I'll contact an old friend of mine in the Met in London. Aren't we required to report the death of a British national to the British authorities?'

'Yes we are, but I assume Junge will do that as he has all the files now.'

* * * * * * *

Junge opened the package and removed the contents. He read Julia's reports - very thorough and as professional as ever. Hopefully that will be the end of it, he thought. He completed his report, removed all of Julia's pages and handed the incident file to his secretary who sent the document to the central archive. He took Julia's paper documents to the shredder room and disposed of them. He then heavily scratched the surface of the disc and left the building. Once in the street, he dropped it into a rubbish bin and called Wunsche from a telephone kiosk.

'There is no indication as to who the other people are except that the woman is an English journalist called Emma Swift' he told him. 'I have taken over the investigation and I have all the documentation. It will all be buried and the file will be closed as a gang-related killing.'

'Make sure there are no loose ends, no paper trails. I'll take it from here. Well done Karl.' Wunsche rang off and called Emmerich.

'It's Wunsche. I have spoken with our man in Nuremberg and he has confirmed that the incident is being viewed as gang-related. He also confirmed that there were only three bodies in the car. One was a woman and the forensic people have confirmed from a press pass that it is Swift. We now know that Cunningham flew back to London on a BA flight from Munich.'

'Good, now find me Cunningham.' Emmerich rang off.

FSB Headquarters

Ivan Terpinski entered Organov's office.

'Cunningham is alive. London has reported that he logged on to the internet and has been researching the Amber Room again. We've tracked him to a London address.' He looked at his notes. 'The home of a Martin Hunt, he's a journalist with the *Independent* newspaper. I've diverted half of team Kilo from surveillance of Cunningham's apartment and they are now positioned outside Hunt's building. I must assume that Cunningham is staying with Hunt. What do you want us to do next, Vladimir?'

Organov stood up and paced up and down in front of his desk, rubbing the top of his head.

'Keep the teams on surveillance in both locations. It will only be a matter of time before Totenkopf pick up on Cunningham. I wouldn't be at all surprised if they have people watching his flat as we speak. Warn the teams and ensure everyone is armed. We must assume that Cunningham has something from the Nuremberg bank, but what? I want Cunningham lifted as soon as possible and, if he is with Hunt, take him as well. I want no rough stuff, they're not our enemy, and we need Cunningham's cooperation. Brief Uri to have them taken to the Chelsea safe house; tell him I'm going to London. Get him to meet me at the airport. Have we still got that telephone tap on Eberle?'

'Yes, do you want us to up the surveillance on him?' Ivan asked.

'Let's do that just in case Cunningham knows about Eberle.'

The FSB had discovered some five years previously that Eberle was a member of the original Verglas team, and had kept him under constant surveillance ever since. They were principally after the officers of the Verglas group and were hoping he might be contacted by one of them. But they had searched his house twice and found nothing related to Verglas.

New Scotland Yard, Headquarters of the Metropolitan Police

Detective Chief Superintendent Richard White returned to his office having just left a boring and unproductive meeting on community policing where he had had to listen to some bleeding-heart liberal fast-tracked woman Commander pontificate on softly-softly policing. Although only in his late thirties, Richard was considered an outstanding policeman. He was no liberal and believed in tough policing. He thought the Met was going soft. He grabbed a mug of coffee and returned to his desk.

Richard was head of the Trident Operational Command Unit (OCU), dealing with gun-related activity within London's communities. So far it was targeting only gun-related murders in the black community.

He picked up a message left on his desk. An Inspektor Klaus Schmidt had called from Germany, a telephone number was scrawled beneath the name. He hadn't seen Klaus since the time he had spent a month in Hamburg on a fact-finding mission to see how the Bundespolizei was handling gang crime. They had both got on really well but had only maintained sporadic contact. He rang the Nuremberg number.

'Inspektor Klaus Schmidt speaking.'

'Klaus, its Richard White, how are you?'

'I'm very well. It's good to hear from you.'

After a short chat, Klaus raised the Emma Swift issue and outlined what had happened at Engel.

'It's very strange, Richard. There is almost a cover-up going on, and there's an obsession that the whole thing is gang-related. Sure we have a gang problem but this was much more sophisticated. There were no identity documents on any of those killed with the exception of one person, who we identified as Emma Swift, a British journalist. Her press card was badly damaged but we have the last few digits. They are 456Z.'

Richard took note of the number. 'I'll get it checked out for you. Do you want me to follow it up?'

'If you can I would be very grateful. We just don't know how she got involved in all of this.' They rang off.

White tasked one of his officers to track down details of Emma Swift. It only took an hour and a few phone calls to confirm that Emma worked for the *Independent*. Richard rang the newspaper and was eventually connected to Mike Whittle, the Editor.

'Mr Whittle, I'm Detective Chief Superintendent Richard White of the Met. Can you confirm if Emma Swift works for your newspaper?'

'Yes she does. What's this all about, is she in trouble?'

'Emma Swift was shot dead two days ago in an incident in a village in Germany.'

'Oh my God, how dreadful! What happened?'

'At this stage I can't give you any more information as it is currently under investigation by the German police. Do you have any details of her next of kin?'

'I know that both her parents are dead and I'm not aware of any other relatives. She was an only child and was not married or in any long-term romantic relationship. Probably the closest person to a relative was a friend of hers, another journalist, Jack Cunningham. I don't have an address for him but I may well have his mobile number; he's done some work for us in the past.'

Whittle found the number and gave it to Richard.

'Mr Whittle, do you know why Miss Swift was in Germany?'

'Yes I do. She was following a lead about Second World War Nazi gold. You may be aware that it's rumoured that at the close of the war the Nazis secreted large quantities of looted Jewish gold. Emma had a lead. Do you think this could be related?'

'I don't know Mr Whittle, but you have been most helpful. I may need to get back to you.'

Richard White rang off and called Jack's number, only getting his answering service. He left a message asking to be called. He then rang Klaus and recounted what Whittle had told him.

'This makes more sense, Richard' said Klaus. 'So she was researching Nazi gold. It has long been thought that the rumours of gold hoards were true but none have been discovered. Thanks for all this, I owe you. Perhaps I can get over to London in the not-too-distant future and between us we can destroy a few brain cells.' Klaus fondly remembered the very social times he and Richard had had in Hamburg. 'I'll be in touch and thank you again.'

Münich

Frederic Kleinfurt walked out of the corporate headquarters of IG Garben, one of the worlds largest pharmaceutical companies, and climbed into his chauffeur-driven black Bentley. He settled back into the black leather upholstery, opened his briefcase and extracted some business papers.

Frederic Kleinfurt was a very powerful and wealthy man. As Chairman of IG Garben he was on speaking terms with the German Chancellor and other heads of state within Europe. He moved in very important business and social circles and had been listed by *Der Spiegel* as one of Europe's most influential people. When Frederic spoke, people listened.

What people didn't know was that he was also head of the Totenkopf organisation; Wunsche knew him as Emmerich.

Frederic picked up a phone from the centre console. This was no ordinary phone. It had a scramble capability, and whenever a call was made to it or from it, the call would be routed via a minimum of five locations. Anyone who was able to successfully monitor the call would eventually track it to an address in Düsseldorf which had been a house and was now a small car park. Frederic dialled a number.

'Wunsche speaking.'

'Franz it's Emmerich, have you found Cunningham yet?'

'We have two teams in London, one on standby and the other watching his apartment building. Nothing to report as yet.'

'I'm sending you another team. I want you to go to London immediately and run the operation from there. I want Cunningham found and just watched for the present, do not try to snatch him. I am going to try a different approach, so I am also sending the Cleaner to London. Call me when you are in London and as soon as you spot Cunningham.'

Frederic replaced the handset. Wunsche knew about the Cleaner and so there was nothing more to be said. The Cleaner's true identity was not known to Wunsche. He didn't even know whether the Cleaner was a man or woman. What he did know was that the Cleaner was only called in if there was something serious going on.

Frederic spoke to his chauffeur. 'Wolf, let's go meet Fräulein Balmer. The usual place.'

At the age of 65, Frederic was too young to have served in the war. He had been born just after the end of it. Kleinfurt was not his real surname. His father was Panzer Glick, one of the most highly-decorated SS Panzer commanders in the Adolf Hitler Liebstandarte Regiment. He had been killed during the Ardennes offensive, unaware that his wife was pregnant.

Every member of the Totenkopf had to be a member of the wartime SS, although most of these were now dead, or to have had a direct blood-line to a member. Wolf, his driver, was the grandson of an SS Hauptscharführer who had served with Glick. Frederic had risen as rapidly through the ranks of the Totenkopf as he had in business. A combination of Totenkopf influence in the background and his own considerable talents had taken him into investment banking and on to become the youngest chairman in IG Garben's history where he had reigned supreme for some ten years.

He stood just under six feet, had a lean body and was immaculately clothed in a dark grey bespoke suit from Savile Row in London. His shirt was made for him by Turnbull and Asser, also in London, and his tie was Hermés. He sported a 1940s Patek Philippe wristwatch. Frederic was a very urbane and elegant man.

The car stopped outside Boettners' restaurant which had been at number 9 Pfisterstrasse since it had been founded in 1901. It was Frederic's favourite restaurant and he had dined there regularly since his wife had died from breast cancer four years earlier. He was greeted by the Maître d'Hôte, Willi Schmidt.

'Herr Kleinfurt, always a pleasure to see you. Your usual table is ready and your guest has arrived and is seated. I took the liberty of giving her a glass of champagne I hope that is in order. Your normal burgundy, sir? '

'As always, very considerate of you Willi but I think we'll stick to champagne. Would you please bring us a bottle of the Gosset Celebris Brut Rosé.'

Frederic went to his table and greeted his guest. 'Deborah, how wonderful to see you, and as radiant as ever. Thank you for coming at such short notice.' He kissed her on both cheeks.

Deborah was 35, with short blonde hair and eyes of aquamarine. She was about five feet ten and had a superb figure. Her stunning looks had not gone unnoticed by the other male diners. She was more than just a beauty; she was also a very successful international lawyer who specialised in mergers and acquisitions. Her job took her all around the world, which was very useful as a cover for a member of the Totenkopf.

Her grandfather, Johann Hartenstein, had been Himmler's personal architect and the brain behind the reconstruction of Wewelsburg. Deborah Balmer's respected position in the Totenkopf was the result of Kleinfurt's mentoring of her and the natural skills and enthusiasm she displayed during her training at a Totenkopf camp. Her instructors were deeply impressed by her ability with unarmed combat. It was one thing to be adept with weapons but to kill required mental detachment and ruthlessness.

Deborah's first test had been to kill a German journalist who was getting a little too interested in Totenkopf activities. While her instructors shadowed her from a distance, she used her feminine charms and picked up the journalist at a bar in the Reeperbahn in Hamburg. He had suggested they went to his apartment, so they walked to a dimly-lit side street where he had parked his car. As he was opening the car door with his back to her, she took out a long thin stiletto blade and drove it into the base of his skull and up into his brain. She wiped the blade clean on the dead man's jacket and then calmly walked to the main street where she hailed a cab and went to the airport to take a flight back to München. From that first job she had been used on numerous assignments to 'sort things out' for her masters. Now only Totenkopf's inner circle of five knew that Deborah was the woman known to the rest of the organisation as the Cleaner.

The champagne arrived and they ordered lunch. Their conversation throughout lunch was very general. Once coffee had been served and the waiters had withdrawn, Frederic turned to the matter at hand.

'Deborah, I want you to go to London immediately and await my call.' Frederic then briefed her on the events of the last week and also about the Verglas file.

'I want you to recover the file and tie up any loose ends. As we speak, Wunsche should be on his way to London. I will have an additional team in place by tomorrow. He knows you are coming.'

Deborah rose from the table. 'I'll call you when I get to London.' She kissed Frederic on his cheek and left the restaurant, Frederic following shortly after.

London

Jack picked up the message from Richard White on his cell phone. He was sitting at the kitchen table with Martin nursing a hangover. Much of the previous evening had been spent drowning his sorrows and being, Martin thought, understandably maudlin over Emma.

'That's blown it,' he said. 'I have a message from a Chief Superintendent who wants to speak to me about Emma. Sounds as though the Germans have identified her body and contacted the Met.'

'You can't tell him the truth because he'll wonder why you left the country and why you didn't contact the German police. And what you were doing there in the first place.'

'I know Martin. I think I'll have to plead ignorance and hope they don't check any flight details.'

Jack rang Richard White.

'Chief Superintendent, it's Jack Cunningham. I'm sorry I wasn't available to take your call. Is Emma in trouble?'

'I'm afraid that Miss Swift has been killed. I was told by her newspaper editor that you are the closest to family she has.'

There was a long silence on the phone. Jack's silence was genuine as memories of Emma came flooding back.

'Mr Cunningham?'

'Sorry, Chief Superintendent. You have to understand this is a complete shock. I cared about her very much. Tell me, tell me how she died and where? I haven't actually seen her for a few days. She had gone to Germany on an assignment for her newspaper; something to do with Nazi gold I think.'

'She was shot in an incident in a village, along with a number of other people. So far she is the only one the Germans have been able to identify.'

'Superintendent, do you have a contact so I can try and get

her body repatriated?'

Richard gave Jack Klaus Scmidt's number. 'I'm very sorry Mr Cunningham, I have no more details on the case but I will contact you when I have further information. Inspector Schmidt will probably be able to tell you more.'

Jack rang Klaus immediately he got off the phone.

'Inspector, my name is Jack Cunningham. Chief Superintendent White gave me your number. I've just heard the dreadful news from him about Emma Swift. I'm the closest that Emma has to next of kin. Do you know when I will be able to bring her home?'

'Herr Cunningham, my condolences. I am sure you will appreciate that the circumstances of Miss Swift's death require an autopsy and forensic investigation so, at present, I can't tell you when her body will be released. Give me your contact details including your email address and I will contact you personally when arrangements can be made for Miss Swift's repatriation.'

'Thank you Inspector, I appreciate it.'

'Herr Cunningham, a question, do you know where Miss Swift went to in Germany?'

'Not really, but I knew she flew to Düsseldorf. I don't know when she left.'

'Thank you Herr Cunningham, I will call you in due course. Goodbye.'

Jack turned to Martin and breathed a sigh of relief .

'I think that went OK. The inspector said he would contact me when Emma's body can be returned to the UK.'

Klaus thought it rather strange that Cunningham had not asked for more details as to what had happened to Miss Swift, particularly as he was a journalist. He called Willi over.

'We've got confirmation from the Brits about Emma Swift. She's a journalist with the *Independent* in London. The really interesting bit is that she was in Germany researching Nazi gold.'

'Maybe she had found out something that resulted in her death, which would make more sense than it being gang-related. We've come up with nothing on the other bodies; it's as if they never existed.'

'Willi, get someone to trawl the hotels and try and establish when she entered the country. She flew into Düsseldorf. Don't you have links on *Der Spiegel*? I vaguely remember an article on Nazi gold and a post-war Nazi underground movement.'

'Leave it with me. My cousin is a journalist on the newspaper.'

★ ★ ★ ★ ★ ★ ★

Martin got up from the table and, slipping on his jacket, said 'I've got to go to the office. I'll be back about six.'

'I have a better idea,' said Jack. 'After last night, I really need the hair of the dog. Let's meet at Donovan's.' Martin waved an acknowledgement as he left. Jack spent the rest of the afternoon trying to do further research on the SS and its link to the Teutonic knights. He found it difficult to concentrate as his mind constantly wandered back to times he had spent with Emma. He looked at his phone, at the last text message she had sent him, and realised it was almost out of power. He tried Martin's charger but it was incompatible. What a bloody nuisance, he thought. He'd left his main charger in the hotel room at Nuremberg. Why hadn't somebody invented a universal charger? His spare one was in his flat. He had no choice but to get it.

He left Martin's apartment and hailed a black cab to take him to his apartment block in Knightsbridge. He didn't notice a dark blue Audi with two men in it parked outside the block.

Jack asked the cab to wait and nipped into his apartment, grabbed the charger and was back in the cab in less than five minutes. He didn't see the Audi slip in behind the cab as he headed for Mayfair and Brown's Hotel. Nor did he notice a Ford Fiesta which was following the cab ahead of the FSB Alpha team in the Audi. The second FSB team, Golf, had seen the Fiesta and passed this information to the Alpha team. They called Roly at the safe house.

'We've picked up a potential threat. Team Alpha is following Cunningham, but there's another party involved. We are following them.'

Roly relayed this information to Organov, who had only just arrived from Moscow and was now seated beside him. They also knew that Cunningham had contacted Eberle, and they now had his cellphone number.

The men in the Fiesta had reported into Wunsche who ordered another team to take over from the Fiesta when Cunningham reached his destination.

Deborah had just arrived in London and was at the Lanesborough Hotel. She always stayed there when she was in London. She liked the Library Bar and found the hotel convenient for the City and the West End.

Her cell phone rang. 'It's Wunsche. Cunningham has just arrived at Donovan's Bar, Brown's Hotel. He's alone.'

Jack entered Donovan's Bar. Ted greeted him with a smile. 'Hello stranger, it's been at least a week my friend. How are you?

Jack climbed on to a stool at the end of bar. 'God Jack,' Ted said, 'You look like shit!'

'Yup, I feel like it as well.' Jack looked at the mirror behind the bar. His eyes were bloodshot and there were dark shadows under his eyes. Anticipating Jack's needs, Ted pulled down the Bombay Sapphire and Lillet. Jack handed over his cell phone and charger and asked Ted if he would charge it for him.

'No problem. Emma joining you?'

'Not tonight.' He felt a great wave of emotion flood over him as he realised she would never join him here again. He wasn't ready to tell Ted about Emma. 'I'm going gay tonight. Martin is joining me at six.'

Ted placed a martini, straight up with three queen olives, on the bar. 'There you go, one heart starter.' He turned away to deal with an order from one of the waitresses. This suited Jack for the moment, as he wanted to collect his thoughts. He had asked the concierge on the way in to book a table for him and Martin at Chez Gérard for eight. They frequently dined there, as they cooked the best steak frites in the area.

Emma had often been with them. His mind turned back to her and to the events of the last few days. He suddenly felt very weary.

Wunsche had left an envelope for Deborah in the reception of the Lanesborough with photographs and biographical details of Cunningham and Hunt. She had memorised the data and shredded the material in the hotel's business centre. She hailed a cab and fifteen minutes later she was walking through the entrance of Brown's.

'Penny for your thoughts,' said Ted. 'You haven't touched your martini.'

Jack smiled and picked up his drink. He had been so preoccupied that he hadn't noticed the woman who was now seated some two stools away from him. She was quite stunning with short blonde hair and very elegantly dressed.

Ted approached her. 'Good evening madam. What may I get for you?' He might be offhand with his friends, but with other customers he was never over-familiar. He was the consummate professional and extremely charming, even more so in the presence of an attractive woman.

She sighed. 'I've had a pretty tough day. What would you recommend to lift my spirits?' Jack noticed a slight accent to her English.

'Always champagne, madam.'

'I agree, but on this occasion I fancy something stronger; a martini perhaps. Do you have T10?'

'Of course.' Ted reached for the tall, slim green bottle.

'Perfect, then let it be a T10, straight up with a twist.'

The lady knows her gin, thought Jack and said, 'May I compliment you on your choice of gin?'

The blonde turned to face Jack. He was struck by her ice-blue eyes.

'Thank you.' She looked at his glass. 'I take it you're not drinking a vodka martini?'

'Absolutely not. I prefer Sapphire T10 is too oily for me. Are you staying at the hotel?'

'No, I'm at the Lanesborough but Donovan's was recommended to me by a colleague.'

'The Library Bar at the Lanesborough is excellent, so it must have been quite a recommendation for you to come here.'

'It makes a pleasant change. Are you a guest here?'

Ted interjected. 'He might as well be with the amount of time he spends here. Jack is one of my best customers. He probably keeps the British gin industry in business.'

'I'm not sure that's a compliment' said the blonde, smiling.

'Rapidly changing the subject,' Jack said, 'I take it you are in London on business?'

'Yes I am. I visit London at least once a month.'

'And the rest of the time? '

'I'm often in New York but I live in München. I'm a corporate lawyer and I spend a lot of time on the road. Fortunately my clients are based in interesting cities and are very generous with expenses.'

'Forgive me, I'm being very nosy. My name is Jack Cunningham.' Jack proffered his hand.

'Deborah, Deborah Balmer. How do you do, Jack Cunningham. What brings you to Donovan's?'

She really is quite gorgeous, thought Jack. He noticed a very nice emerald ring. There was no wedding ring.

'Best watering hole in London with one of the best mixologists in the business although I think even Ted would have to take second place to Salvatore Calabrese. Salvatore used to run the Library. He is probably the king of cocktails. I live and work in London.'

Ted gave Deborah her martini. 'Be careful with Jack, he is an investigative journalist and very inquisitive.'

Deborah smiled and sipped her martini. 'Excellent, truly excellent; really hits the spot. Thank you Ted.' She paused and turned back to Jack. 'Jack Cunningham… didn't you write a major piece on corruption in the city a few years ago?'

The brief left at her hotel had provided a potted history of Cunningham and even included a précis of the said article. Jack was impressed.

'That's me, I'm interested that you read it, and even more so that you have remembered it. I made a lot of enemies. It scuppered any future access to the City.'

'I didn't say I liked it, Mr Cunningham!' She smiled.

I like this woman, thought Jack. She's sassy, intelligent and very sexy.

Deborah moved to the stool beside him and they verbally sparred their way through another martini. Jack's cell phone rang, and Ted handed it to him. Jack excused himself and went to the lobby.

It was Martin. He was stuck in the office and would probably have to meet Jack back at the apartment.

Jack returned to the bar. 'Sorry about that, my date has just stood me up, friend of mine, a fellow journalist.' Ted was making floppy wrist signals to Deborah who started to laugh. Jack quickly turned around to catch Ted's camp display. He turned back to Deborah.

'Don't worry, I'm not gay but I can't say the same about Ted.' He smiled and stuck his tongue out at the barman. 'Bitch!' hissed Ted, turning to take an order from one of the waitresses.

Jack and Deborah continued their animated conversation. She was certainly very good company and just what he needed at the moment.

'I know you might think it a bit forward but I have a table booked at a nearby restaurant and, as my friend can't make it and I don't like dining alone, would you care to join me as my guest?'

'I'd be delighted, Mr Cunningham.' She was still grinning at Ted. 'Sorry Ted, it looks like the gay man gets the girl.' Jack laughed. 'The restaurant is just around the corner, it's a short walk.'

'It will do me good to get some fresh air after this amount of gin, I usually only have one martini. Let me pay for the drinks.' She offered cash to Ted and told him to keep the change.

Deborah was always very careful about paying with a card. Cards could be traced, so apart from her legitimate activities as a lawyer, she paid for most things using cash. She never left any unnecessary electronic or paper trails.

They said their farewells to Ted and stepped out into the cool and refreshing night air. Brown's was on Albemarle Street, and Chez Gérard was in Dover Street, which ran parallel. As they walked down the road, Deborah slipped her arm through Jack's.

Behind them, a man got out of a BMW and followed, keeping ten metres back. The street was just crowded enough to ensure he did not look obvious. The BMW drove off and went around the corner at the end of the street.

Wunsche had kept Emmerich fully apprised of the developing situation and was instructed to kidnap Cunningham and the woman. Emmerich had not told Wunsche that the woman was the Cleaner but he had made it clear that no one was to be hurt. He didn't want a repeat of the débâcle in Engels.

Jack and Deborah reached the end of Albemarle Street and turned left down Grafton Street, Deborah on the outside. The BMW had parked on the left side of the street, and, as Deborah and Jack came alongside, the rear left door of the car was flung open blocking Deborah's way.

A man in the rear of the car pointed a gun at Deborah's stomach and told her to get in. Jack suddenly felt a hard object jammed against his spine as the man who had been following them positioned himself immediately behind him. The object was a Glock automatic. The man pressed it harder into Jack's back and told him to get into the car. The door was closed and the man got into the front left passenger seat.

The BMW slowly pulled away from the kerb and proceeded down Hay Hill, stopping at the lights at the junction with Berkeley Street.

The man in the back of the car pressed his gun into Deborah's side. 'Please don't try anything foolish Mr Cunningham, it will take only a split second for me to destroy this woman's spine. We want you and we don't care what happens to this woman. I'm sure you don't want another woman's death on your conscience.'

Jack said nothing, thinking furiously. These men were clearly involved with what had happened in Engels. He stared straight ahead as the car turned right into Berkeley Street and then left into Berkeley Square, which was as busy as usual for that time of the night. They turned into Fitzmaurice Street, passing the old MI5 headquarters. Following them about 30 metres behind was the FSB Alpha team in the Audi.

The BMW drove into Bolton Street and headed towards Piccadilly and Green Park.

The Alpha team leader was in contact with Organov.

'Where are they heading?'

'Piccadilly, but I am not sure whether they will go east or west.' He paused. 'Hang on, they've turned right, they're going towards Hyde Park Corner, Knightsbridge way.'

Organov instructed Roly to place Golf team in reserve and to instruct another surveillance team, who were in a blacked-out Range Rover in The Mall in St James's, to proceed up Constitution Hill towards Hyde Park Corner. There were four men in the Range Rover, heavily armed with non-Russian weapons and equipment. The team were fluent in English with no trace of a foreign accent and their clothes were Western made. In order that they could not be identified as Russian, their dental work had been completely redone. Everyone was an expert in his respective field and all had served at one time with Spetsnaz, Russia's Special Forces.

The BMW proceeded down Piccadilly, keeping pace with the other traffic.

Organov instructed the two teams to tail the BMW, each team leapfrogging the other. Under normal circumstances a good vehicle surveillance team might use up to five cars so that the target could not easily pick up the fact that someone was following. They didn't have that luxury but, with so much traffic, they hoped they might be lucky and remain undetected even though the traffic also made it difficult to maintain contact with the target. Organov was pretty sure that Cunningham and the woman were being kept alive until whatever Cunningham knew had been extracted by Totenkopf and, after that, they would be killed. Provided luck stayed with them, the FSB would be able to track the BMW to its final destination.

The BMW entered the Hyde Park underpass just as the Range Rover reached Hyde Park Corner. The Audi team directed the Range Rover towards Knightsbridge where, as they passed the Lanesborough Hotel, the BMW exited the underpass. The Range Rover team leader communicated that the target had been spotted and took the lead while Alpha team's Audi pulled back behind the Rover. As the lead vehicle, the Range Rover team leader maintained a running commentary in order that everyone knew where the target vehicle was heading. This enabled any other teams to join the operation easily.

At the top of Sloane Street the BMW took the road towards High Street Kensington. The Rover followed and the

Audi continued into Knightsbridge where there was little traffic, accelerating as they passed Harrods. The Alpha team leader told the Rover team that he would take over the lead position just beyond the Albert Hall.

The BMW continued past Knightsbridge Barracks but slowed down because of heavy traffic, not helped by roadworks at the junction with Trevor Place. No one spoke inside the BMW and Jack gave a reassuring squeeze to Deborah's hand, although he had no idea where they were going or what was going to happen to them.

The Audi made excellent progress, executing a right turn by the Victoria & Albert Museum and accelerating up Exhibition Road. They stopped at the traffic lights at the top of the hill and looked for the BMW.

'Damn,' said the leader, 'the target is to our right.' The last thing he wanted was to be ahead of the target. It would mean they would have to allow the BMW to pass them, with the potential threat of discovery.

The lights turned green and the Audi turned left as the Rover team confirmed that the BMW was approaching the Royal Geographical Society building, and the Audi being ahead of them. As if they were dropping off or picking someone up, the Audi pulled up outside the Baglioni Hotel. The BMW passed them and the front passenger casually looked to his left, briefly catching the eye of the Audi driver. There was no hint of recognition, even though the Audi driver recognised the passenger from the stakeout at Jack's apartment.

The Audi team leader decided that it would be better if the Range Rover maintained pole position. They could leapfrog them later.

The BMW proceeded down High Street Kensington and

headed towards Hammersmith Broadway. For no apparent reason the traffic suddenly cleared, and the Audi and Range Rover found that they were now in very light traffic and potentially exposed to discovery. Both vehicles dropped back far enough to enable them to see the BMW.

The Audi now took pole position. The BMW was travelling at 30 mph in a 40 mph zone, a deliberate tactic to see if anyone was tailing them. Traffic was overtaking the BMW, leaving both the Range Rover and the Audi in view.

The Audi team leader spoke with Organov. 'They have slowed right down and there is little traffic. We've also had to slow down. It can't be long before the target spots us.'

Organov told the Range Rover team to break off, go south and run parallel on the Cromwell Road, heading for Hammersmith Broadway. The Audi leader continued a running commentary so that the Range Rover could get in position to take over the surveillance. He hoped that the traffic would become heavier so the BMW wouldn't see them. They were approaching Hammersmith Broadway and the Audi was getting dangerously close to the BMW.

Suddenly, a cyclist rode off the pavement and across a zebra crossing in front of the BMW, causing the driver to brake hard. There was much swearing and waving of fists by the cyclist who continued on his way, mounting the pavement and nearly hitting a pedestrian, resulting in a stand up row with more expletives.

The sudden braking of the BMW had caught the Audi driver off guard and he had to brake hard to avoid hitting the BMW. The driver of the BMW looked in his rear-view mirror and recognised the Audi. He spoke to the team leader.

'It may be nothing but there is an Audi behind us and he

has been with us since we passed the Baglioni Hotel. I noticed it parked outside a hotel and then he pulled out behind us. It may be just a coincidence.' The team leader adjusted his wing mirror so he could see the Audi.

'OK, let's test him. Do a U-turn and then turn right at the next set of lights. It will take us down to the Talgarth Road and then head for the M40.'

The BMW moved forward slowly. The driver suddenly did a U-turn and accelerated away.

'Fuck, we've been rumbled,' said the Audi team leader. He spoke on the net. 'Target is now heading east at speed, he's clocked us. He has just turned right down Edith Road and is heading your way. I am blocked in and will have to continue to Hammersmith Broadway. I just hope the target will continue in that direction.'

'So do I,' responded the Range Rover team leader. 'I am west of Edith Road and can't do a U-turn there's a central barrier.'

Organov interrupted. 'We mustn't lose them.' He instructed the Audi to break cover and continue the pursuit with a view to intercepting the BMW. To hell with the final destination, they mustn't lose Cunningham.

The Audi was boxed in to its right by a Mini which, even with the Audi indicating right, had no intention of relinquishing its place in the traffic. 'Fuck her, said the Audi driver as he cut across the front of the Mini tearing off the left wing, much to the shock of the brunette who was driving it. The Audi increased its speed and turned right at the lights, ignoring the red signal and narrowly missing two cyclists. They caught sight of the BMW in the distance as it turned east into Talgarth Road. The Audi leapt forward down the narrow street, removing the wing mirrors from a couple of parked cars.

They ignored the red light at the junction and turned left in pursuit of the BMW, colliding side-on with another car and pushing it into a van.

At this point they could see the BMW some 300 metres ahead. They accelerated to 60 mph. Fortunately the traffic was light so they were closing the distance between themselves and the BMW very rapidly. The team leader kept up his commentary. The Range Rover had reached Hammersmith Broadway but was now stuck in heavy traffic.

The BMW driver spotted the Audi and accelerated. 'Continue towards the M40' said the BMW team leader. The driver turned left into Warwick Road and headed north towards the Shepherd's Bush roundabout. The Audi followed as the BMW weaved its way through the increasingly heavy traffic.

'I'm going to take a gamble that the BMW will try to head west again' said the Audi team leader. 'Hang on. He's crossed the Shepherd's Bush roundabout and is heading for the M40.' He instructed the Range Rover to clear Hammersmith Broadway and head north to join the M40 at Hanger Lane. With luck he would pick up the BMW there.

Organov ordered a 'cleaning' team which had been positioned in a white van in Chiswick to head for the same junction on the M40. The task was to intercept the BMW, eliminate the team in it and rescue Cunningham and the woman he had with him.

The BMW was travelling in excess of 70 mph as it headed towards the M40 junction. As it passed the exit from the Westfield shopping mall the driver intentionally struck a motorcyclist a glancing blow, making him lose control and career into the cars that had just left the exit ramp.

The BMW driver smiled as he looked in his mirror and saw

the mayhem he had created. 'That should slow the Audi down,' he muttered as they entered the ramp for the M40, travelling west.

The Audi was now out of their sight but they were unaware that it had managed to avoid the accident and had also seen them joining the M40 westbound. The FSB team leader relayed this to the Range Rover team and Organov, who came on air.

'I want you to box in the BMW and take it out, and keep up your commentary as the cleaners are also heading for the M40. You will have to take out the BMW before the Hanger Lane junction, and as close as possible to it. Zulu Alpha, all call signs acknowledge.'

'Zulu Alpha' was the code for the destruction of all evidence, including the elimination of the targets. The teams acknowledged the instruction as the Audi joined the M40 and the Range Rover pulled over on to the hard shoulder of the up-ramp of the M40 junction at White City. The Range Rover was positioned low enough so that it would not be seen by the BMW as it passed. The white van was approximately five minutes away from the Hanger Lane junction.

The BMW was now doing in excess of 80 mph, but the Audi was catching up. As the BMW passed the White City junction, the Range Rover accelerated rapidly to get alongside it. They had less than a mile before they reached the Hanger Lane junction. The BMW had to slow down as the traffic got heavier which enabled both the Audi and the Range Rover to close the gap.

The Range Rover was only 20 metres from the BMW on its offside with the Audi some 30 metres to the rear. The rear side window of the Range Rover was wound down and two short bursts were fired from a suppressed Heckler & Koch 2013 automatic weapon. The 2013 fired caseless ammunition which left no empty cartridge cases as evidence. The bullets shredded both nearside tyres of the BMW making the driver swerve sideways into the traffic. The Audi rammed the front passenger side, driving the BMW into the central reservation where it skidded for about 30 metres with the Audi embedded in its side. The Range Rover switched on its hazard warning lights and skidded to a halt sideways across the first two lanes, totally blocking the motorway.

Two of the Range Rover team got out of the vehicle on the blind side and out of sight of the traffic behind them. They were less than 100 metres from the off ramp to the Hanger Lane junction where a white van was being driven down the exit ramp heading towards the crash site.

The impact had destroyed the BMW's front passenger door and most of the front left wing, both vehicles were write-offs. Deborah had been knocked forward, hitting the side of her head against the driver's headrest. Jack felt a sharp pain in his left knee where it had collided with the inside of his door. All of the BMW's airbags had activated.

Most of the impact had been taken by the front passenger who had been killed instantly. The driver had cracked his head against the side bulkhead and blood was streaming from a cut above his right eye. The other man had been jammed up against Deborah by the side-impact air bag. He had dropped his gun in the foot well and the airbag was preventing him retrieving it.

Jack's door was suddenly flung open and he and Deborah were wrenched out of the car and taken to the back of the white van which was now parked immediately behind the

Range Rover. Traffic had stopped on the road and people were getting out of their vehicles, some using their cell phones to call the emergency services.

Jack had had all the wind knocked out of him and he was unable to put up any resistance as he and Deborah were pushed into the van. He looked back and saw two men lean into the BMW; both were armed with silenced handguns. He guessed what assistance the passengers of the car were getting.

He and Deborah were seated on a bench running the length of the van. There was a man sitting opposite. The man who had got them out of the car climbed into the van, closing the doors behind him. The seated man was holding a small sub-machine gun in the crook of his arm.

The van pulled away and went up the ramp exiting the motorway before turning down a side street; it was soon clear of the crash site. The two FSB men from the Audi walked away from the crash site and climbed into the Range Rover.

As the first onlookers walked towards the crashed vehicles, they saw them explode with a low *kerrump*. The other FSB men had set off two Thermate-TH3 grenades, which comprised a mixture of thermite and pyrotechnic additives, greatly superior to standard thermite for incendiary purposes. To all intents and purposes the fuel tanks had ignited, destroying both the BMW and the Audi and burning the three bodies beyond recognition. Subsequent autopsies would reveal that the men had been shot, but by then it would not matter, and there was nothing that could identify them.

The Range Rover was soon clear of the area and following the white van up the exit ramp. The sound of sirens could be heard in the distance.

Jack slowly got his breath back. Recovering his senses, he looked at Deborah who was very pale. Blood was running down the side of her face. One of the men handed Jack a first-aid kit which he used to dress Deborah's wound; it did not appear as bad as the bleeding suggested.

He turned to the man. 'Who are you people, where are you taking us?'

He got no response. The rear of the van was windowless and the driver's compartment was isolated, so Jack had no idea where they were, let alone where they were going.

After some 35 minutes the van stopped and the rear doors were flung open. They found they were in a large space under a railway arch, confirmed by the sound of a train passing overhead. Jack guessed that it was probably an Underground train.

The space where they had stopped was like so many industrial units you found around London. They could have been anywhere in the city. In fact they were near Parsons Green, just off the Fulham Road.

They were marched into an office-type area lit by strip lighting. Apart from a girlie calendar which was three years out of date, there was nothing else on the walls. The furniture was all utilitarian.

One man took Jack's arm and directed him to a door at the end of the office, while the other took Deborah in the opposite direction and through another door.

'Hey, where are you taking her?' Jack said. He pulled himself away from the man and tried to follow Deborah, but was instantly pole-axed by a blow to his solar plexus which knocked all of the air out of him.

'Please Mr Cunningham, there is nothing to fear.' A man was standing in the doorway. 'The lady is going to receive treatment for her injury. I will have a medic with her shortly.'

The man helped Jack get up from his knees and escorted him through a door into a small office with a table and three chairs.

'Please take a seat, Mr Cunningham,' he said sitting down in a chair opposite Jack.

Jack could see a stainless steel thermos flask, two mugs, a couple of glasses, a bottle of Lagavullan malt whisky, a jar of Marmite and some savoury biscuits. The man poured whisky into the two tumblers and slid one to Jack.

'Are you all right, Mr Cunningham? I notice you are limping, do you need any medical assistance'?

Jack shook his head. 'I'm fine. A few explanations might be in order.'

'All in good time.' The man sipped his whisky. 'I do love Islay malts. Do have a drink Mr Cunningham. Or may I call you Jack?'

The man didn't pause to give Jack a chance to reply. 'Let me introduce myself. I am General Vladimir Organov and I'm a senior member of the FSB, the KGB as you once knew it. Please be assured that we wish you no harm. The crash and the shootings in Germany were part of our actions to protect you. I am very sorry about Miss Swift but I also lost four of my people that night.'

'What's this all about, who were the other people?' Jack gulped at his whisky and poured himself another.

'You don't mind do you?' He winced as the alcohol made contact with a small cut inside his mouth. He put a finger inside his mouth and it came out bloody.

'Before we go any further Jack, do you wish this lady, whose name I don't know, to join us?'

'That won't be necessary I only met her a few hours ago and I am not sure you need to know her name. She's an innocent bystander who just happened to be in the wrong place at the wrong time.'

'As you wish.' Organov rose and went to the door opening it slightly. He spoke briefly to a man standing outside. Then he returned to his seat, poured some more whisky for the two of them and began to tell Jack all about his department and their interest in the Amber Room.

'So you see Jack, we only wish to recover what rightfully belongs to Russia. The problem is that you have stumbled upon something that is not only of interest to us but also to the Totenkopf.' Although Jack already knew a lot about the Totenkopf he didn't want Organov to know that.

'Whilst we know a great deal about the Totenkopf, it is an extremely difficult organisation to penetrate. It operates very cleverly in discreet cells, very similar to the way your own Provisional IRA operated insofar that if one cell is compromised there is no link to any other. As a result the operators in each cell only know details about their specific cell. Totenkopf is also very wealthy and has access to considerable funds at very short notice. It has members who are at the highest levels in the German government, business, the police and security services. We suspect that there is a small group that controls the Totenkopf and that it may be based in Münich. Who these people are we have no idea. The people who shot Miss Swift and my people were Totenkopf, as were the people who abducted you this evening.'

A man entered the room and placed a basket covered with a linen napkin on the table.

'Are you hungry, Jack?' Organov lifted the napkin, revealing freshly buttered toast. Jack declined.

'What do want from me?'

'I just love your English toast with Marmite.' Organov spread the dark paste over the toast. 'It's one of my only weaknesses. Jack, I know that you were given something in Nuremberg. I don't know what exactly, and you may not be aware of its full significance, but I believe it will lead us to the Amber Room which I know you have been researching. Totenkopf also want what you have, otherwise it would have had you killed ages ago. Miss Swift's death was an accident and unintended. We also know that you have been investigating Wewelsburg and the Spear of Longinus as well. I would appreciate your help in locating the whereabouts of the Amber Room so that we may return it to Russia. We know of the Totenkopf's objectives to create a new Fourth Reich and our research shows that it is also interested in the Spear of Longinus or, as they call it, the Spear of Destiny. That may also be why it believes you have information on this and perhaps other artefacts. Do you Jack? Do you have information?'

Jack took another sip of his whisky. 'How do I know I can trust you and you are who you say you are? How do I know you are not Totenkopf? You speak Russian, but that means nothing.'

'You don't know Jack and, on current experiences you would be right not to trust us. Two strangers enter a restaurant and get you involved in a gun fight, and your friend loses her life. Now here we are in London involving you yet again with death and an unexplained conspiracy. Sometimes you do need to take things on trust. I will leave it at that for the moment.' He turned to the door. 'Roly?'

The door opened and a man entered. Organov slipped a piece of paper to Jack. 'This gentleman is Roly, and this is his cell phone number. If and when you are ready to help us or need assistance, call Roly on this number, any time of the day or night. You now know what Roly looks like, and he will be the only person you will deal with. Any strangers that he sends to assist you will make themselves known with the code word 'Parkinson.' We will continue to keep you and Mr Hunt under surveillance and my men have strict instructions to protect you, or you can agree to cooperate with us now and I will have you taken to a safe house until this affair is concluded.'

Jack thought for a moment and then said. 'I think I would prefer to run free for the present.' He stood up.

Organov also stood and held out his hand.

'You are at liberty to go.' Jack shook his hand.

'Your companion is waiting for you. Her injury is minor, although she will probably have a headache. Please look for signs of shock as I suspect that the past few hours are not an everyday experience for her. I will now return you to the van as you will appreciate that we cannot have you knowing our location. Goodnight Jack, I do hope we can get to a point where we can cooperate for mutual benefit.'

Roly escorted Jack to the van where Deborah was waiting for him.

'Are you all right?' he asked.

'Yes, I'm fine. But what's this all about?'

'I'll tell you later.'

A man climbed into the van with them and the doors were closed. They sat in silence until the van stopped and they were dropped off in a side street just off the Gloucester Road, near the University. Jack hailed a cab.

As they headed towards the Lanesborough, Jack apologised to Deborah. 'I'm really sorry that you've got involved in this. The least I can do is offer you an explanation if you want. I just don't want you exposed to any further danger.'

Deborah smiled. She seemed remarkably composed.

'I think this has been one of the more interesting evenings I have ever spent. I think we should talk about it over a drink at my hotel and you can tell me all about it'. She squeezed his hand.

A green Volvo estate followed the cab to the Lanesborough. On arrival a man and a woman got out of the car and followed Deborah and Jack into the hotel. Organov was very keen to identify who Deborah was, and had tasked the man and woman to keep tabs on both of them.

Jack and Deborah went into the Library Bar. Although it was now past eleven o'clock, in typical style the staff rustled up some sandwiches for them. A couple of glasses of a fine Oregon pinot noir helped them start to relax.

Jack told Deborah the story in outline. He did not report his exact conversation with Organo although he did let slip Organov's connection with the FSB. He described his relationship with Emma and explained who Martin was. He gave Deborah no indication as to the file's location, nor did he say that copies had been made.

It was after midnight when Jack had finished talking. Deborah had asked the odd question and had shown genuine concern for his welfare. He asked the waiter for the bill. 'I better get on my way, I'll call you in the morning to make sure you're OK.' Deborah took the bill. 'I'll get it, I'll put it on the room' she said. Jack stood to go. She placed her hand on his.

'Please don't go' she said, looking up at him. Jack paused and looked back at her. There was sadness in his eyes. "I'm not ready for this, Deborah, it's too soon after Emma's death. If you'll forgive me I must go.'

'Of course. I understand.' She placed her hand on his arm and gently kissed him on the cheek. 'Emma must have been very special.'

Jack walked her to the lift and left the hotel, followed by Organov's man. He joined his female companion who was now waiting outside the hotel in the car. She called Vladimir who instructed her to keep a tail on Cunningham. He also instructed them to keep their eyes open for any Totenkopf personnel.

Organov sent another team to the hotel to keep an eye on Deborah Balmer. He had not yet been able to find out who she was but it would only be a matter of time before he would have her full profile.

FSB, London safe house

Uri briefed Vladimir. 'The woman is Deborah Balmer. She is 35 years of age and a German national born in Stuttgart. Both her parents are deceased and she is an only child. We have no details on them other than her father was wealthy and before he retired had been a freelance architect. He was in his sixties when she was born. He was old enough to have served during the Great Patriotic War, but there is no record of his military service. She is an M&A lawyer for Macklin & Schweinfort GMBH.'

'M&A, Uri what the hell is that'? Organov sipped his tea. He was on his third slice of toast and Marmite.

'Sorry sir, Mergers & Acquisitions. Her company is based in Münich but it has offices in all the major financial cities in the world. It is considered one of the top M&A firms. They have an office in the City.'

Uri consulted his notes. 'It's in Rood Lane where her cab dropped her. Nikolai and Vanya are on her. We have no more information on Balmer, but Central is checking out her company and will track down her home address and do the usual search. Do you want her address in Münich searched?'

Organov was naturally suspicious and never took anything for granted. 'Yes, search her place. Good, Uri, it's now just a waiting game; I do hope Cunningham sees sense. If Totenkopf get him it will find out his secret and then he's a dead man. Where is he at the moment?'

'He stayed overnight at Hunt's apartment. Andrei is tracking him and he is currently following him across Hyde Park. Katya is back-up for Andrei. The team at Cunningham's apartment reports that there is a Totenkopf team in the street.'

'I am concerned that we've not been able to infiltrate Totenkopf. If we lose Cunningham we will be running blind. We might not be so lucky if it attempts to lift him again. Activate the Fire Brigade. I want it no more than five minutes away from Cunningham.'

The Fire Brigade was the name given to the Range Rover team which had been involved in the M40 incident.

Macklin & Schweinfort GMBH

Deborah spoke with Frederic over the secure phone in her office. Macklin & Schweinfort was a legitimate company, and none of the core employees were members of the Totenkopf. The office Deborah used was permanently locked, with access only available to Totenkopf personnel; not even the building's facility manager had access. No one thought this level of security unusual as the M&A world was built on secrecy.

Deborah briefed him fully on her progress. The communication equipment was the same state-of-the-art system Frederic used in Münich and was totally secure.

'So the FSB are our unknown rivals. But why would they be interested in Verglas?' Frederic asked.

'I think it's the Amber Room connection.'

'Of course. Despite the replica which our stupid government gave their president they have a dedicated department looking for looted art material. I know it's a department within the FSB, but not a very important one. It is only commanded by a colonel with limited staff and certainly not with the capability we saw in Germany that evening and in London. The job they did on you and our team last night was expertly done. I smell a rat. This has now got more complicated.'

Deborah said,' I'm getting close to Cunningham. He phoned me this morning and I'm seeing him tonight for dinner. I think it's time to pull out Wunsche's teams. We must presume that the FSB are also watching Cunningham. They will certainly do a check on me and the company, but they will find nothing. I think we need to watch my apartment in Munich. I'm sure they will get the address and search the place. I can't stay in London too long, no more than a few more days. I could stretch it to the weekend and leave on Sunday evening.'

Frederic said, 'Find out as much as you can about this Hunt man Cunningham told you about. Is he just a friend of Cunningham? How much does he know? Depending on what you find out from Cunningham we may have to eliminate Hunt.'

Frederic rang off and called Wunsche. 'Your rivals are FSB, so be careful, they're professionals. The Cleaner wants the teams pulled off and placed on standby. The Cleaner has got close to Cunningham.'

'Do you think it wise to pull the teams back? What are our

Russian friends doing? Won't they get suspicious that we are no longer watching Cunningham?'

'A good point Franz, good thinking, but for the moment pull the teams back. Have all of the teams at a high state of readiness, we must be able to respond quickly.'

London

Martin had been asleep when Jack had returned to the apartment. He got up early without waking his friend and wrote a note to him to meet him at the local Caffè Nero at midday. Jack left the apartment and went for a long walk in Hyde Park trying to collect his thoughts.

He arrived at Caffè Nero early, ordered a latte and took a corner table. He chose the table so that his back was to the wall and he could observe the whole café and its single entrance. The place was not very busy, so he had an uninterrupted view of the whole area.

He had just taken his first sip of coffee when Martin entered. He waved to Jack and went to the counter to order a double espresso. He sat down next to Jack and drank his coffee.

'I bloody needed that. So tell me, what's the latest?'

Jack told him about Deborah and the events of the previous evening. 'I really don't know what to make of the Russians. They have saved my life on two occasions now, and I wouldn't be at all surprised if one of them is in this café as we speak.'

Martin looked around the café. 'It sounds as though they are only interested in the Amber Room; it does after all belong to them. I've been checking out the Totenkopf. Details are pretty sketchy but I spoke to George Price, you know, ex-*Guardian*, he has become a bit of a Nazi expert. You may remember he did a series of articles on the Odessa a few years back.' Martin looked at his notebook. 'The Odessa, *Organisation der ehemaligen SS-Angehörigen*, Organization of Former SS Members, is believed to have been an international underground organisation created to protect members of the old Nazi régime. It was the Odessa who set up escape routes for the Nazis out of Germany and Austria. Most of them went either to South America and the Middle East. George told me that Totenkopf was created from the Odessa by the more extreme elements of the SS. He reckons the reason so little is known about it is that it has no outsiders in the organisation. I suspect that there are very few original members of the SS alive. It is the sons, daughters and grandchildren of the SS who make up Totenkopf. They are organised as discrete cells, none knowing the other cells. He believes that Totenkopf is much more powerful than we could ever imagine, having penetrated all levels of the German government, security services and industry and often at very senior levels.'

Jack drank his coffee. 'The FSB and Totenkopf clearly know we have something, but not how useless the file is without Appendix B. You know, we're at a dead end and in a pretty perilous situation. We have nothing more to go on and no bargaining chips. The only lead we have is Eberle and unless we can speak to him, we're buggered. We've got his address, do you think we should visit him?'

'If we're being watched then all we would do is lead them to him. Does anyone else know about the file?'

'I had to tell Deborah. After all, I accidentally dragged her into this whole affair, so it was the least I could do. I didn't tell her about the missing appendix.'

'So there are now three of us at risk.'

'Martin, I'm really sorry for dragging you into this.'

'Actually Jack, I don't think I've had as much fun for a long time, all this intrigue and with Nazis as well. Fancy another coffee? My shout.' Martin headed off to place his order.

Jack's cell phone rang. 'Mr Cunningham, it's Hans Eberle. My daughter gave me your message. I have often wondered how long my true identity would remain a secret. What can I do for you?'

Jack spoke briefly of his link to Helmut and explained that he had died.

'Ah the Obergruppenführer. He was a good man. I presume then that I am the last of the group alive?'

'Yes you are, Herr Eberle.'

'What do you intend to do with this information, Mr Cunningham?'

'Nothing that will cause you harm, but I do believe that you might be the last part of the puzzle.'

'I'm not sure that I will be the solution you seek. I'm an old man and with probably not many years left on the clock, but if I can help you I will.'

Martin returned with the coffees fit to explode about the slow service he'd just received but Jack pointed to his phone.

'Would it be possible to meet, Herr Eberle?' He looked at Martin, who raised an eyebrow.

'I am not very mobile these days Mr Cunningham, but my daughter takes me out to lunch every Thursday so perhaps we can meet then. My daughter knows nothing of my past other than my publishing life. Maybe it is time that she was told the truth. We always go to an Italian restaurant nearby, it's called Due Fratelli. I presume you know my address, so one o'clock this Thursday. You may pick up the bill.' Eberle chuckled. 'Until then Mr Cunningham, goodbye.'

'Well that was a turn-up for the books' said Martin as he handed Jack his coffee.

'Has he agreed to meet?'

'Yes, lunch on Thursday.'

'Great. Now how about dinner tonight? I missed out on steak frites last night.'

'So did I. I'm meeting Deborah tonight, so join us.'

The three of them met at La Brasserie, a comfortable restaurant on the Brompton Road near Jack's apartment. Deborah was charming and, Jack could see, captivated Martin. Conversation was lively, with no mention of the Verglas file. Deborah chose not to refer to the previous evening and Jack's revelations with respect to the file. She hoped that either Jack, or more likely Martin, who was quite merry, would eventually raise the issue.

Another bottle of red wine had the desired effect.

'I have to say, Deborah,' said Martin sipping his wine, 'you're an amazing woman, and in remarkably good form given your adventures last night.'

She smiled. 'On the outside I may appear calm and collected, but inside...' she let the words trail off. 'It does help having a martini, an excellent meal and god knows how much red wine.' She had to be careful not to appear too much at ease and in control of herself.

Martin continued, 'I know Jack told you about the file. What do you think?'

'It is all pretty fantastic, but even though I am German, the object you mentioned, the spear thing, what was it called?'

'The Spear of Longinus' said Jack.

'You have to understand that the Nazi period was never really taught in schools or discussion encouraged. Of course we all knew about Hitler and Himmler and the SS and the atrocities my nation committed but the things Jack mentioned to me, I'm totally ignorant of. I can't really comment on the file - I'm really out of my depth. So what do you think you're going to do next?'

Martin mentioned the earlier phone call with Eberle, and said Jack was meeting him on Thursday at a restaurant called Due Fratelli for lunch.

Jack thought Martin had said rather too much. He answered Deborah's question.

'Not sure, actually. The file is probably of historical significance but I think the Russians are barking up the wrong tree. As for the Nazis, well I suppose after last night's events someone seems serious about it, but I don't know the significance of the file or what to do with it.' He didn't want Deborah involved. The less she knew the safer she would be.

'I assume you have the file in a secure location?'

'Yes we do but it's better for your safety that you know as little as possible. I suppose, though, that your legal mind cannot resist wanting to know more.' Deborah smiled.

'I don't know about you two, but I am not only very tired but pretty pissed. I'm off to the loo' said Martin. He stood up shakily and wandered off.

Jack called for the bill and looked at the beautiful woman sitting opposite him. 'So what are your plans for the rest of the evening, Deborah?'

'Jack, it's already 11.30 and some of us have to work tomorrow!'

Martin returned just as Jack had finished paying the bill. He looked at them both. 'I'm getting a cab. Are you coming with me?'

Jack said 'No, I'll see Deborah back to her hotel and join you later.'

'OK, I'll therefore bid you adieu.'

They watched Martin manoeuvre his way between the tables. As they followed they saw him climb into the back of a black cab blowing kisses to a pretty assistant who had hailed the cab for him.

Deborah turned to Jack. 'You're very fond of each other, aren't you?'

'We've been friends for a long time. Martin might play the buffoon but he's no fool, and he is also a highly accomplished journalist. He is one of life's 'cup half full' people. Nothing's impossible until you prove it is, and even then, try again.'

It was beginning to rain, so Jack hailed a cab taking Deborah to the Lanesborough. He was oblivious to the FSB and Totenkopf watchers. Martin had also been unaware of his own watchers, although in his current inebriated state they could have probably travelled in the cab with him and he wouldn't have noticed.

At the hotel entrance Deborah gave Jack a brief hug before turning and entering the hotel. Jack climbed back into the cab and returned to Martin's apartment where he fell into bed and slept fitfully until the alarm woke him at seven.

He was on his second mug of coffee when the phone rang, it was Deborah. 'Jack, I've just had an urgent message from my office concerning a deal I'm involved in which appears to be falling apart. I have to go back to München this evening and I'm not sure when I'll be returning to London.'

Jack felt a pang of disappointment 'What a shame, can I drive you to the airport. What time is your flight?'

'That's sweet of you, but I have a car collecting me from the office.'

'You could cancel it.'

'Actually I may be travelling to the airport with one of my American colleagues who's returning to New York this evening so perhaps not.' She paused and looked at her watch. 'Look, I must go. I'll call you.'

Deborah checked out of the hotel and then took a cab to her office. Leonid, one of the FSB men who had trailed Jack and Deborah to the hotel the night before, followed her into the City. The FSB team had already clocked their Totenkopf shadows, but Leonid was surprised that when he separated from the team to follow Deborah no one from Totenkopf did likewise. He called Control.

'I'm onto the woman; she's checked out of the hotel and she's in a cab with her luggage' he said. 'Looks like she's heading for the City. It may be nothing, but for some reason the opposition isn't trailing her, although they have whenever she's been with Cunningham.' Vladimir was listening on the speaker. He reflected on the information. 'Uri, tell Leonid to keep close to her. I want to know her every movement and, where possible, who she meets or speaks to, even if it appears trivial. Send another operator to support him.'

Organov's success had been predicated on having an incisive mind and a natural suspicion. For him there was no such thing as coincidence, there was a reason for everything. He turned to Uri. 'I need to know more about this woman. Get Ivan to put Section 6 on to it. I want them to delve deeper into her parents' background.'

He also gave Uri instructions to check outbound flights to Münich to see if Miss Balmer was booked on a flight, and if that failed, to widen the search to other European cities. The FSB had always had full access to all airline booking systems, so unless a person was using a false name tracking was straightforward. In less than 30 minutes he had learned that Deborah was booked on a BA flight to München departing from Heathrow Terminal 1 at 1935 hours.

He rang Ivan in Moscow on the secure link, briefed him on progress and instructed him to get a team into München for her arrival. Ivan told him that the search of her apartment had revealed nothing. Miss Balmer might be a total innocent, but Organov's instincts were usually pretty spot on. They had kept him alive all these years.

Deborah assumed that she was being followed, but as yet had not spotted her shadow. She entered Macklin & Schweinfort and went directly to the secure office to call Emmerich. She only used his real name when she was in his presence, and even then only when they were alone or with his immediate personal staff.

'Cunningham and Hunt know a lot more than they are telling me. I have to go slowly and not sound too interested. Hunt let slip they had spoken with a man called Eberle. I don't know who he is and what the connection is, but Cunningham made a pretty unsubtle move to change the subject. Hunt said Cunningham is having lunch with Eberle this Thursday at a restaurant called Due Fratelli, in Putney. I've given the details to Wunsche. I know Cunningham has the file in a secure place. These guys are not stupid so we must assume they have made a copy; probably a digital one.'

'I'll get Eberle checked out' replied Emmerich. 'His name rings a bell. Wolf will collect you from the airport. I am otherwise engaged tonight, but call me from the car on your arrival. We must assume that the FSB will continue their surveillance on you so don't drop your guard.' Emmerich knew that Deborah was too much of a professional to do such a thing, but he liked to assert his authority. He rang off and summoned his personal assistant, also a member of the Totenkopf.

'Henry, contact the Curator and get him to look at the Verglas II file and see if Eberle is mentioned' he ordered.

The Curator was, as his title suggested, a curator but for an extremely important archive of Nazi activities which included the Totenkopf. The archive was held in a 16th century schloss some 40 kilometres outside Munich near the town of Bad Tölz. The Verglas II file was the administration element of the two files. Verglas I was the operation order, while II covered logistics and administrative details, but nothing in detail of the contents of the Verglas hoard or its location. Verglas I had that important detail and this was the file that Kautenberg had and which the Totenkopf so desperately wanted. Henry came back about twenty minutes later.

'Eberle was a Hauptscharführer on the Verglas team. He was Kautenberg's personal driver.'

Emmerich rang Wunsche in London, gave him this information and instructed him to abduct Eberle and Cunningham.

Deborah's flight arrived on time and she was met by Henry who escorted her to the Bentley where Wolf was waiting. Henry climbed into the front. Neither had noticed the FSB woman who followed them out and climbed into an Opel parked nearby.

Wolf turned around. 'Welcome back, Fraulein Balmer. Just tell me when you wish to be connected to Herr Kleinfurt. There's some hot coffee in a flask in the cabinet, please help yourself.'

'Thank you Wolf, it is always so nice to return home.'

She poured herself a mug of coffee and settled into the leather upholstery. 'Thank you, yes please connect me now' she said. Wolf pulled away from the kerbside and headed for the airport exit and the autobahn for Munich. As the phone rang Henry pressed a button which raised a screen between the driver and passenger compartments.

The Bentley pulled away from the kerbside and the Opel followed some three cars back. Wolf intentionally took a slightly convoluted route, constantly checking for anything unusual.

Henry's presence wasn't just a 'meet and greet' service. He was also part of the security. He had a loaded Glock in a shoulder holster and an MP5K machine pistol housed underneath his seat.

Wolf entered a roundabout and travelled all the way round, exiting where he had entered. The Opel also entered the roundabout, noted Wolf's manoeuvre and took the first exit. The Bentley headed for the autobahn. As Wolf drove down the entry ramp he failed to notice a Mercedes taxi following them. The Bentley's number plate and photos of both Wolf and Henry had been transmitted to Major Terpinski in Moscow.

It took little time for the car and the two men to be identified and for the information to be relayed to Terpinski, who then rang Organov.

'The two men are Wolf Koenig and Henry Munch. Koenig is 35 years old and Munch is 28. Both are long-term employees of a man called Frederic Kleinfurt, who is Chairman of IG Garben, but they are not employed by the company.'

Organov thought this a little strange. 'Ivan, carry out a more detailed background search of these two.'

'I've already set this in motion, but it could take at least 36 hours.'

Organov thanked Ivan and rang off. He turned to Uri.

'Uri, this Frederic Kleinfurt, Chairman of IG Garben, is a serious industrialist, a man who moves in the highest circles. We have a number of options. Balmer with her M&A expertise may have a professional relationship with Kleinfurt. He is a widower so there may be a romantic connection. Or... ' His voice trailed off. 'Uri, get Ivan back again, I think we are running out of surveillance teams. We will need to redeploy teams from Italy immediately.'

* * * * * * *

In the Bentley Deborah picked up the ringing phone. 'Hello Deborah. Thank you for calling me; just to give you an update we have tracked down Eberle. He was part of the original Verglas team. I have told Wunsche to pick him and Cunningham up on Thursday. We must keep Cunningham and, for that matter, Hunt alive until we have all of the elements of the file. Tell me more about how your relationship with Cunningham. Does he suspect anything?'

Frederic had always been attracted to Deborah and the thought of another man, any man, being with her angered him. Deborah knew this, but she also knew that to tease Frederic would be extremely unwise.

'Our relationship is developing; he finds me attractive, but we're not yet close enough for him to trust me totally.'

'Look we'll await the outcome of Wunsche's efforts with Eberle. He'll get an answer. Wunsche may be an unpleasant and an unsophisticated man, so much like his father, but he is a highly effective interrogator. When do you expect to return to London?'

'I don't want to return too quickly. If I can I'll try and get Cunningham to come to Münich.'

'Keep contact with him, but don't appear to be overkeen. We don't want him to back off.'

Frederic ended the call just as the Bentley entered the outskirts of Münich. The Mercedes taxi had been replaced by another cab. Wolf dropped Deborah off at her apartment.

London

By the time the emergency services had arrived at the crash scene on the M40 on the night of Jack and Deborah's abduction, the BMW and Audi were total wrecks. The Thermate grenades had generated an intense heat which had quickly ignited the fuel tanks. The bodies were burned beyond recognition; in fact the heat had been so intense that the bodies had almost crumbled to dust.

The police quickly ascertained that this was no ordinary road accident. Witnesses spoke of a white van and armed men, so the incident escalated to the crime detection desk where it was decided that the incident could be terrorist-related. As a result, Commander Jolyon Hunt, head of SO15 Counter Terrorism Command, was called. He despatched Chief Inspector Don Grant to the scene.

Don was in his early forties and considered to be one of the sharpest operators in the unit which was the reason Commander Hunt sent him. Grant and Hunt were old friends and had joined the Met together. Don had previously been in the Marines and Jolyon had joined straight from university on the graduate programme.

Don spoke first with the senior fire officer at the scene.

'What do you make of this mess? It looks pretty devastating.'

'This was no ordinary fire; it took us a long time to extinguish it. There is nothing that would naturally cause this level of incineration. The bodies are almost dust, which is an indicator of the intensity of the heat. Even the road has melted. You don't get that from burning fuel alone. Forensics might be able to work out the cause of the fire but I would be surprised; there is unlikely to be any chemical residue.'

Don spoke with the traffic police, who confirmed that a black Range Rover and a white van had left the M40 travelling the wrong way up the down ramp. Witnesses had said that they had heard two muted explosions and then the two cars had caught fire. The whole incident had happened very quickly.

Don had two detectives with him, who were speaking to witnesses. He called one of them over.

'George, what time did the incident take place?'

'Around ten o'clock, boss. I've got all the stuff I need from here. The forensic boys are on their way and Mike is nearly finished.'

'Get over to the Yard, grab Smith. I want the pair of you to look at the surveillance tapes for this area. Go out for a radius of 500 metres and for the period 21.30 hours to 22.30. I'm looking for a black Range Rover and a white panel van.'

There was little point in Don hanging around; he had seen everything he needed to. He turned to the fire officer.

'Where will you take the wrecks?'

'They are going to the Docklands quarantine depot after the forensic guys have had their initial look-see.'

Don thanked the fire officer and drove to Scotland Yard.

On the way he called Commander Hunt.

'Jol, forensics will shortly be all over the scene. We have confirmed that armed men were involved and there may have been a couple of explosions. George Andrews is pulling the surveillance tapes for the area. We're looking for a black Range Rover and a white panel van.'

'What do you think, Don?'

'Well it may be terrorist or gang related. Either way it was all done very professionally and was certainly no accident.'

'Keep me posted.'

Don rang the head of the Scotland Yard press office and said that they wanted to put a lid on the M40 incident for the moment If any of the press made enquiries it was to be explained as two sets of racing joy riders.

It was just after one in the morning when George rang Don Grant.

'Boss, we're lucky that there were two surveillance cameras on that stretch of road, one looking east and the other west. We've got the whole incident on tape. Before you say anything, I've extended the search radius to two miles, so we might get lucky and find out where the vehicles came from and went to or at least the direction they were travelling.'

It took Don less than five minutes to get to the control room. He found George and Smithy surrounded by empty coffee cups and biscuit wrappers.

'OK George, what have you got?' Grant slumped into the chair next to George.

'The westbound camera picked up the Range Rover coming close to the BMW. It didn't touch the BMW, but for some reason the car hit the central reservation and bounced out and then was hit by an Audi. You can see the Range Rover deliberately going side on and blocking the carriageway and our view of the BMW and the Audi. If you look up to the left,' George pointed to the screen, 'you can see the white van coming down the up ramp. 'It's the eastbound camera that picks up the really interesting stuff. The Audi is part of the incident. Smithy, play the other tape.'

Smith played the tape from the eastbound camera. Don saw two men exit the Range Rover carrying semi-automatic weapons fitted with suppressors, and then fire into the BMW. He noted that each gunman fired just two shots; very professional, he thought. He saw two men from the Audi grab a man and woman from the rear of the BMW and take them to the white van which had just pulled up by the Range Rover.

'If you look closely, 'said Smithy, 'it looks like two grenades are thrown into the BMW and the Audi.'

There was a blinding light and an intense explosion. By this time the Rover and the van could be seen exiting the motorway and heading south.

'Well done you two. Get me copies of the tapes and send them to the techies. Get Harold on to it. I want the registration numbers of the vehicles. This was a slick operation, so I won't be surprised if the numbers are false, but we may get lucky. I know you have been at it for a number of hours; are you both OK to continue to look at the expanded area?'

'No problem. It's a bit like watching a Bruce Willis movie.'

Don chuckled. 'George, narrow your search to south of the motorway. I want to know where the vehicles went. Smithy, extend your search eastwards. Let's see where these guys came from. I'll get you some more people as soon as I can.'

Having briefed his boss, Don decided to stay in his office and use the camp bed that he kept in the corner. Sleeping in his office had become a regular feature in his life; terrorists never respected normal working hours. He always kept a change of clothes and spare washing kit in his office because of this.

By 7 am George had tracked the Range Rover and the van to the Fulham Road near Parson's Green, where the vehicles had turned off into an area with no surveillance cameras. This was unusual, as London probably has more surveillance cameras than any other capital city in the world.

George called Don and informed him as to what he had found. He also told him that Smith had managed to track the BMW, the Range Rover and the Audi. The Audi and BMW had joined the M40 by the Westfield shopping mall and the Range Rover had joined it at Shepherds Bush. He decided to extend his search as he had two more people assisting him, so it was just a matter of time before they had the full picture.

'Well done George, and thanks Smithy. Quarantine all tapes for central London between 2030 hours until 2230 hours. Take as many people as you need. Meet me in the briefing room at 10.00.'

Don rang off and instructed his assistant to call a meeting for 10.00. He had just started the meeting when Detective Al Green entered and gave Don a series of photo enlargements which had a high enough resolution to identify all the people as well as the number plates of the vehicles. He gave them back to Al, who pinned them on the operations board.

'Ok, Al what have you got?'

'Not a great deal on the cars, I'm afraid. The number plates on all the vehicles are false. SO19 has confirmed that the weapons are state-of-the-art Heckler & Koch 2013 sub-machine guns fitted with suppressors. The guys really rate these weapons. They said they fire caseless ammunition, which is why we didn't find any empty cartridge cases at the scene. What is interesting is that these weapons are very difficult to acquire and they tend to be used by Special Forces. It's going to take time to identify the people.'

George then briefed everyone on what he had found. Don stood up.

'George, if you lead on the camera surveillance? Get someone to focus on the Fulham/Parsons Green area. See if the Rover or the van reappears. Harry, get some men on the ground in Fulham as soon as you can. Al, see what the forensic team has found. Sue, you lead on getting identities. OK guys let's rock and roll.'

As the team left the briefing room Don called Sue Andrews, one of his better detectives, back.

'Sue, you're the key to this. George may get lucky with the CCTV coverage, but if we are going anywhere I want to know who in particular the man and the woman are. Concentrate your efforts on them. It's not clear whether they were being rescued or kidnapped.'

'Will do boss, but it could take some time.'

It took George's team to the early hours of the following day to pick up the white van again as it entered CCTV coverage, just an hour after it had disappeared. He tracked it to the Gloucester Road, where the man and the woman were dropped off. So it was a rescue job, thought Don. The van retraced its steps back to Parson's Green. The break came when he saw the man and the woman hail a cab and drop off outside the Lanesborough Hotel.

'George you're a fucking marvel. Contact Sue and get her to check out the Lanesborough. See if you can give Sue the best resolution photos of the man and woman.'

152

Using a camera coverage map they were able to identify an area in Parsons Green approximately 300 metres square where there was no camera coverage. Don tasked a team to walk the area.

Sue Andrews rang Don about two hours later.

'I've got a positive ID on the woman but not the man. Her name is Deborah Balmer. She's a German national and a regular at the Lanesborough. They think she works in the City. Unfortunately she has checked out of the hotel and the concierge confirmed that she was returning to Munich.'

'Sue, see if you can track down her London address and any addresses in Munich.'

'OK, boss.'

London, Thursday

Jack returned to his apartment early in the morning to get some fresh clothes for his meeting with Eberle. When he left he made his way to Harrods aware that he was probably being followed. He entered the store by the entrance opposite Starbucks, and having walked through the men's designer clothes section went into the perfumery and turned left into the food halls. He had selected his route wisely, because, as usual, the food halls were packed with shoppers and tourists. Jack moved quickly and exited by the Underground station.

The street was packed with people. His instinct was right; he was being followed. He thought he had picked up someone who he believed was trailing him, but he had failed to notice the FSB man and woman paralleling his track. He had lost the first man in the melée in the store, but the man and woman were still with him.

Jack walked up Knightsbridge towards Sloane Street and stopped outside Russell & Bromley, looking at the window display. The man walked past Jack unnoticed, while the woman stopped outside Bally, also window shopping. Jack turned around, retraced his steps and continued westwards. He knew there was a bus stop just before the Brompton Oratory. The woman followed and spoke into her cell phone; another FSB man across the road was paralleling her track.

Jack walked across Beauchamp Place and stopped by a bus stop. He couldn't see any buses. He began to feel apprehensive; the longer he stood where he was, the more likely he was to be discovered. The woman also joined the bus queue. She looked just like any other person waiting for a bus.

A number 14 bus for Putney Heath approached and Jack climbed on board and went upstairs to the back so he could have a clear view of the people on that deck. The woman stayed on the lower deck, where she could observe the stairs to the upper level. The days when you could just hop on and off a bus were long gone, which made her job easier. If Cunningham got off it would have to be at a bus stop, so she could easily follow him without arousing suspicion.

As the bus departed the man ran across the road, speaking into his cell phone. He was immediately picked up by a Volkswagen Golf.

Jack could have stayed on the bus all the way to Putney, but he decided that he would get off at South Kensington tube station and continue his journey by Underground.

The Golf followed the bus. At South Kensington Jack got off the bus and entered the Underground station, heading for the District Line. He used his pre-paid Oyster card to speed his way through the barriers. The woman followed him.

Jack had specifically chosen South Kensington station

because the platform was at ground level and served the eastbound and westbound routes of the District and Circle Lines and down some stairs was the Piccadilly line. He stood in the middle of the platform and looked around. He did not notice the woman, who was now seated on one of the benches reading a copy of *Hello* magazine.

The Golf pulled into a parking space near the station and one of the men in it got out and entered the station. As instructed by the woman, he went straight to the District and Circle Line platform. He saw Cunningham and the woman and placing himself about 20 feet away, opened a copy of *The Times*.

A Circle Line train entered the station, and Jack climbed on board. The woman stood up and entered the same carriage, but as the doors started to close Jack stepped back on to the platform. The woman made no attempt to follow him and continued reading her magazine. She knew her team mate had Cunningham covered.

Jack walked quickly down the stairs to the Piccadilly Line and boarded a train heading westwards; the man followed. The woman got off her train at Gloucester Road, stayed on the eastbound platform and waited for the next train, which was a District Line train for Upminster. She positioned herself at the western end of the platform, enabling her to see into every carriage as it passed. Luckily the train was largely empty, so she could see that Cunningham was not on it.

She waited for the next train and, again, there was no sign of Cunningham. As she had not heard from Nicolai and, noting that her cell phone had no signal, she decided to leave the station.

Exiting on to the Gloucester Road her phone rang, it was Nicolai. He told her that Jack had changed trains at Earls

Court and taken a District Line train heading towards Wimbledon. Jack intended to get off at Putney Bridge and take the footbridge that ran beside the railway line over the Thames to Putney.

'We are on a District Line train heading towards Wimbledon. We're just passing through Parsons Green.' The woman relayed the information to Uri just as the Golf arrived to pick her up. Uri contacted the two-man team watching Eberle's house in Deodar Road. He was sure Cunningham was going to make contact with the old man.

Eberle and his daughter left his house at the usual time for his weekly lunch at Due Fratelli. Despite his age Eberle walked erect and with the stride of a man who had seen service in the military. Apart from a heart murmur and a minor stroke which had laid him low some two years earlier, he was still a fit man. He was also a good-looking man, noted for his charm and wit, particularly with women. He had owned and run a very profitable educational publishing company from his house in an office above his garage until he had been bought out by the Random House publishing group. He had been assisted by his daughter who, after the sale, had moved on to forge a very successful career, also in publishing. Their weekly lunch date was almost sacrosanct, so she was mildly irritated when her father told her they were being joined by a stranger.

One of the FSB men, part of the team that had maintained a permanent surveillance of Eberle, followed them at a discreet distance. Notwithstanding the heightened state of interest in Eberle, he still considered his job mind-numbingly boring. His partner, contrary to their instructions to retain the integrity of the team, had gone to a bank in Putney High Street, leaving him on his own.

The FSB man watched Smith and his daughter enter Due Fratelli. He moved to Café Rouge across the way which would give him an uninterrupted view of the entrance to the main restaurant as well as the adjoining café, part of Due Fratelli.

Eberle was a regular at the restaurant, and the FSB man had become a regular at Café Rouge. But he would rather have reversed the situation. While Due Fratelli's reputation for good food had got better, it was the reverse for Café Rouge where the food had got depressingly worse.

He settled down at his usual table, which gave him an unrestricted view of the entrance to Due Fratelli. He had not seen Jack Cunningham enter the café part of the restaurant some 15 minutes earlier.

As Eberle and his daughter entered the restaurant they were warmly greeted by Roberto, the owner, and ushered to their usual table where Roberto had already seated Jack. Fortunately the table was in an alcove and not visible from the street.

Jack stood as the couple approached. Eberle was a big man with a neatly trimmed beard and a full head of hair, albeit now grey in places. He had piercing blue eyes, which Jack thought looked cold and unfeeling. He offered his hand to Eberle.

'Mr Smith, I'm Jack Cunningham.' Jack turned to Eberle's daughter, 'Miss Smith, a pleasure to meet you, I apologise for the intrusion.' He eyed her admiringly, noting her blonde hair and trim figure. Her eyes were the same piercing blue as her father's. She was wearing tailored jeans and a cream shirt, and her only jewellery was a pearl necklace and a pair of pearl earrings. He thought she was probably in her early fifties, perhaps younger. All in all, he found her a very attractive woman.

She warmed to Jack's good manners and soon forgot her

resentment at his presence. 'My father told me you were joining us but not why, so I'm rather intrigued,' she said. 'Please call me Penny.'

Eberle directed them to sit. 'Shall we have some wine? I hope you don't mind, Mr Cunningham, or may I call you Jack?' He didn't wait for Jack to reply. 'I am a creature of habit so I trust you like my choice of white wine; it's an Albarino.'

Roberto had anticipated Eberle's choice and had already opened a bottle of Albarino. He poured the wine. Having given Roberto their food orders, the trio continued their small talk. Eberle decided it was time to address the reason why Jack was present.

'Shall we get to the point of our meeting?' He turned to Penny and told her his story. He was somewhat economical with the truth, but Jack saw no reason to complicate matters by interrupting him. Eberle told her that he had been a member of the SS during the war and because after the war all ex-members of the SS were considered to be war criminals regardless of whether they were or not, he had taken a false identity. He went to some lengths to explain that he was not part of the SS which had been involved with atrocities and that he had been an ordinary driver working for a senior officer in army administration. In fact he had never served outside Germany. He talked for about ten minutes.

Jack thought that what he had said was hardly revelatory and that most of his confession was bald lies. He was not warming to Eberle.

Penny was clearly shaken. 'Did Mummy know?' she asked her father.

Eberle sipped his wine. 'She didn't. As far as she knew, I was a refugee from the war and my name was Schmidt. Over time, as my English lost its accent, I changed my name to Smith. The reason Jack is here is because he was carrying out research on Germany for a book he is writing. He accidentally discovered my true identity.'

Jack interjected. 'I'm a freelance journalist and I'm working on a history book. Part of my research covers a General Kautenberg, who your father used to drive for. He gave me your father's details but, before I could carry out a detailed interview with the General, he passed away.'

It was now Jack's turn to look directly at Eberle. The lie was complete.

'The General had given me a file, but it's missing an appendix. I wondered if your father could shed some light as to its whereabouts.'

'I'm afraid I cannot help you there-I didn't even know of the existence of such a file' the German responded. 'I haven't been in touch with Kautenberg for at least 50 years.'

'Has he ever sent you anything?'

'No, nothing.' He paused. 'Hang on though, I was sent a book some six weeks ago from Germany, no letter with it, just a book on birds. I'm not even interested in the subject. I do remember the return address on the package was in Paderborn, but I don't know anyone who lives there.'

Jack kept it to himself that Paderborn was where Kautenberg had lived.

'Have you still got the book?'

Eberle thought for a moment. 'I think it's in my study, in a pile of books behind the door. Penny, be a darling and get it for me?'

Penny responded light-heartedly. 'Only after I've finished eating, you selfish old fool.'

It was an excellent lunch and Jack was well aware that when he had departed there would be a lot of talking between Eberle and his daughter. Eberle ordered coffee while Penny made the short walk to the house. The FSB man saw her leave the restaurant but stayed where he was; his target was Smith.

Penny arrived at the house oblivious to a white Transit van parked across the street. She found the book easily and returned to the restaurant. The Transit van had now turned into Deodar Road. A man got out, crossed the road and entered the café part of Due Fratelli. He recognised the woman and assumed that the elderly man with him must be Eberle. There was no sign of Jack as he had gone to the loo. The man was not observant enough to notice that the table was set for three persons.

The van moved forward and positioned itself on Deodar Road, at the junction with Putney Bridge Road. The van was just outside the view of the FSB man, who hadn't noticed the man cross the road and enter the café. The man spoke with the owner.

'It may be just a coincidence, but the elderly man over there in the alcove, I think I know him.'

'It is Mr Smith' the café owner responded. 'He's a regular guest. That's his daughter with him. He lives nearby.'

'Thank you, I thought it was him, I haven't seen him in ages, but I won't interrupt their lunch. I'll catch them later.'

The FSB man paid no attention to the man as he crossed the road, and did not see him climb into the white van. The man telephoned Wunsche. "There's no sign of Cunningham; he's not there. There's only Smith and his daughter. What do want us to do?"

Wunsche was losing his patience. "Damn, where the hell is that fuck Cunningham? No matter; lift Smith and the woman and take them to the warehouse."

Jack returned to the table and Eberle handed him the book. 'You are welcome to keep it. It is of no value to me. I am feeling tired and I think our meeting is over so, if you will excuse us, I'm sure that you will understand that Penny and I have a lot to talk about. I will leave you with the bill and I trust that this will be the last time we meet'.

He shook Jack's hand, said goodbye to Roberto, and walked towards the exit. Jack kissed Penny on both cheeks. 'Maybe we might bump into each other again,' he said. She murmured, 'Yes, perhaps,' as she left with her father.

Jack sat back at the table and ordered another coffee. He thought he would stay for at least another 30 minutes so that he could avoid any potential surveillance. He started turning the pages of the book, looking for clues. He was pretty sure that Kautenberg had sent the book to Eberle so there must be something, some clue.

Eberle and his daughter crossed the road and entered Deodar Road. The FSB man got up to follow but he had forgotten to pay his bill and had to return to the table. This short delay to his departure would be critical.

As Eberle came alongside the white van, a man came up to Penny and thrust a pistol into her side. The side door of the van slid open and another man, also armed, spoke.

'Smith, get into the van or we'll kill your daughter.' Smith and Penny were pushed into the van and the door was closed. Penny and her father were seated together on a bench. While one man sat opposite pointing his gun at them, the other tied their wrists behind their backs with plasticuffs and taped their mouths shut with duck tape.

The FSB man came around the corner just as the van

pulled slowly away from the kerb and turned into Putney Bridge Road and headed east. He could not see his charges and was sharp enough to know that there had not been enough time for Eberle to have reached his house. His partner was nowhere to be seen.

He made the correct assumption that they had been abducted and could see that the only vehicle nearby was the white van. He turned, but the van was accelerating away. There was no chance he could catch up on foot but he did have the presence of mind to make a note of the van's number plate which he relayed to Control.

At this point, his partner turned up. 'What is it?' he asked.

'Fuck, we're in the shit now. I think Smith and his daughter are in that white van.' He pointed into the distance as the van accelerated and was soon out of sight. 'Uri is going to kill us.'

Jack, in the meantime, was sitting in blissful ignorance of the events unfolding on the street. His focus had been on the book, which despite his having turned every page had revealed nothing of interest. He then realised his stupidity. The last book clue he had found had been in the spine.

He bent the book backwards to try and release any item in the spine. This didn't work, so he took a table knife and cut open the spine.

Taped to the inside was a wax package similar to the one he had found in the other book. He opened it and unfolded a small piece of paper.

Not more bloody riddles, he thought as he looked at the paper. He rang Martin and told him what he had found and arranged to meet him as soon as possible. Jack paid the bill and left the restaurant.

FSB, London

A man entered the control room and spoke with Uri. After he had left the room, Uri turned to Organov.

'Cunningham has reappeared. He had given us the slip for at least three hours but he is now with Hunt in a pub in Chelsea. These guys really like their drink. We have no more news on Eberle and his daughter and we have confirmed the white van plates were false. So unless we are very lucky...'

'We must assume that Totenkopf has them, but why? I need to speak to Cunningham. I think we'll go and join them.'

Nuremberg

Because of Germany's reputation as a country obsessed by bureaucracy and, in particular, record keeping, it had not taken Klaus' team long to track down Emma Swift's movements. Willi briefed Klaus.

'Swift booked into a hotel in Paderborn two days before the shooting. She was not alone.' Willi looked at his notebook. 'She was with a man called Jack Cunningham. She left with him for...'

'Hold it Willi. Did you say Jack Cunningham?'

'Yes. He travelled with Swift to Nuremberg where they checked into a hotel. What is it?'

'Continue, Willi.'

'Helmut spoke to the concierge in Paderborn, who told him that Cunningham had rung him to arrange for their luggage to be stored in the hotel in Nuremberg. It seems the concierge is very friendly with his counterpart in the hotel in Nuremberg. Cunningham had told the concierge he and Swift had to return to London immediately and there was no time to check out. This all happened on the day after the shooting.'

'So Cunningham was there after all.'

'What do you mean boss? Do you know Cunningham?'

'Willi, I've spoken with Jack Cunningham. He told me Swift had gone to Germany by herself. Our Mr Cunningham is a liar. Any news on the Nazis?'

'No, I left a message with my cousin.'

'Find out when and where Cunningham left the country. Also check if he hired a car.'

It didn't take long to establish that Jack had left for London on a BA flight out of Munich and that he had used a hire car from Hertz, which he had dropped off at Munich airport. Klaus made a quick call to a friend in the Münich police and in no time a forensic team was all over the car. Luckily the car was still parked with Hertz and had not been rented since Cunningham had returned it.

It was not long before the forensic team, with their usual efficiency, reported that they had found blood samples on the upholstery and that these had been sent for DNA testing. Five hours later the results were sent to Julia in Nuremberg.

'Klaus, it's Julia. The DNA sample from Münich matches the DNA of Emma Swift.' She gave him all the details and he then rang Richard White.

'Richard, it's Klaus. We have confirmed that Jack Cunningham was in Germany with Miss Swift. We have matched her DNA with blood samples from a car hired by Cunningham. Cunningham told me Swift had gone to Germany on her own. What worries me is why, if Cunningham is an innocent party, he didn't contact the police. Unless he was implicated in the killing of Swift, or possibly he found himself in a complex situation which meant he had to leave Germany quickly.'

'I think it's time we had a face-to-face with Mr Cunningham. It's not strictly my area, but I'll talk to one of my colleagues as to the right department to handle this. I'll let you know how it goes as soon as possible. Thanks Klaus.'

London

Sue Andrews was with SO19, meeting with Inspector Mike Shepherd. SO19was Scotland Yard's specialist firearms unit, an élite cadre of highly-trained police officers who responded to any armed incident in London. Shepherd was an expert on firearms, particularly those weapons he referred to as 'exotic'.

Sue and Mike were running through the footage of the M40 shoot out. It had been Mike who had identified the weapons used at the incident and although it was probably a long shot, Sue was hoping he might be able to identify the gunmen.

'These are real professionals, Sue. You just have to look at the way they hold their weapons and how they move. I would certainly say they are ex-military or specialist police. As I told you guys, these weapons are state of the art. I would put 100% on it that gangs can't get hold of this sort of weaponry. This smacks of government, though not ours. Look at the grenades they throw into the vehicles.' He zoomed in and paused the recording, pointing to the grenades. 'They look like Thermate and the explosion confirms this. Thermate generates enormously high temperatures which would explain the damage reported. Let's play it again. We'll slow it down and enlarge it as much as we can.'

Sue rewound the recording and managed to get a magnification of 5 before the resolution deteriorated. They slowly scanned the imagery until Mike hit the pause button.

'Stop there, Sue. Go back to the two people being removed from the car. I think I've seen the man before.'

Sue rewound and froze the best image she had of the man, which was just as the man looked up.

'Bugger me, it's Jack Cunningham' said Mike. 'We were in the Regiment together.'

'What do you mean, the Regiment?'

'Sorry Sue, the RAF Regiment. The RAF has its own private army, so to speak. Best-kept secret on the block. Next to Special Forces, the Marines and Paras, they have had troops on operations solidly since the Second World War. Jack was an officer, a good operator, with a very promising future ahead of him. I was with him in Bosnia, but I think he got disillusioned and left. We kept briefly in contact but I suppose we weren't the greatest of friends- he was more an acquaintance. I seem to remember that he became a journalist. He wrote a few articles on Bosnia; they were pretty good. I wonder what he's doing there.'

Sue was already on the phone to Don Grant.

'Boss, we've had another break. Inspector Mike Shepherd, you know, from SO19? I popped in to chat about the weapons that were used on the off chance he might recognise the guys, and he did. Shepherd was previously in the military and in particular', she looked at her notebook, 'the RAF Regiment. Never heard of them; seems the RAF has its own army. Anyway, Mike served with our man. He identified him as Jack Cunningham. He's a freelance journalist.'

'Great stuff Sue, well done.'

It didn't take long to track down Cunningham's home address, 14A Kensington Mews. Don called over Bill Bright.

'Bill, grab Lucy and go over to Cunningham's place.

Martin is getting some photographs of Cunningham. If he's there, lift him. If not, just keep the place under surveillance. See if you can get some telephone numbers for him – home and mobile.'

In due course the team reported that Cunningham was not at home and the porter had confirmed that he had not seen him for a few days.

It was 7 pm when Don left the office to go home. In the lift, he found Richard White.

'Hello Don. How are you? I understand you have a bit of a mess on the M40.'

Don and Richard were great friends and had played rugby for the Met. They held each other in high regard.

'Yes, it's a mess but we've had a few breaks over the last hour or so.'

'Fancy a quick beer? There's something that has accidentally come my way and it's not strictly Trident business.'

'Yeah, sure. It's been a long day.'

They went to the Dog and Feather in nearby Norton Street, a regular watering hole for the New Scotland Yard lot. Don bought them a couple of pints and they settled at an empty table at the back of the pub.

'You remember that secondment I had to Hamburg about 18 months ago with the Gang Task Force? Well I worked with a really good operator called Klaus Schmidt. He now heads up a similar unit in Nuremberg. He rang me because there had been a serious shoot-out on his patch, initially thought to be gang-related, but now he's not so sure. The weapons used were too sophisticated, Special Forces stuff, state of the art and not the sort of hardware that gangs could normally get their hands on.

'A woman journalist, a Brit, was killed and we discovered

she was accompanied by another Brit journalist who I've spoken to; he's basically her next of kin. At no time did he give an indication to either Klaus or myself that he was in Germany with her. In fact he went so far as to say she went to Germany on her own, but Klaus has confirmed he was in Germany with her. All a bit fishy. His name is Jack Cunningham. I'm not sure whose department should handle this.'

Don sipped his beer. 'I think you can give this one to me Rick. We've identified Jack Cunningham as one of the people in the M40 incident, also involving some pretty sophisticated weaponry. Busy little bugger, by the sound of it.'

Richard gave Don Klaus's contact details. They had another beer before Don returned to his office, having rung his wife to tell her not to expect him home that evening.

Don rang Klaus's cell phone. It was now 9 pm London time, 10 pm in Germany. He explained briefly that they had a mutual interest in Jack Cunningham and they agreed they would have a more detailed chat first thing in the morning.

London, The Builder's Arms

Before Jack met Martin at the pub, he photocopied the slip of paper he had found in Eberle's book and mailed the original to Martin at his office address. They were on their second glass of wine and Martin had scrutinised the paper managing to translate the word 'krypta' as Crypt, but he said that the rest was gobbledygook to him.

Martin picked up his wine glass. 'It looks very much like a clock face with the hands set at four o'clock. What the letters and symbols mean is anyone's guess. Kautenberg knows how to make life difficult. God I hope it's all going to be worth it in the end.'

'Do you mind if I join you gentlemen?' Organov pulled up a chair and sat down with them. 'Is the white wine all right? I must say I prefer whisky. Mr Hunt, would you be so kind? An Islay malt if they have it, a double, no ice and just a little water.'

Martin was about to protest when Jack gently said. 'Martin, please get the General his whisky.'

Martin stood up, pocketing the slip of paper. Organov turned to Jack. 'I presume Hunt knows everything?'

'He does.'

'Then I will wait until he returns before I speak.'

Martin soon returned with the whisky and a bottle of white wine. 'Economy of effort, and I have a strange feeling we are going to need this.' He topped up his and Jack's wine glasses.

Organov raised his glass. 'Cheers, gentlemen. With your drinking habits you could both be Russian.'

Jack introduced Martin to the General. Organov sipped his whisky.

'I will get to the point. Jack, you expertly evaded our surveillance today, and I congratulate you. Please be assured that I am not your enemy; my people are there to protect you. I need your co-operation. Now tell me, did you meet Smith today? Please don't lie. It's imperative I know, because this afternoon Totenkopf snatched both Smith and his daughter as they returned from a restaurant.'

'Do you know where they are? Are they safe?' Jack was thinking about Penny.

'I am afraid I don't know- the vehicle that was used had false plates. My people are still looking, but our options are extremely limited.'

'Yes, I did meet with them. I was with them at lunch.'

'Why?'

'Smith is the last surviving member of the Verglas group and I needed to know if Kautenberg had contacted him.'

Organov took another sip of his whisky. 'Excellent, thank you Martin. So had Kautenberg contacted Eberle?'

'No.'

'Come come, Jack. I suspect he gave you or told you something. And I suppose the slip of paper that Martin so ineptly pocketed is unrelated? As I have said before, I am only interested in recovering the Amber Room. I can assure you that once Totenkopf has the file they will kill you both; they will leave no loose ends. You should perhaps consider me to be your friend at this juncture.'

'Kautenberg had sent Smith a book, and the paper was hidden in the spine of it. Martin, show him.' Martin handed the paper to Organov.

'Neither of us has any idea as to its meaning except that 'krypta' means crypt. Apart from it looking like a clock face set at four o'clock, that's it.'

Organov handed the paper back to Martin. 'Perhaps when you do find out you might let me know. Does Smith know what you have found?'

'No. I found it after they had left me.'

'Very well Jack. Work with me; I am your ally, and I have access to enormous resources. I cannot guarantee your safety if you keep evading my people. Once Totenkopf has you... and, by the way, be very circumspect about what you tell Miss Balmer. She may be just an innocent but I am having her checked out so, until I give you the all clear, treat everyone with suspicion. A pleasure meeting you Mr Hunt, and thank you for the drink.'

Organov stood up, finished his whisky and left the pub. Uri was waiting for him outside with a small security team.

'You know Martin, I have no idea how to play this. How do we know the General can be trusted? It may be the new Russia, but no matter how you dress it up or change names, the KGB is still the KGB, and the General is old enough to have been in the old one as well as the new. Both he and the Totenkopf want what we have, and frankly we currently have nothing unless we can decipher this piece of paper. The Eberle thing is a bit worrying. I didn't warm to him, but his daughter really is an innocent party. Let me look at the paper again.'

Martin placed the paper on the table, and as he withdrew his hand he accidentally knocked Jack's wine glass over, soaking the paper.

Jack grabbed the paper. 'Sod it. At least the ink hasn't run.' He shook the paper to remove some of the liquid, holding it up to the light.

'Hang on, hold it there' said Martin. 'Well, bugger me.'

He was looking at the paper from the reverse side. He took the paper from Jack, wiped the table's glass surface with his handkerchief and placed the paper face down on the glass. A symbol had appeared. Martin took out a pen and messily traced it.

'It's that simple. What we thought were a mix of symbols and letters are in fact just letters written in reverse. It reads WEWELSBURG. It makes sense - Crypt, Wewelsburg and the clock face. But is the time four o'clock or eight? I suspect if we can get into the crypt at Wewelsburg we'll find a clock face.'

'Fucking genius, Martin! You're not just a pretty face. Let me pour you another glass.'

Martin was grinning from ear to ear. 'Rather clever of me, wasn't it. Should we tell the General?'

'No we don't or at least not for the moment. It looks like another trip to Wewelsburg.'

'So when do we go?'

'We'll need to fly to Düsseldorf and then drive over to Paderborn.'

'I've only got a few things I have to complete at the newspaper but can probably manage tomorrow morning. I'll book the flights and car through our travel agent, and you know a hotel where we can stay.'

Jack picked up the sodden paper and crumpled it up, placing it in the ashtray on the table. 'We don't need this any more. I think we can remember the contents.'

They both stood up and left the pub. Jack went back to Martin's apartment to pick up his stuff as he had decided that it was time to go home and give Martin some brief breathing space. Martin went on to his office. Neither of them saw a woman move across the pub to their table and retrieve the paper. She left shortly afterwards and climbed into a Ford Fiesta parked nearby. The woman rang Wunsche. "Hunt and Cunningham left behind a piece of mashed up paper. We were only able to make out the word "Wewelsberg".'

Jack got back to his apartment and while he was unpacking he checked his cell phone for messages; Deborah had called. Though less than 36 hours had passed since he had last seen her he found that he was missing her company and realised how much it had helped him meeting her when he did. Coping with Emma's death that is. He poured himself a glass of red wine and called her cell phone.

'Jack, how lovely to hear from you.' She was sitting in Frederic's apartment with a glass of champagne. Jack could hear music in the background. 'Hang on let me turn the music off.' Frederic moved towards the hi-fi and accidentally bumped into the coffee table, knocking a pile of books on to the floor.

'What was that? Is someone else there?'

'I'm alone of course. You're not jealous are you?' She teased. 'I just caught the coffee table and knocked some books off.'

'Sorry Deborah, I'm just missing you. How was your journey?'

They continued chatting. Frederic sat patiently across from Deborah, occasionally sipping his champagne.

'So, are you any closer to solving your mystery?' said Deborah. But just then Frederic's cell phone rang.

'Hang on Jack, the apartment telephone has just rung. It's OK, it's clicked on to the answering machine.'

Frederic stood up and moved quickly and silently to the bedroom.

'Deborah, I think we've cracked the next clue. Martin and I are flying to Düsseldorf tomorrow.'

'That's wonderful, I'm so pleased. Call me when you are there. Why not then join me in München and we can spend some time together.'

'Let me call you once I know how everything pans out and hopefully I will be able to join you on Saturday.'

'Marvellous; just be careful, both of you. Look I must fly, I have a dinner engagement.' She paused. 'With a girlfriend.'

She hung up just as Frederic re-entered the room.

'Cunningham is going to Düsseldorf tomorrow with Hunt. They have discovered another element of Verglas, although he wasn't specific about exactly where they are going.'

'That was Wunsche. Eberle has confirmed that he met with Cunningham and that he gave him a book which he believed had been sent to him by Kautenberg. Cunningham is going to Wewelsburg.'

'How do you know that?'

'He very helpfully left a piece of paper in a pub ashtray which had 'Wewelsburg' written on it. The paper was too damaged for them to read what else was written. I assume he found it in the book Eberle gave him. Apart from that Eberle knows nothing. Threatening violence to someone's daughter tends to loosen the tongue.'

'I am sending Wunsche and a team to Wewelsburg. Wunsche can't leave London until early tomorrow, so I'll get a team to meet him at Düsseldorf airport.'

'What will you do with Eberle and his daughter?'

'Sadly they will perish in a domestic fire at Eberle's house sometime later this evening. Shall we go for dinner?'

Jack was about to have a shower when his phone rang. It was Martin.

'I'm afraid you'll have to go to Wewelsburg on your own. My mother's had a fall and been taken to hospital. It looks as though she has broken her ankle. I'll have to be with her when she comes out of the hospital.'

'Oh I'm so sorry to hear that but I totally understand. Give her my love.' Jack liked Martin's mother. He had met her several times and knew that at the age of 79 she was still a very game lady.

'I will. Anyway I've booked you on BA0938 leaving Heathrow at 09.40. It gets you into Düsseldorf around midday. I know you have a Hertz Gold card, so I've arranged a car for you; I just need your passport details. Email them to me and I'll get the booking references over to you and you can check in on line. Let me know how you get on. And be careful.'

Jack rang the Landhotel in Paderborn, where he and

Emma had stayed and arranged with the concierge for the transfer of his and Emma's luggage from Nuremberg. If everything went well he would drive down to München early on Saturday. His biggest problem would be dumping the people who were tailing him.

He rang Ted on his cell phone. 'Ted, I need a favour. Are you at Donovans?'

'No I'm at home.'

'Are you working tonight and if so, could you come over beforehand and bring a sports bag or a holdall that would pass muster for airport hand luggage? Put stuff in it so it looks full.'

'Sure Jack, nothing like intrigue. I'm not due at Donovans until seven so I could pop in about half an hour if that suits?'

Forty minutes later Ted arrived at the apartment with the holdall. Jack emptied the contents of the holdall and replaced them with his own belongings. They agreed that Ted would drop the bag off with the concierge at the hotel and Jack would collect it next morning. Luckily Jack was well known by all the concierges at Brown's.

Early next morning Jack left the apartment block dressed in jogging kit, catching his watchers completely by surprise. He ran down a side alley and took a route where for the most part no car could follow. Then he made his way to Brown's, recovered the holdall and changed in the men's loo. He stuffed his running kit into a plastic bag and left it with the concierge for Ted to collect. Then he hailed a cab and made his way to Heathrow.

What he didn't know was that Wunsche had already withdrawn his team. Organov was furious that Jack had evaded his men again, so he focused his efforts on Hunt, Kleinfurt and Balmer.

Over at Jack's apartment block the FSB team on station

noted that a police car had turned up. Two policemen in plain clothes entered the building and less than five minutes later returned to their car. The concierge had told them that Jack had gone on a run. The detectives waited in their car for nearly an hour before deciding to leave, having called for an unmarked car to keep a watch on the entrance.

The FSB team were now getting concerned that Jack had not returned, and called Roly. It took until 1700 hours for both Don Grant and Roly to separately establish that Cunningham had flown to Düsseldorf that morning. By the time that Don got hold of Klaus it was nearly 2100 hours German time.

Wewelsburg

Jack arrived in Paderborn mid afternoon. The concierge at the Landhotel remembered him.

'Welcome back Herr Cunningham. I take it that Fraulein Swift is not with you?'

'I'm afraid not, she has to stay in London this time.'

'I see you are staying with us for two nights. I've placed your and Fraulein Swift's luggage in your room. If there is anything else I can do for you please do not hesitate to ask.'

'Thank you. In fact there is something you can do for me I would greatly appreciate it if you let me know if anyone asks after me.'

'Of course sir, I fully understand.' Jack slipped the concierge a 50 Euro note. 'Thank you for arranging the luggage. There is something else you can do for me. Do you know if there is a DIY or hardware store located nearby?'

'Yes sir, there's a large store just on the outskirts of the town, not far at all.' He showed Jack the store on a town map.

Having unpacked, Jack drove the short distance to the store, where he purchased a heavy-duty torch and a pocket torch, masking tape, a small crowbar and a pair of work gloves. He drove to the castle to get his bearings and reconnoitre the area in daylight. Just in front of the castle there was a track which ran into a heavily-wooded area just below the ramparts.

He drove about 300 metres down the track and found an area just off the road where he could park. He had learned from the concierge that Wewelsburg was going through a major renovation and was currently closed. Apparently it was to become a museum specialising in the SS. The idea was to demystify the SS, which had become a focus for far-right extremists.

There was scaffolding all over the castle's outer wall, which would give Jack easy access to the inner courtyard and the main buildings. With a bit of luck he would be able to force one of the lower windows. He knew he would be taking a gamble that the place was not alarmed.

He returned to the car and drove back to the hotel. He reckoned that it would be fully dark at around 9 pm and noted that at present it was a cloudless sky. This would help his movement through the undergrowth.

Jack ate in the hotel restaurant, and at 8.45 pm he drove back to the spot where he had originally parked.

Wunsche had taken the first available flight from London, which left Heathrow at 12.20, arriving in Düsseldorf at 14.40. He was met by two members of Totenkopf and during the journey to Paderborn he briefed them on the situation. They had come heavily armed, and gave him a Glock 9 mm pistol with a suppressor and shoulder holster.

Henry called Wunsche to tell him that Cunningham had arrived in Dusseldorf at midday and had hired a black Mercedes from Hertz. Although he had a two-hour start on them it was unlikely that he would have had the time to get into Wewelsburg. He also confirmed that Cunningham had booked into the Landhotel and gave Wunsche the address as well as the car registration number. Wunsche asked after the man who was supposed to be with Cunningham. Henry said he had no details on any other person.

They parked the van near the hotel car park and one of the team confirmed that Cunningham's car was there. While one of the team went for some food, the other two maintained surveillance on the car.

At 8.45 pm they spotted Cunningham leaving the hotel and followed him towards Wewelsburg. There was heavy traffic on the main roads, so the dark blue van they were driving did not look out of place. They saw Cunningham turn down a track near the castle, and decided not to follow as their lights would give them away.

Wunsche instructed the driver to pull over, just off the main road. The driver stayed in the vehicle with the lights off while

Wunsche and the other man went on foot down the edge of the track. They could see the headlights of the Mercedes in the distance and the brake lights as the car stopped. Then the lights went off. The car was about 300 metres down the track.

The second man pulled out a small passive night vision scope through which he observed the Mercedes. He handed the scope to Wunsche and they drew their weapons. There was no sign of Cunningham.

As they approached the Mercedes, Wunsche instructed the third man to drive down the track with his lights off, park 50 metres from the Mercedes and remain with the van.

Jack climbed the scaffolding with ease and descended into the main courtyard. He sat in the shadows of the wall and scanned the area for any activity. The ground floor windows to the main building were all at head height and difficult to reach.

Then he spotted a pile of wooden pallets in the corner. Dragging them over one at a time, he managed to build a stand which enabled him to reach one of the windows. He tried to open the leaded window with the crowbar, but it wouldn't budge.

He moved the pallets to the next window where he managed to open a small window within the main structure. He pulled himself through the window, falling unceremoniously into the great hall. He picked himself up and switched on the large torch. To reduce the chance of discovery he had taped over the lens so that it emitted a very narrow beam, just enough to see by.

He was in a large hall with four exits, each with a big wooden door. The third door he checked opened on to a set of spiral steps which descended into the bowels of the castle. Jack closed the door behind him and went down the steps. He must have descended at least 20 feet when the steps opened into a small chamber, at the end of which was a substantial set of double wooden doors. He opened the doors and stood at the top of a short flight of stone steps leading down to a large chamber.

This room was windowless so Jack removed the tape from the torch and scanned the room. It was circular and vaulted, and there was a sunken pit in the centre some twenty feet across with what seemed like a series of stone seats equally spaced around the edge of the pit. He supposed that this must be the crypt.

At the back of the crypt was a low circular stone affair with a metal structure above it. Jack thought it was probably a well. He descended the steps and walked over to the pit, which was about two feet deep. A highly-polished black circular stone was inset in the centre. There were twelve seats equally positioned around the edge of the depression, each engraved with SS runes. One of the seats had a higher back than the others and was more elaborately carved.

Jack went over to the other stone structure and confirmed that it was a well. He picked up a small stone chip from the floor and dropped it into the well. Four seconds later there came a faint splash; it was deep.

Jack looked again at the room. There was no sign of any clock or anything vaguely resembling a clock face. Perhaps there was another crypt. He glanced at his watch, it was 10.15 pm.

He decided to see if there was another underground chamber. He climbed the steps to the door and turned for one last scan of the room. It then dawned on him that, of course, the circle had twelve positions - it was a clock face. He descended the stairs and stood in the centre of the circle. If the larger seat represented 12, then was it the fourth or the eighth seat that had been signified on the slip of paper?

He went to the fourth seat and examined it thoroughly. He found inset into the back of the seat a stone, about six inches square. SS runes were carved on the face of the stone. He looked at the seats either side; each also had a small stone inset in the back.

He inserted the crowbar into a slit above the inset and carefully teased the stone out of the back of the fourth seat.

Jack had been concentrating so hard on the stone that he had failed to hear the two men who had come down the steps into the crypt.

'Good evening Mr Cunningham.' Wunsche approached him. The other man was pointing a pistol at Jack.

'Where is Hunt?' said Wunsche.

Jack thought this was a strange question. If these are Totenkopf, they would certainly have had Martin under surveillance.

'He's back in London as far as I know. I'm here alone.'

'Shall we see what you have uncovered? Step away from the seat, Mr Cunningham. Schumaker, check the recess.' Wunsche pulled out his pistol and Schumaker shouldered his gun and went to the seat. He bent down and shone a torch into the recess, then placed his hand inside.

'There is nothing here, it's empty.'

Wunsche turned to face the man. This was Jack's moment. He flung the crowbar at Wunsche, hitting his shoulder and causing him to drop his gun. Before Schumaker could rise Jack kicked him twice in the side of his head. Schumaker collapsed unconscious over the seat.

Jack leapt at Wunsche, forcing him to the ground. With his fists he rained blows to Wunsche's head. Wunsche managed to retrieve the automatic but Jack was holding his wrist, preventing him turning the gun on him. But Wunsche was very strong. Slowly the barrel of the gun turned towards Jack's chest.

Jack managed to get his right hand over the rear of the gun, jamming his little finger into the gap between the hammer and the firing plate. Wunsche pulled the trigger, but Jack's hand was preventing the hammer reaching the cartridge. Jack released his left hand from the gun, keeping his right hand on the hammer. He then drove two of his fingers into Wunsche's eyes and twisted his fingers in the eye sockets.

Wunsche screamed and released his hold of the gun. The hammer fell and the gun fired, the bullet ricocheting around the room. Jack grabbed the now blinded Wunsche and propelled him to the edge of the well. With a great heave he tipped him in.

Jack turned just as the other man was rising unsteadily from the floor. He grabbed the heavy Maglite torch and hit the man hard on the head, repeatedly. He slumped to the floor.

Jack noted dispassionately that there was very little blood, although his own hands were sticky with Wunsche's blood.

He searched the man's body and retrieved a wallet, which had about 300 Euros in it. There was nothing else, no credit cards or anything that could identify the man. Jack also noted that there were no labels on his clothing. He removed the man's shoulder holster which carried two spare clips of ammunition and a suppressor. He found a cell phone in the man's jacket pocket. Jack now had two loaded Glocks and two spare magazines. He fitted the suppressor to one of the Glocks and put on the shoulder holster. He checked that both the guns were loaded, each with a round chambered and the safety catch on.

Adrenalin was still pumping through his body as Jack dragged the man to the well and tipped him into the abyss. He didn't care whether the man was alive or dead. Using the man's jacket Jack wiped up the blood on the crypt floor. Having checked that there were no other tell-tale signs of their presence, he wiped his hands on the jacket and then tossed it into the well.

Jack looked into the recess and checked that there was nothing in it. He replaced the stone and walked over to the eighth seat. Then, using the crowbar, he removed the stone inset. He put his hand into the recess and felt something soft; a folded leather package. He withdrew it and replaced the stone.

There was no time to lose; other Totenkopf men could be following. After a quick final check that the room was as clean and clear as it could be, Jack ascended the stairs in darkness, allowing his night vision to develop. He held the Glock in his right hand and the switched off torch in the other. As he got to the great hall there was enough moonlight to enable him to see clearly and to reach the window where he had entered the castle.

He climbed out of the window and carefully descended to the cobbled courtyard below. He moved into deep shadow and remained there for a few minutes scanning the area to his front for any sign of activity. He was temporarily spooked by an owl which swooped down past him to take some small creature. He now felt very calm and focused; his former military training and experience clicked in as he moved out of the shadows and made his way rapidly and silently towards the forest edge, staying in shadow as much as he could.

There was a full moon which was a nuisance but at least it assisted his movement. He slipped in between the trees and moved slowly and deliberately, feeling his way with his feet. It was a still night and he knew any noise would carry. The last thing he wanted to do was snap a twig. He kept his mouth open, knowing it sharpened the hearing.

He began to head towards the road where his car was located, offsetting his route to the right so that he would hit the road just above where the car was parked.

After a few minutes he stopped at the edge of the forest and lay down on a carpet of pine needles. Here he spent a good ten minutes scanning the area around his car. He was just about to move when he caught sight of the glow from a cigarette, some fifty metres down from his car. Stupid bugger, he thought. A basic art of field craft was that you never smoked at night unless you were fully shaded, and even then it was unwise because of the smell of the smoke.

He pulled back. Then, taking a wide route through the forest, he circled around until he was about thirty feet from the smoker. He now knew why he hadn't seen the man before; he had been shielded by a dark van parked on the edge of the road. Jack moved closer until he was about 10 feet away. The man was of heavy build and there was no obvious sign of any weapons, but Jack had to assume he was armed.

He stepped on to the road and walked rapidly towards the man. The man heard Jack and turned, but before he could retrieve his weapon Jack shot him in the head at point blank range. The only noise was the muted crack of the suppressed Glock and the man's body falling to the ground.

Jack quickly checked the van; there was no one else. He moved to the edge of the track, slipped into the undergrowth and sat on his haunches, scanning the area to look for any activity. He could not hear or see anything but, to be sure, he stayed in position for another ten minutes before returning to the van.

He pocketed the man's handgun and searched the body. As with the man in the schloss, there was no form of identification, but Jack found a further 250 Euros to add to his funds plus another cell phone. He had a good look inside the van and found a holdall in which there were two MP5K automatic weapons, a bag of ammunition and what looked like stun grenades. He took the holdall to his car, placed it in the boot, and returned to the man. He locked the van and pocketed the keys, then dragged the man into the forest for about 30 metres and covered him with pine needles and branches. He tossed the keys deep into the forest and returned to his car. He desperately wanted to see what was in the package but he knew that, first, he needed to clear the area and get to a place of relative safety.

He got into his car and drove towards Paderborn. Once there he found a quiet residential street and stopped the car. He turned on the courtesy light and took the package out of his pocket; it was waxed, like the one they had found in the book in Helmut's flat. Inside were two tightly-folded sheets of paper, roughly A4 in size and brown with age.

Both sheets were in German. The top one bore a number of place names Jack recognised, and what looked like a twelve-figure map grid reference. The other sheet appeared to be a sketch of a tunnel system. He had found the missing Appendix B.

Jack looked at his watch; it was now 1 am. He decided he would not go to München but would return straight to London. He knew there was a flight from Düsseldorf which departed at 12.35 pm, so he drove back to the hotel, went on line and booked the flight. With the excuse that he had been called back to London, he checked out of the hotel and drove for a couple of hours. Desperate for sleep he parked in a Rasthof on the autobahn, and woke at six after sleeping fitfully. He bought a coffee and a bratwurst roll from the Rasthof and thought about his next move. He knew he had to get rid of the weapons as there was no way he could sneak them past security at the airport. Yet he needed to hang on to them in some way.

He also needed to get rid of the cell phones. Leaving them switched on, he placed them on separate lorries parked nearby. Hopefully the trucks would be going to distant destinations, so if the phones had tracking devices they would certainly screw up the Totenkopf.

He rang Martin and told him which flight he was going to catch. For security reasons they agreed that Martin would not pick him up from Heathrow but that Jack would travel by underground to Osterley and Martin would meet him at the station. Martin sounded as excited as a small boy when Jack told him what he had found.

It was just after 9 am when Klaus's team were provided with the details of Jack's hotel. Much to Klaus's annoyance the Research team tasked with tracking down the hotel had gone home early the previous evening; they were civilians and stuck to their employment hours rigidly. The police had yet again lost Jack. Klaus rang Don Grant apprising him of the situation.

Before he went to the airport, Jack drove first to Düsseldorf's main rail station and deposited the holdall and the weapons and explosives in a left-luggage locker ready for collection when he returned to Germany. Reaching the airport he rang Martin to tell him the flight was on time As he boarded the aircraft, he briefly telephoned Deborah to tell her that he couldn't make it to Münich as he had to return to London. She sounded upset but seemed understanding about Jack's decision.

By the time Klaus had established which flight Jack was on,

the aircraft had landed at Heathrow and Jack was on the Underground heading to Osterley where Martin was waiting. As they travelled back to London, Jack told Martin what had happened.

'It was strange. They were expecting you to be with me' said Jack. 'I have no idea how they would know that.' He had forgotten that he had mentioned Martin in his conversation with Deborah when she had been at Frederic's apartment.

'Neither do I, I hadn't told anyone. Only you and I knew you were even going to Germany, and, even if someone managed to get the flight details, they would have seen I wasn't with you. If you were followed they still wouldn't have seen me.'

The pair went straight to Martin's office at the *Independent,* where they made one photocopy of the two pages, scanning them to two discs, and then placing one disc with the original documents in the Chelsea Flower Show file. The Verglas file was now complete.

Totenkopf, München

Ernst Meyer, the leader of the Dortmund team, was briefing Frederic Kleinfurt over the secure line from Paderborn. When Wunsche had failed to report in, Meyer had despatched the Dortmund team to check out his last known location; Wewelsburg. They had also carried out a location check on Schumaker's cell phone, but this had placed him heading into France until the battery ran out and they lost contact. A second cell phone was tracked to Berlin before it also became silent. Nothing made sense.

'We can't find Wunsche and Schumaker, they have vanished off the face of the earth. I must assume they are dead or Cunningham has them. We've recovered the van which was empty. We found Schmidt's body concealed in the woods. He had been shot in the head at close range.'

Frederic was slowly losing patience. 'It would seem our Mr Cunningham is a resourceful and lucky man' he said. 'I think we may have underestimated him. Ernst, I want you to take over Wunsche's role. I will ensure everyone knows that you are now head of operations. We must find Cunningham. Use our contacts in the airline and car hire industry. We know he entered the country and hired a car at Düsseldorf Airport. We cannot guarantee he will return to London via the same airport, but I am positive he will return. We must also assume that he found what he was looking for in Wewelsburg. Increase the surveillance on Hunt. I am going to send the Cleaner back to London.'

Frederic rang off and immediately called Deborah telling her all that Ernst had told him. He instructed her to return to London and connect as soon as possible with Cunningham. 'We must bring this matter to a close. I want the Verglas file. You know what to do once you have it.'

London

Jack and Martin had left the newspaper building and had gone to a pub in St Katherine's Dock. They found themselves a booth where they could not be overheard. Martin went to the bar and Jack opened the *Telegraph* much to Martin's annoyance as he returned clutching two pints of bitter.

'You have no bloody loyalty, you bastard' said Martin. 'Particularly as you're expecting me to translate these documents for you!' Jack promised to convert to the *Independent* but continued to read his *Telegraph* while Martin translated the papers, occasionally muttering under his breath. 'Disloyal bugger.'

Jack was thinking about Martin's comments during their journey into town. He remembered now that he had told Deborah that Martin and he were going to Düsseldorf, though she did not know about Martin's mother. It must be a coincidence. Or perhaps the General was right in being cautious.

It took Martin about an hour to translate the documents. 'Well, that was fairly straightforward' he announced. 'Your hunch was right. Page One is a set of instructions and directions to a mine entrance in the Oberfälzer Wald, about 100 kilometres east of Nuremberg. The second sheet is a map of a mine, or tunnel complex, which ends in a chamber at the end of the system. I reckon the chamber is located about half a kilometre into the hill. The chamber is marked Verglas, so I suppose we can safely presume that is where we'll find all or some of the items listed in Appendix A. This is gripping stuff Jack; straight out of a Dan Brown novel. What next, mein Führer?'

Jack sipped his beer. 'Well we've hidden the original documents and one of the discs somewhere safe. I think I know where I'll send the second disc and this copy. You remember the bank Emma and I went to where we got the original file? I'm tempted to send them there. However, we'll need another copy as when I go to Germany I'll need one for myself of Appendix B.'

'Bugger that. You're not leaving me behind this time, and I think I'll be able to leave my mother for a couple of days. Anyway you'll need a babysitter to keep you out of trouble. Before you say anything, I am totally aware of the risks. I may not be an ex-soldier, but I can still handle myself. Have you got the Nuremberg bank details to hand? I can send the disc and papers by secure courier via the newspaper plus do another copy for us.'

Fortunately Jack had both the details of the bank and the account number, so, while Martin rushed back to the newspaper, he ordered another pint and started to formulate a plan.

His thoughts were interrupted by a text message from Deborah saying she would be back in London the following night for a few days and wanted to see him. Somewhat surprised as he'd only spoken to her that morning from the airport but pleased, he texted her back to meet him in the Library Bar at the Lanesborough and said he'd call her room when he arrived.

On Martin's return they discussed the plan. They would fly to Düsseldorf with only hand luggage, hire a car and collect the weapons from the railway station. They would then drive to Bayreuth, purchase the additional clothing and kit they would need afterwards travelling to where they would stay at that night. In the interim Jack would see if he could get a map of the area where the mine was located - at least a 1:50,000 scale and if possible a 1:25,000.

'Stanfords in Convent Garden is probably your best bet for the maps,' suggested Martin. They decided they would leave London in three days' time. Jack didn't tell Martin that this was partly to enable him to see Deborah.

At 7:30 pm, the following evening, Jack was sitting in the Library Bar at the Lanesborough, nursing a martini waiting for Deborah. She entered the bar some thirty minutes later wearing a tailored black dress set off by a grey pearl necklace and diamond studs, looking fabulous. Her entrance as usual had turned a few heads. He looked at her as he stood up to greet her and thought, surely, she couldn't be the one to have betrayed us.

The waiter approached them and he ordered a T10 martini for Deborah. Pleased that he had remembered, she asked him what had been happening and why he had chosen to fly back to London rather than coming to see her in Munich. She teased him, 'If the mountain won't come to Mohammed....'

He told her that he and Martin were flying to Düsseldorf on Tuesday and then driving south to Bayreuth.

'But why don't you fly to a closer airport?' she asked.

'Martin has to meet some journo friend in Düsseldorf related to his work, so we thought we could kill two birds with one stone.'

Jack didn't want to tell Deborah about the weapons cache at Düsseldorf Railway Station. He had decided to be more circumspect about what he told her as he was not at all sure whether to trust her. But he did find her very sexy.

Deborah looked at him as if she could read his mind. 'Why don't we have dinner in my room?' she said softly. As they travelled up in the lift, Deborah moved close to Jack and Jack, thinking only fleetingly of Emma, kissed her. The lift stopped and they moved towards her room. Deborah fumbled with her room card, eventually opening the door.

Their lovemaking was urgent and passionate as they explored each other's bodies until they both reached orgasm. Afterwards they lay back in bed exhausted. Deborah stroked Jack's hair and murmured "I think we deserve some champagne." She slid out of the bed and took a chilled bottle of Perrier Jouet from a bucket on a table close by. She opened it and poured two glasses.

"Prosit, Jack" she said, raising her glass. She turned to Jack, and without saying anything, she stroked his penis gently until he became hard again. They made love once more, this time with greater tenderness, eventually falling asleep in each others' arms.

Jack awoke to find that Deborah was out of bed taking a shower. She came into the bedroom drying her hair and wearing an oversized white towelling robe. She went over to him and kissed him gently once on each eyelid.

'I feel rather deprived. I seem to have missed out on dinner. Mind you, there were compensations.'

Jack caught her wrist and dragged her down on top of him. "No no" she said, sounding reluctant. 'There's no time.'

'How disappointing. So what instead, Deborah?"

'I think some breakfast - I'm absolutely famished' she said, walking over to the telephone. She rang room service and turned back to Jack.

'You still owe me dinner and I'm in meetings all day from ten. Why don't we meet at Donovan's and try to finish the evening we started? Preferably without all those Russians and Germans!'

Jack showered as she dressed, and after breakfast they went down to the lobby. Neither of them noticed the woman sitting in the lobby reading a newspaper.

The doorman called a cab. 'Can I drop you anywhere?' Deborah asked as the doorman opened the cab door for her.

'No thanks it's such a nice day I think I'll take a walk.' She kissed him gently on the lips. 'I'll see you at seven.'

'Yes I'll see you then. We'll finish the evening properly this time,' Jack smiled as he closed the cab door for her.

Jack walked through the subway by the hotel towards Hyde Park, entered the park and headed towards the Albert

Memorial. He was not ready to return to his apartment which he was sure was being watched.

Behind him, a green Volvo stopped and a man got out. The woman who had been reading the paper in the hotel climbed in and it drove off, pulling into the traffic behind Deborah's cab.

Jack rang Martin and they agreed to meet for lunch at the Red Lion near Martin's flat. There, they made their final plans for their trip, Martin confirming that the disc and documents had arrived at the German bank. He gave Jack three maps covering the area in Germany where they would be travelling.

Deborah had, meanwhile, contacted Frederic and briefed him on what Cunningham had told her.

'I need you to go to Nuremberg, to the safe house, as soon as you can' said Frederic. 'I want you to coordinate activities from there. I will send four teams; three to track Cunningham and Hunt's route from Düsseldorf airport to Bayreuth, and the other team to Bayreuth. I don't want Hunt and Cunningham harmed until we are 100 per cent sure we have the complete file.'

Having booked a Lufthansa flight leaving Heathrow at 13.20, which would get her into Munich at 16.10, Deborah took a cab to the hotel, checked out and went straight to the airport. Then she rang Jack.

'Jack, it's Deborah, I have to go back to Munich immediately-another crisis. That deal I told you about is definitely falling apart. I'll call you tonight when I get back home.'

Jack said he totally understood but in fact was quite relieved as he really didn't have the time to see her that evening as he and Martin still had to work out how they could leave London without their minders.

Scotland Yard

Don Grant was getting increasingly frustrated by events. This Cunningham is like a will o' the wisp, he thought. He's always one step ahead of us. He voiced his concerns to his team.

'Ladies and gentlemen, boys and girls, Jack Cunningham is running fucking rings around us. He gave the Germans the slip on his recent foray over there. He's either very clever or bloody lucky. With his experience in covert ops with 14 Intelligence Company in Ulster, I suspect the former.'

If Grant had only known the truth; Jack had been lucky. So far.

'Dan, I want you and George to start checking all Cunningham's known associates. Sue, help Dan. Keep up the surveillance of Cunningham's apartment block and if he turns up, lift him.' He paused. 'I'm convinced Cunningham is the key to this whole case. Harry, anything from the Parson's Green search?'

'No boss, there are a load of vacant business units under the arches beneath the rail line and the occupied ones all check out as legit. There's one that's been empty for five years.' He checked his notes. 'It's leased by a Finnish export/import company. I spoke with them and they seem to be kosher. They have a great deal on the lease so they've just hung onto it.' Harry did not know that the person he had spoken to was Roly.

Don stood up. 'I think we are now totally reliant on finding people linked with Cunningham. Either that or we get lucky and he sticks his head above the parapet. Thanks people.'

Don then rang Klaus. 'Klaus, it's Don Grant. As you let me know, we're not having much luck at our end either. I'll call you as soon as something further happens.' They rang off.

London, FSB

It was 5 am when Ivan Terpinski in Moscow called control in London. The duty officer immediately went to Organov's room, where he was sleeping on a camp bed. 'General!' He gently shook Organov. 'It's Colonel Terpinski. He needs to speak with you urgently.'

Organov woke from a very deep sleep, his mouth tasting like a bear's jock strap. Too much whisky.

'Thank you Travkin, just give me a few minutes.'

Organov rolled out of bed, put on his dressing gown and trudged down the corridor to the bathroom, thinking he was perhaps too old for this game. He relieved himself and cleaned his teeth. At least he had got rid of the taste of stale whisky. Still wearing his dressing gown, he went to the control room in the basement. He sat down at the desk and picked up the secure phone. Travkin placed a mug of fresh coffee by his elbow. Organov sipped the coffee and nodded in appreciation.

'Ivan, what is it?' Organov knew that Ivan would only call him if it was important.

'Vladimir, I am sorry it has taken us so long but we've had a break. It was in our own archive! It goes back to an operation we did in 1989 involving a member of the Stasi - you may remember, his name was Johann Hartenstein. He had tried to offer the Amber Room on the open market and even had a fragment of Amber as proof.'

'I remember. Wasn't he killed under suspicious circumstances before we could get to him?'

'That's correct. He was found alone in a car at the bottom of a cliff. He was in the driver's seat, which was strange because Hartenstein couldn't drive. In trying to follow up on any links and to see if we could sort out his death we obviously checked with the family and known associates. Hartenstein had a son and daughter, and he got them to live with one of his wife's brothers. You will remember in the Sixties things were beginning to turn nasty for the Stasi as Mossad were tracking down war criminals who were protected by the East German regime. It would seem he wanted to have his children disassociated from him. Well the daughter eventually grew up and married and had children... '

Organov interrupted. 'You're going to tell me that Frau Hartenstein's maiden name is Balmer and that this is the same Deborah Balmer we are dealing with.'

It was a minor frustration for Ivan that Organov was always ahead of him in his reasoning. 'Correct. She was christened Margareta Deborah and now only uses Deborah. Hartenstein was a member of the Nazi party and SS and was Himmler's personal architect. His major project was the creation of the SS College at Wewelsburg. The West still think he's alive and there is an open warrant for crimes against humanity as he oversaw the death of some 3900 concentration camp prisoners who worked on Wewelsburg. I am transmitting a photograph of her. It's of her as a teenager. Unfortunately it's the only one we could find.'

Travkin was already bringing up the image on his computer, alongside a current photo they had taken of her. Using a software package for face recognition and comparison he soon confirmed that there was an 83% match; it was the same woman.

'We have our woman Ivan, well done. Any more news on Kleinfurt?'

'No but we're working on it.'

'Thank you Ivan.' Organov hung up and turned to Travkin. 'Where are Cunningham and Hunt?'

'Cunningham is at his apartment and Hunt is staying at the hospital where his mother is being kept. It seems what they thought was a minor fracture of her ankle developed a blood clot which has caused problems. There is nothing life threatening, but she is being kept under observation.'

'Call Cunningham, I wish to speak with him.'

Travkin called Jack's number. 'There's no reply. His cell phone is off and his house phone keeps diverting to the answer machine.'

'Leave a message on his machine for him to contact Roly immediately. Cunningham has his number.'

What the General didn't know was that Jack had slipped out of his apartment with the help of his concierge, who was only too happy to assist him after he had been told he was being watched by private detectives working for the jealous husband of his lover. Jack had left with a bunch of removal men who were emptying one of the apartments.

At the hospital Martin had stolen a doctor's white coat and a stethoscope, which he placed around his neck. He left the hospital through the very busy and crowded A&E department. Jack and Martin had rendezvoused at Heathrow, where they had checked into the Radisson Edwardian. At the time the General was trying to contact Jack they had just checked out of their hotel and were on their way to Terminal 1 for their 7.20 flight to Düsseldorf.

'Travkin, I don't trust these buggers. Run an airline check on them both, German destinations only, and get me Uri.'

By 7 am Organov had the flight details, but there was insufficient time for him to get a team to Düsseldorf before

Jack and Martin's flight arrived there.

'Damn, we've lost them, the fools. Give me Cunningham's cell phone number. It's too late to call him as he will be on his flight but I can send him a text.' Travkin handed him the phone. 'Get me on the next available flight back to Moscow, I'll run the operation from there.'

Düsseldorf, Germany

The BA flight landed at Düsseldorf airport at 9.45. As they only had hand luggage, Martin and Jack had cleared the airport quickly and collected their hire car, a black Mercedes, with no hassle. Martin drove them to the main railway station where Jack recovered the bag from the locker. From there they set off on the 500-kilometre journey to Bayreuth.

Martin reckoned, depending on traffic and rest breaks, it would take them between four and five hours to get there. Jack thought he would ring Deborah and tell her of their progress but found his cell phone battery was out of power; he would have to wait until they got to Bayreuth to recharge it. At least he remembered her number. 'Martin, lend me your phone' he said. 'I'm out of power.'

Jack called Deborah but got her answering service so he left her a message that they were on the road and he would call her when they got to Bayreuth.

The reason Jack was unable to contact Deborah was that she was in Nuremberg speaking with the team that was currently trailing Jack and Martin in a green Opel some 200 metres behind them. A second car would take over around Frankfurt, and if necessary a third would see them through to Bayreuth, where a fourth team had already been deployed.

Jack and Martin arrived in Bayreuth around 3.30 pm and checked into the Grunau Hotel which was a short distance from the E51 Autobahn. Because they were planning to leave early next morning they decided to pay their bills up front. Leaving the hotel they drove into the city where they purchased, from an outdoor activities centre, various items of equipment including protective clothing, all green in colour, climbing helmets, rope, two rock hammers, thermos flasks, head torches, sleeping bags, cooking equipment, emergency dry rations and two rucksacks.

Martin went off to buy a digital camera, and Jack went to a hunting shop and bought gun cleaning material. A charger for his cell phone was the next priority. All this was observed by the Totenkopf team and relayed to Deborah. She instructed the first two surveillance teams to redeploy to Nuremberg and the third team to support the team in Bayreuth.

Due to the checks he had put in place, Don Grant now knew that Martin Hunt was a close friend of Cunningham. Both Cunningham and he had disappeared and, after checking with the airlines, he discovered that Cunningham and Hunt had travelled to Düsseldorf together that morning. He rang Klaus and informed him of this development.

Jack and Martin returned to the hotel. While Martin sorted out the kit, Jack put his phone on charge and then cleaned and checked the weapons. They had three Glock 9 mm semi-automatic pistols with three spare magazines, each magazine holding seventeen rounds and a total of one hundred rounds of ammunition. There were two MP5Ks, each loaded with thirty rounds of 9mm ammunition, plus a further four spare magazines. They now had something like three hundred rounds of ammunition and six stun grenades.

Martin looked at the weapons Jack had placed on the bed. 'We've got enough to start a small war. We really are in the proverbial if we have to use this lot.'

'Well if we do, I'd better show you how to use them.'

Jack then spent the next hour putting Martin through his paces, including aiming and stoppage drills accompanied by lots of swearing from Martin as he grazed his hands reloading.

Jack still couldn't guarantee that they hadn't been followed so, when they had finished, he unscrewed the air-conditioning vent and stashed the weapons and ammunition behind the grille. He retained one of the Glocks, which he placed in a shoulder holster.

The concierge had earlier recommended the Lömuhle, a restaurant noted for its Franconian cuisine and had made a reservation for them. They were not disappointed. They were given a table on the terrace overlooking the Mühlbach River, and dined on some excellent trout. They talked at length about the next few days and contingencies if they were discovered and followed. Despite having been out the military for a number of years, Jack remembered his tactical training. It felt good that he had not completely lost his edge.

They returned to the hotel, had a nightcap and then retired to their rooms. Before going out Jack had positioned a couple of items, a book on his bedside table and a pen on the desk and had marked their position with small pencil marks. He noted that each had been moved, albeit only slightly. He rang the front desk and asked if housekeeping had visited his room.

'No one has been in your room Herr Cunningham, but if there is a problem?'

'No, thank you, everything is fine.'

So someone had searched his room. He had to assume they had also searched Martin's.

He checked the vent. He had placed a hair across the side of it, secured with dabs of toothpaste. The hair was intact. He withdrew the bag and examined the contents. They had not been tampered with and he returned the bag to the vent. Thank God he had kept the copy of the appendix with him. He rang Martin.

'We've had company. We must assume we're being watched.'

They agreed to get up early and, as they had only about 80 kilometres to drive to their final destination, they could catch breakfast at a Rasthof en route.

Putting down the phone, Jack sat for a moment thinking and then, on impulse, went to Martin's room and handed him a loaded Glock with a suppressor fitted. 'Just in case our friends plan any more visits. I know it sounds a bit melodramatic but don't answer your door unless you know it's me. I'll knock twice, pause for five seconds and then knock a further three times. You do the same routine when you visit my room.'

Just as he got back to his room Jack's cell phone rang. It was Deborah. 'Jack, I'm so sorry I missed you. Is everything OK?'

'Everything's fine. We're in our hotel and we've just had an excellent dinner. We'll be leaving rather early tomorrow. It's lovely to hear from you but I'm pretty exhausted - particularly after the other night.' She laughed and Jack thought that she had the sexiest laugh. He said rather reluctantly, 'I really do need to go to bed.'

They talked for a few more minutes and agreed that Jack would ring her once there were any further developments. He stripped off and was about to climb into the bed when his phone beeped; he had been sent a text message. He opened his inbox.

'Jack. Important you contact me. Deborah is Totenkopf. Call Roly ASAP. Vladimir.'

Jack couldn't believe it. He took a bottle of whisky from his luggage, poured a large shot and contemplated what Organov had told him. He felt like a fool but the more he thought about it, the more he realised it was the truth. He was now under no delusion. There had been too many unexplained coincidences, all linked in some way to Deborah. He called Roly, who connected him to the General. 'Jack, I'm sorry, she is Totenkopf.' Organov then briefed Jack fully on what they had discovered. Jack told him where they were and explained that in the morning they would be driving in the direction of Weiden. Roly checked the proximity of Bayreuth to Weiden and Münich, which was the location of the nearest FSB team. The team was instructed to deploy to Weiden immediately.

'Jack, listen to me, I'm sending a team to Weiden tonight. They'll have your cell phone number and will call you in the morning. They will use the password 'Eiswein'. I will get more people on the ground, but it's going to take time; I need 24 hours. Jack you must let us help you, we can provide security. Do the Totenkopf know where you are?'

'I think my room had been searched so I must assume there are Totenkopf nearby. I have told Deborah my current location, but nothing more. Only Martin and I know where we're going.'

Jack was still absorbing the information about Deborah, but he knew he had to trust someone.

'OK General, we'll cooperate with your people.'
They rang off immediately and Jack called Martin who took some time to answer and asked him to come to his room.

Martin arrived wearing a dressing gown looking as if he'd been dragged from a deep sleep – which he had - and sat on the bed. Jack poured each of them a whisky and removed the bag with the weapons from behind the vent. He told Martin about his conversation with the General.

'We're on the final leg. It'll be dangerous. Because of me, Deborah knows we have the appendix and that we're going to the place identified in it. We're about to become expendable. The General is sending his people to protect us, but he needs 24 hours to get them all in position. I'm not sure we have that luxury. Deborah doesn't know we now know of her link with Totenkopf, so I could feed her some false information. But once she realises she's been duped... ' He poured them each another whisky. 'We have to assume the hotel is being watched and they probably know which car is ours, so our next challenge is to get out of here without them knowing. Martin, go back to your room and get dressed and packed.' It was just past midnight. 'Meet me back here at 1 am; I've a couple of things I need to do.'

'Like what?' Martin stood up.

'I'm going to see if I can spot our followers. It's something I need to do on my own. No offence old mate, but this is one area you are not skilled in.' He wrote Roly's phone number on a piece of paper and handed it to Martin. 'Take this. If I don't come back, call the General.'

'Will do.' Martin finished his drink and went back to his room.

Jack got dressed and then packed. He put on the shoulder holster, checked the Glock, fitted the suppressor and cocked the action. He placed a spare magazine in his jacket pocket and slipped out of the room taking the elevator to the first floor where he got out and took the stairs to the lobby. He opened the door to the lobby slightly to enable him to see into the area. He could hear music coming from the office behind reception but there was no one in the lobby. He was about to step out when a man appeared from the toilet across the lobby, so he held back and watched the man sit down. Luckily the man had his back to Jack and was facing the lift entrance.

He had to be the enemy. Who else would sit on their own in a hotel lobby at this time of night?

Jack opened the door and moved rapidly towards the man, the sound of his footsteps masked by the carpet. The man turned just as Jack placed the barrel of his gun in the man's neck and gripped his shoulder. Jack said nothing but indicated for the man to stand. Then he led him through the door into the stairwell. Here Jack removed a gun from the man's shoulder holster before directing him to go down the stairs to the basement level.

As they neared the bottom the man stumbled, taking Jack off guard. In that moment the man swept his right arm around, hitting the back of Jack's right knee and sweeping him off his feet. He tumbled the last few steps, falling over the man and landing on his back.

The man pulled out a switchblade. Jack lashed out with his right leg and hit the man's thigh, knocking him down. Jack leapt on top of him, holding the man's knife hand by the wrist, and hit him repeatedly around the head with the butt of his pistol. The man lost consciousness.

Jack dragged the body into a basement corridor and then into a store room containing cleaning equipment. He pulled the man to the back of the room, where he looked around for something to tie him up. There was nothing.

'Oh sod it,' he muttered. He shot the man once through

the forehead, pocketed the switchblade and searched the body. He found some Euros which he also pocketed. He placed the body behind some boxes and left the store room.

Jack returned to the basement corridor and exited the hotel via a service entrance. There was no one about. The car park was lined with trees so he used them for cover, quickly moving from tree to tree and keeping in the shadows. There were a dozen cars in the car park and Jack slowly scanned each one. He was about to look away when he saw that tell-tale glint of a cigarette from one of the cars. Did these guys never learn?

The car was a red Audi and there was a man in the driver's seat. Jack approached the car at an angle and to the rear, so the man couldn't see him in the car's mirrors. The window was open. At less than six feet, he fired a single shot into the man's head.

He dragged the body from the car and searched it. The man was armed but had no identity documents on him, just more cash, which Jack took. He placed the body in the boot, locked the car and threw the keys into the undergrowth.

Jack returned to the hotel and entered through the lobby; the night porter was too engrossed with his television to notice him.

At the agreed time Martin came to Jack's room and Jack explained what had happened.

'Jesus, you don't fuck about, do you?' Martin exclaimed as they left the room. They went through the lobby just as the night porter came out of the office. Jack gave him their keys - the porter had been briefed on their planned early departure. He did a quick check of his records to confirm there were no more charges and wished them a safe journey before returning to his television, clearly annoyed that his viewing had been interrupted.

Martin drove the car onto route 22 and they headed towards Weiden. At the edge of the Naturpark Steinwald, just beyond Erbendorf, they pulled off the road and drove about a kilometre into the forest, where they parked. They both desperately needed some rest.

At 3 am Deborah was woken to be told that nothing had been heard from the team at Jack's hotel. She ordered another team to be sent to check on the team at the hotel. Thirty minutes later they confirmed that one of the team was missing and the other had been found dead in the boot of the car, shot in the head. She instructed them to remove the car and body and dispose of them both. They didn't have the time to search for the missing man.

Damn, she had lost them. They were clearly more resourceful than she had thought. She turned to one of the operatives. 'I presume the idiots didn't put a tracking device on their car?' The operator just shook his head.

'Do we have a cell phone tracking capability?'

'Yes we do, and we have the capability to track incoming calls to cell phones. If you call them we can also track them.'

Deborah gave the operator Jack's number. 'Let me know his location if he uses his phone before 10am. I will call him after that.' She felt a bit happier now that she was regaining the initiative but not a lot.

Jack and Martin awoke at around six. Having stretched their stiff and aching limbs they drove back onto the 22 and entered Weiden, where they found a café and had breakfast.

At about 7.30 Jack's phone rang. 'Mr Cunningham, I am Tatiana Pushkin. Eiswein. I have a team in Weiden as we speak.'

Jack told her they were also in Weiden and gave her their

location. Some 15 minutes later a petite, attractive woman with long black hair walked into the café. They were the only two men together in the café, so she came directly to their table.

'Miss Pushkin.' Jack invited her to take a seat. They all shook hands and she sat down.

'Please call me Tati.' She was attractive, but Martin couldn't take his eyes off her very black and substantial eyebrows.

'Yes they are distinctive, Mr Hunt' she said, smiling. Martin blushed with embarrassment. In fluent German she ordered more coffee.

'I am expecting another team later today. They are on the road as we speak. My job is to ensure your safety. You know what our ultimate aim is and I have been told by the Colonel to reassure you that you are in no danger from us.'

Jack told her about the incident at the hotel and said it was their plan to head south immediately after leaving the café. Tati pointed out a silver Mercedes parked just down the road.

'I have two colleagues with me, and if you are in agreement we will follow at a discreet distance' she said. She pulled out a handset from her bag, gave it to Jack and showed him how to use it. 'It has a range of five kilometres but reception is not good in valleys or mountainous areas where we do not have good line of sight. The battery has about twelve hours' life.' She finished her coffee. 'I will wait for you in my car.' She left the café.

While Martin paid the bill and bought some ham and cheese rolls, Jack went back to the car and returned to the café with two stainless steel flasks, which the café owner obligingly, but not cheaply, filled with coffee. They returned to the car and after studying a map of the area they thought they would stay on the 22 until they reached Ober-Viechtach some 30 kilometres away.

In Nuremberg, Totenkopf had managed to pinpoint the call Tati had made to Jack to the town of Weiden, but she had not been on the phone long enough to allow a more accurate fix. Deborah despatched one team towards Weiden, a second to Leuchtenberg, just south of Weiden, and a third by the E50 autobahn near Schwandorf, 30 kilometres south of Weiden. She then called Jack.

'Jack darling, I hope I'm not calling you too early.' It was now 9.30. 'I'm so missing you. The sooner this file thing is over the sooner we can spend more time together.' She needed to keep him on the phone as long as possible. 'I have some great news. You remember I had to return to Münich because of that deal which was unravelling? Well it's all been resolved to everyone's satisfaction. My chairman is so pleased that he 's given me a month off. A great opportunity to, maybe, go on a relaxing holiday together. How does the Caribbean sound?'

'Yes, interesting. I've missed you too, darling.' Martin rolled his eyes as he listened to Jack's hypocrisy matching Deborah's. 'Look I'm driving at the moment and the road is pretty twisty. Can I call you later?'

'OK. Great.' She rang off.

One of the operators turned to Deborah. 'The car is heading slightly east of south on route 22.' Deborah went to a wall where there was a large map. She directed Team Two to get ahead of Jack and Team Three to get in behind them. She sent the fourth team north to Nabburg and instructed them to hold there. Then she called Frederic and briefed him on the situation.

Jack turned to Martin. 'That was a strange conversation - almost too gushing. She didn't ask where we were or what we were doing; almost as if she doesn't care. I suspect they may have a phone tracking capability, which means they are only able to track us at the moment via my cell phone.' He called Tati on the radio. 'Tati, I think they can track us via my cell phone. Tell Vladimir if he wishes to speak to me not to use my cell phone number but to go through you. We're heading towards Ober-Viechtach. Out.'

Jack was approaching Lauchtenberg on the edge of the Oberpfälzer Wald, a large forest region that ran along the border between Germany and the Czech Republic. Tati's team were 500 metres behind them. Now that Jack had told her where they were going, Tati had dropped back. They would close up as they neared Ober-Viechtach.

The road followed a wide sweep as it navigated the valley around a large hill feature to the west. Jack's car had been spotted by Totenkopf, and a black Passat pulled out behind them and overtook. Martin crossed the junction of the 22 and the 14 and continued south just as a green Audi overtook the FSB car.

Tati couldn't help but notice that the Audi had three male passengers and the number plate was from München. Her driver accelerated as she called Jack. 'It looks like you have a tail, a green Audi. I want you to slow down to no more than 70 kph.'

The road was wide enough for overtaking, and Tati reckoned that travelling at 70kph would force the Audi to overtake Jack. She was right. As they rounded a bend she saw the Audi break to enable it to come in behind him. No attempt was made to overtake Jack, even though the road was wide enough.

Tati's team knew exactly what to do. While she called Organov, the man in the rear passenger seat pulled out a Heckler & Koch MPK-2020, a caseless assault sub-machine gun, a model which had become the mainstay of anti-terrorism and Special Forces units in Europe. The caseless ammunition left no empty cartridge cases and therefore no evidence. Tati called Jack. 'We will take care of your tail; accelerate when I tell you.'

Deborah was now aware that two of her teams were in position, having bracketed Cunningham and Hunt she directed the third team to head towards Ober-Viechtach. She was unaware that there was an FSB team in place, and that another had just passed Pilsen and would cross the German border near Waidhaus in under two hours. Organov had instructed Tati to take out the Audi and the Mercedes accelerated towards it.

Tati lowered all the windows and pulled out an MPK9, the caseless ammunition variant of the MP5K. The rear passenger positioned himself to be ready when they overtook. The driver prepared to overtake, but had to brake hard for a van which had just turned into the road, narrowly avoiding a head-on collision.

The FSB had now lost the element of surprise. The Germans had spotted the Mercedes and Tati could see the passengers winding down the windows and preparing weapons. She had to regain the initiative, and quickly.

She told the driver to ram the rear of the Audi, brake and then immediately overtake. It was a windy road with a high risk of oncoming traffic, but it was a risk she had to take.

The Mercedes hit the rear of the Audi heavily, causing the man in the rear to lose his balance and drop his weapon. The Audi swerved from the impact and in that instant the Mercedes overtook. Just before they came alongside the Audi, the FSB team opened fire.

The 2020 had a 60-round magazine with a high rate of fire and this, coupled with the firepower of Tati's MPK9, tore into the Audi. In a matter of seconds 60 rounds had entered the car, killing the occupants instantly. The Audi hit the crash barrier and spun out of control across the road before tumbling and careering over the opposite barrier into the forest.

Tati and the other FSB crew coolly reloaded their weapons and she closed the windows. She then told Jack that the threat had been eliminated and he could accelerate to a more normal driving speed.

The Audi team had not had the time before the attack to tell Deborah of the situation so she assumed it was still in position behind Jack. She was still unaware of the FSB vehicle.

Jack and Martin had been travelling around a wide bend when the attack had taken place which meant they hadn't seen it. They were now about eight kilometres from Ober-Viechtach where they would be turning off to the east. Ahead of them, and in sight, was the black VW Passat.

The Passat team leader called Deborah. 'We have lost contact with team Tango. I don't think it's a communications problem because we are in contact with the Golf team.' She instructed the Lima team to allow Cunningham to overtake them.

The Passat slowed down enough to allow Jack to overtake. He overtook the Passat, quickly followed by the FSB Mercedes. Tati was not expecting another enemy car so close and had failed to notice the three occupants in the Passat.

The Germans didn't miss the Russians, and they could see the damage to the front of the Mercedes. They relayed this information to Deborah who passed the details to the Golf team instructing them to intercept the Mercedes. The Golf team were in a Range Rover, parked with the engine running in a side road, where they had a clear view of the road Jack and Martin were travelling on.

In no time they could see Jack's car and the Mercedes about 200 metres behind. The Range Rover team let Jack pass then, as the Mercedes approached, they turned onto the main road, forcing the Mercedes to brake hard, with flashing headlights and a volley of curses from the FSB driver.

Before the FSB realised what was happening the rear window of the Range Rover had opened. A man holding a US-made MM-1 40mm multi-shot grenade launcher opened fire at their windscreen. A mix of four high explosive and incendiary rounds entered the Mercedes, turning it into an inferno. Its fuel tank exploded.

The Range Rover accelerated away, shortly followed by Team Lima. Jack saw the explosion in his rear-view mirror but didn't know the implications; us or them, he wondered? Martin called Tati but there was no reply so he quickly turned off the road and entered the village of Ober-Viechtach. Driving into a side street, he parked up and waited for some 15 minutes.

Teams Lima and Golf had not seen Jack turn off but, as there were few side roads, it would only be a matter of time before they would realise that their quarry had stopped somewhere. It was now 11.30 am.

Jack was right about his followers. The Germans had gone about two kilometres south before stopping, Lima continuing further south and Golf turning around and retracing their route. There were only two turn-offs, one east towards Ober-Viechtach and the other west towards Murach.

Jack and Martin drove out of Ober-Viechtach towards Pirkhof and then Pullenreid. The road gradually became narrower as the pine forest encroached on each side.

Jack decided to take a chance and called the General on his cell phone. The signal was weak, but he managed to tell him that he believed Tati's team had been destroyed. Organov confirmed they had lost contact with her and Jack told him they were going to Tröbes probably continuing on foot if there were no suitable tracks. After he rang off, Organov passed on their location to his other team. Tröbes was not far from where they would cross the border but they were at least an hour away.

Jack's brief call enabled Deborah to place him between Pirkhof and Pullenreid and this was relayed to teams Lima and Golf. By this time, fire engines and police were all over the scene of the two 'accidents'. This, coupled with the discovery of a body in the Grunau hotel and a burned-out vehicle outside Weiden suddenly made this relatively quiet backwater of great interest to many people.

As they drove deeper into the forest Jack and Martin lost the signal coverage on their cell phones. Just before Tröbes they stopped the car and consulted the 1:25.000 scale map of the area. They were now less than a kilometre from their objective.

Jack pointed towards the hills. 'It looks like there should be a trail just ahead which should take us to within 500 metres of the mine entrance; that's assuming the car can make it. Bugger, I should have thought earlier and hired an off-road vehicle.'

They found the track indicated on the map. It was a gentle climb and the going was sufficiently easy for the car. It was a logging track, as attested by the felled timber stacked by the side of the track. Luckily, despite some recent rain, they made good progress, and after about 300 metres the track ended in a clearing from which a number of smaller tracks radiated.

They parked the car, unloaded their equipment and changed into their outdoor clothing. They put on their shoulder holsters and placed the MP5Ks on slings around their necks. Using the map and Jack's compass, they headed up one of the tracks.

After about 50 metres, out of sight of the clearing, they stopped and checked their bearings. They ate the rolls and high energy bars and drank coffee in silence.

Martin, who had not broached the subject when they were driving, suddenly spoke. 'Jack, I'm really sorry that you had to find out what Deborah was all about. I know you liked her but....'

'Jesus, Martin, there's no real emotion involved. I wasn't close to her in that sense - it was just a fuck. Frankly, Emma is, was, the woman I loved. Yes, of course, it's been a pretty ghastly discovery that she's not at all what she seemed but, when I remove my ego from the situation and let my brain take over, it all makes sense. There were too many coincidences.' He stood up and shouldered his rucksack. 'Let's get going.'

The ground became steeper as they went deeper into the forest and soon they had to leave the track and move off on a compass bearing. Initially they had to find their way through quite heavy undergrowth but then the ground cleared and they were walking on a thick bed of pine needles lying beneath tall trees.

The ground continued to rise, and after a further 30 minutes climbing they came across an overgrown track about twelve feet wide. They sat down to catch their breath and drink some water.

'If my calculations are correct, and I haven't completely forgotten my training. I reckon we have about 200 metres more to go,' said Jack.

'How will you find the entrance to the mine? We could end up either side of it' said Martin.

'I've offset the bearing we're marching on so we we'll end up to the right of where the mine should be. After we've covered the approximate distance I'll turn left. I'm using a Mils compass which gives a much greater accuracy than a traditional degrees compass.'

'All sounds a load of bollocks to me. Typical military!' scoffed Martin.

In the valley below, the Totenkopf Golf team had entered the hamlet of Tröbes, but had found no sign of the Mercedes. With the Range Rover following, the team retraced their route on foot looking for clues as to where it had gone. They were joined briefly by Team Lima, who were directed to follow the road through Tröbes and search to the north.

Despite the number of trails leading off the road, most were too steep for a Mercedes saloon, and, at first, there were no signs of a vehicle having recently entered a track. But it didn't take long for them to find a track with fresh tyre marks. The Golf team remounted their vehicle and drove up the track until they found the parked Mercedes. The leader tried to contact Lima but he couldn't get a signal, either with the radio or cell phone.

The FSB team had just turned off route 14 and were heading south towards Tröbes. Team Lima had already passed through Tröbes and was heading north towards the FSB.

The Golf team were all heavily armed with suppressed MP-213 sub-machine guns, and they also carried Glock semi-automatic pistols. They searched the clearing, trying to ascertain which way their targets had gone. The leader tried again to contact base as well as the Lima team but to no avail. A combination of the geology of the mountains and the overall topography was not good for any of the more traditional communications. The team leader was frustrated that he had not brought satellite phones. He would definitely raise this at the debriefing.

One of the team spotted a piece of fresh bread on the

ground. They locked the Range Rover and went up the track. Their observation skills were further rewarded when they noticed freshly-broken branches in the undergrowth where Jack and Martin had left the track.

They were unaware of the raging fire fight that was taking place between Team Lima and the FSB in the valley below. Because both the FSB and Totenkopf teams were using suppressed weapons, nothing could be heard higher up in the hills.

It had been the FSB team that had seen the Passat first. The FSB vehicle had stopped on a bend and the team leader had gone forward on foot and using his binoculars scanned the valley below. The Passat had stopped and two men had got out and were looking up a side track. They were both armed. The FSB team leader returned to his car where he briefed the rest of the team on what he had seen. He decided they would set up a linear ambush just above the bend. Ten minutes later and as the Passat rounded the bend it was hit with a hail of bullets, which instantly killed the driver and seriously injured one of the passengers. The rest of the Lima team dismounted and engaged the FSB.

The fight seemed endless but in fact it lasted no more than five minutes. By the time it was over, one of the FSB had been killed. The injured Lima team member had already died of his injuries having bled like a stuck pig; a bullet had severed his carotid artery and the car dashboard was covered in arterial blood that had sprayed from the man's neck. The last Totenkopf team member had tried to escape down the road but was shot by a lone FSB man positioned as a stop.

The FSB team leader tried to contact Control but like everyone else he couldn't get a signal. They placed the Totenkopf bodies in the Passat and one of the FSB managed to drive it off the road and up a track until it was out of sight of the road. He deployed the same type of Thermate-TH3 grenades they had used in London, setting a time delay fuse for 30 minutes before rejoining his leader.

The FSB team placed their dead comrade's body in the boot. Turning their vehicle around, they headed north and then west on the 14 until they obtained a signal on their phones. The team leader briefed Organov. As a single team with only two people they were no longer a viable unit so Organov instructed them to return to Pilsen and await instructions. Organov turned to Ivan.

'Well that's it. Sergei's team has lost a third of its strength but at least we have neutralised another group of Totenkopf. Let's get a team to Pilsen to reinforce Sergei. I'm afraid for the moment Mr Cunningham, you are on your own.'

Up on the mountain, Jack had been right in his navigation. They had moved on for some 200 metres and then turned left. After walking about 40 metres across the slope they came across an area of dense undergrowth at the base of a small cliff. There were the signs of an old track which stopped at the base of the cliff.

Jack and Martin pulled at the undergrowth, which was mostly ivy, until they revealed an entrance to a tunnel. The entrance was about 15 feet wide and high, with a set of iron gates.

Back in Nuremberg, Deborah had lost contact with all her teams and was having to deal with Frederic's regular calls for situation reports. She knew the general area where her remaining teams were, but the signal from the vehicle tracking device on the Range Rover was intermittent and not good enough to pinpoint the exact location of the vehicle. There was no contact with the Passat. She assumed that they were all experiencing the same communication problems.

Team Golf continued their climb up the mountain. They had no map or compass to assist them, but Jack and Martin had left a well defined trail through the pine needles on the forest floor.

Jack shone his torch through the bars of the iron gate, but the beam penetrated only about 50 feet into the tunnel. The gate was secured with a chain and padlock which were very rusty but, using his rock hammer, he was easily able to snap the links on the chain, and with help from Martin, managed to pry open the gates.

They put on their climbing helmets, fitted the head-mounted torches and entered the tunnel. Jack got out the second page of Appendix B, which showed the map of the tunnel complex.

'The first leg is about 200 metres, and then it should veer to the left' he said. Leading the way, he and Martin counted their paces. At 210 paces the tunnel veered to the left, exactly as the map had indicated. They noted that there was a narrow-gauge rail track that ran down the centre of the tunnel.

The tunnel gently sloped downwards. Water dripped from the roof and there was green mould on the walls. The temperature had dropped quite considerably and Jack shivered. 'Should have thought of bringing something warm. How far have we gone since the last leg?'

'I reckon about 100 metres.'

Jack looked at the map. 'According to the map, after 250 metres the tunnel should split three ways.'

Exactly as indicated on the map, after about 250 metres, Jack and Martin came to a three-way junction. They went down the left-hand tunnel for about 30 metres and came to a dead end. They turned around and retraced their steps and entered the next tunnel. This too came to a dead end.

'Well that's it Martin; it must be the third tunnel' said Jack. 'Trust us to get things out of sequence.' They went down the third and last tunnel to find yet another dead end.

'What's the point of this?' frowned Jack. 'I don't understand why there's a dead end at exactly the same distance into each tunnel. There must be a reason. Do we have any coffee left?'

Martin got out the second flask and poured each of them a cup. They were sitting on the tunnel floor in silence, each contemplating their situation, when the silence was interrupted by the sound of metal on metal and what sounded like a curse. Team Golf had found the entrance to the mine.

Jack and Martin immediately switched off their helmet lights and unhooked their MP5Ks. Jack whispered to Martin to grab his rucksack and to follow him. He told him to hang on to his belt in the darkness. Jack picked up his rucksack and the pair went back down the tunnel to the intersection and lay down on the tunnel floor with Martin to Jack's right. Jack hooked his right foot over Martin's left leg. In the pitch dark this was the only way to keep silently in contact with his team mate.

They listened intently. Now they could hear movement. They saw three torch light beams. Someone spoke in German.

Jack cocked his weapon carefully, making little sound, Martin did likewise.

The lights got closer. Jack whispered to Martin not to open fire until he did, and then to fire in short controlled bursts. Jack slipped the safety catch to automatic.

He opened fire, quickly followed by Martin. The noise was deafening as the tunnel amplified the sound. They heard a scream and one of the lights went out.

Jack told Martin to roll over to the other tunnel entrance

and fire from around the corner so he had some protection. Jack did the same on the opposite tunnel entrance, reloading his weapon as he moved. The enemy were now returning fire in controlled bursts. Luckily the rounds were going down the central tunnel.

The two men kept up a withering rate of fire but Jack knew it was unsustainable with the ammunition they had. They were covered in dust from the shooting and he told Martin to cover his ears, open his mouth and close his eyes. He then tossed a stun grenade down the tunnel. The grenade exploded with a flash and an enormous bang; the noise amplified in the confined space.

The objective of a stun grenade was not to kill but to disorientate anyone in close proximity to the explosion for about five seconds. There was a brief silence and then Jack opened fire again with a long burst, emptying the whole clip. He told Martin to stop firing. Suddenly there was a burst of fire from down the tunnel and then Jack saw a light moving. It looked as though someone was running back down the tunnel.

'Martin, stay here. I'm going after him'. Jack pulled out his Glock and, attaching the suppressor, he switched on his helmet light and went down the tunnel where he found two men; they were both dead. He stayed low, hugging the wall and followed the third man. He would have preferred not to have a light on but he had no choice.

As he came closer to the bend in the tunnel the man fired a short burst towards Jack but missed him. Jack got to the bend and turned off his light. Although still in darkness, he could make out the daylight at the tunnel entrance. Using the light as his guide he moved on, stopping at regular intervals to lie low and scan the area ahead of him.

Suddenly the man made a break for it, silhouetting himself against the outside light. Jack fired twice and saw the man twist and fall. He ran up to him and fired another round, this time into the man's head.

He went to the tunnel entrance and sat in the undergrowth, scanning the area outside. Satisfied that there was no one else in the forest, he returned down the tunnel and retrieved the dead man's weapons.

Just by the bend he shouted to Martin that he was coming back. The last thing he wanted was Martin to shoot him by mistake. He retrieved the other two men's weapons, and rejoined Martin. Together they sat slumped on the tunnel floor.

'Fuck me Jack, that's the scariest thing I've ever experienced. I don't think my hearing will ever be the same again. Are they all dead?'

'As far as I can tell there were only three of them and yes, they're all dead. I did have a brief look outside, but that doesn't mean there aren't more people looking for us. We don't know if that bunch had communicated with anyone although, if they've had the same comms problems we've had, we might be in luck. Let's check ammunition and reload; I don't want to be caught out. Then we're going to get the hell out of here. I'm afraid it looks like this is a dry hole.'

He inspected the enemy's weapons. 'That's a bit of luck. They're using the same ammo.'

They checked their weapons and, having reloaded, got ready to leave. Martin stood up.

'I'm sorry but I just can't believe that all this effort, the files, the clues, the maps, would have been done for nothing. I'm going to recheck the spurs.' He went off and, less than five minutes later, called Jack. Jack found Martin by the back wall of the central tunnel.

'Look at this.' Martin pointed to where chunks of rock had been dislodged by bullets that had been fired by the Germans. Jack bent down and felt the rock.

'This isn't rock it's cement,' said Jack. 'Feel it. Rock doesn't crumble like this.' He crumbled the cement into Martin's hand and then, taking his rock hammer from the rucksack, he attacked the rear wall. More cement fell. After about ten minutes of hammering, they could see brickwork.

'It's a sham; the cement is just camouflage,' said Martin. He got out his rock hammer and, for the next fifteen minute, the pair of them attacked the bricks until they had a made a hole about a foot square. They were now completely covered in a fine dust. They let the dust settle and then, taking his hand torch, Jack shone it through the hole into the space beyond.

'It looks like the tunnel extends through and turns to the right. I can't see anything else.'

They removed more bricks until there was enough space for them to climb through. They kept all their equipment; they might need it and didn't want to waste time searching for it if the need came. Jack went through the hole first followed by Martin who stumbled through, having caught his rucksack on the bricks. As they moved off down the tunnel it turned to the right. They continued for a further 30 metres before the tunnel opened into a cavernous room. Shining their torches around the room, they saw that it was about 40 feet square and stank to high heaven. Martin shone his torch towards the ceiling.

Instantly they were enveloped by hundreds of bats. Fortunately the creatures must have sensed the new exit. They carried on flying towards the tunnel the men had just come down.

'Shit, that scared the life out of me' said Martin. 'I'm not sure I can take much more of this sort of fun.' He picked himself off the floor.

They continued their scan of the room. In the centre of the chamber were numerous objects of varying sizes, all covered by tarpaulins. This was the moment of truth. They stood there in silence, almost paralysed as to what to do next.

Martin moved to the tarpaulins and pulled one off, covering himself with dust and bats' droppings. 'Bugger, I hate this job.' He spluttered, spitting out pieces of batshit.

There were two wooden boxes under the first tarpaulin. One box was about two feet long and one foot square at the end and was positioned on top of a larger box. Both had numbers and SS runes stencilled on them.

They lowered the smaller box to the floor and using their rock hammers, prised open the lid. Inside was a container wrapped in heavy duty felt. They lifted it out and peeled off the felt revealing a dark wooden box. Opening it, they found a fine leather bag. Jack undid the drawstring and lifted out a spearhead. It was about 18 inches long, of blackened metal, with gold and silver wiring adorning the shaft.

Jack handed the spearhead to Martin. 'Do you think this is it?'

'You mean the Spear of Destiny; yes, I think so. They looked at in awe. After a few minutes, Martin said,' Let's put this away and open the other boxes. My God, this really is like Christmas.' They were both grinning from ear to ear. They put the spearhead back into its box and opened the next crate.

'Bloody hell' exclaimed Jack as he lifted out a gold ingot from the crate. Martin looked into the crate and counted the top layer. 'There must be at least a hundred ingots in this crate. Looks like we can give up the day jobs.'

He looked around. 'There are another six crates this size.'

He opened one of them and found this too was full of gold ingots. 'I don't remember any gold mentioned in the file.'

'It wasn't, unless this is one of the consignments mentioned in the appendix.' Jack placed the ingot in his rucksack, noticing that it was embossed with the Nazi eagle and SS runes. 'Martin, you take one.' He gave Martin an ingot.

They closed the crates and moved over to another tarpaulin, which revealed a crate with what looked like glass sheets inserted in specially-made grooves. They carefully pulled out one of the sheets and examined the sheets.

'Well, I think we've found the General's Amber Room' said Jack. 'I suspect the rest of the crates all contain parts of it. There looks to be at least twenty crates of the same size.'

Martin had removed another tarpaulin, revealing a black funeral casket with SS runes inset in silver. 'Well I'm not going to open this bugger' he said. Jack came over and looked at the casket.

'A casket was mentioned in the appendix but it didn't say who or what was in it.' He looked at his watch. 'Martin, it's gone six o'clock. I think we should put the tarpaulins back in place and return once we've worked out what to do next. There's no way we can shift this lot on our own. I reckon we're going to have to trust the General after all.'

They packed up, retraced their steps and, having searched all the Germans removing further quantities of Euros and a set of car keys, they left the mine and covered the tunnel entrance with undergrowth as well as they could. Anyone searching for the entrance would have no trouble locating it, but the camouflage would probably fool the casual walker.

The two men were now covered from head to foot in a fine coating of dust and, in the half light, they looked like a pair of ghosts. They retraced their steps to the clearing, where they found the Totenkopf Range Rover parked by their Mercedes hire car. Standing by the cars they discussed their priorities. Get clear of the area, clean themselves up as well as possible and find a hotel for the night.

They drove both vehicles down to the bottom of the valley to a small stream, stripped off their clothes and washed as much of the dust from their bodies as they could. Dressing in the clothes from their rucksacks that they'd originally worn, they looked less like something the cat had dragged in. They looked at the map and decided to head for the nearby town, Schwerzenfeld, about 25 kilometres to the west and close to the E50 autobahn. Jack took the hire car and Martin drove the Range Rover.

They were unaware that as they left the valley the vehicle tracking beacon on the Range Rover had been picked up by the Totenkopf control team in Nuremberg.

The pair reached Schwerzenfeld about 30 minutes later and checked into the hotel Brauerei Gasthof Bauer, a small, family-run and very traditional hotel on the edge of the market square. It suited their needs exactly and enabled Martin to dump the Range Rover in a side street with no parking restrictions. The vehicle had German number plates, so it was unlikely to attract undue attention. What he didn't know was that a Totenkopf team had left Nuremberg and was already en route to Schwerzenfeld.

Having demolished two steins each of pilsner beer which barely touched the sides, Jack and Martin went to the dining room and had an excellent meal of boar sausage, red cabbage and roast potatoes washed down with more beer. Discussing their next moves, they agreed to keep Jack's cell phone off and use Martin's phone instead. Even then this would be only in an emergency. They had fully flexible air tickets which enabled them to fly on any BA flight out of Düsseldorf. It was really a question of when they should leave Germany. They debated whether they should go back to London first and then return to collect the 'loot' or stay.

They decided that they would call the General in the morning but the real question was how to deal with Deborah as it would be only a matter of time before she tried to call Jack. She might even have already tried. He was reluctant to turn on his cell phone if she really was able to track him.

Going to the bar, they continued talking until late, experiencing the German equivalent of a pub lock-in. Their host was a very amiable man who spoke broken English and did not overly intrude on their conversation but he did pour them a few glasses of Himbeergeist, a raspberry-flavoured schnapps.

They retired in good spirits and before finally going to bed, Jack cleaned all the weapons stashing them under his bed. At some stage he would have to dispose of them but, for the moment they might still need them. He also folded the two diagrams of Appendix B and inserted the package into a small gap in the old ceiling beam.

Nuremberg

Sergeant Willi Brandt entered Klaus' office. 'I think we've had a lucky break. I've just had a call from Herman Pitz. You remember Herman? He worked with us on the Pfizer case last year. You wanted him to join the team, but because of family circumstances he preferred to stay at Weiden.'

'Yes, of course I remember Herman, he's a good man. A real shame we couldn't have bagged him.'

'Herman and I are old chums and we keep in regular contact. He was in town the other day so I had a beer with him and we chatted about our little 'non-gang' problem. He has just telephoned and told me his guys attended an incident today which they thought initially was just a series of road traffic accidents on the 22 near Ober Viechtach. That's about 80 kilometres east of us. They found a totally burnt-out vehicle. When they searched it, or rather what was left of it, they found a whole pile of weapons inside. The other car was about a kilometre north. It contained four dead bodies. They had all been shot.

'The interesting thing is that the weapons they found were all sophisticated Heckler & Kochs. Herman said he had never seen this type of weapon before and you know he's a bit of a gun nut. He thinks this may be linked to our incident. The number plates on both vehicles are bogus. Herman is sending the weapons to our forensic guys.'

'Bloody hell, Willi. I suppose Junge will think this is gang-related again. Weiden is within our jurisdiction so I had better tell him. Get some guys over to the scene as soon as you can. Send my best wishes and thanks to Herman.'

His phone rang.

'Klaus, it's Don Grant. Cunningham left the UK yesterday morning on a flight to Düsseldorf. He's travelling with a Martin Hunt; I've just emailed you a photo of Cunningham and will send you Hunt's as soon as I can. They both have open-ended tickets - there is no return booking. I have no further details. '

'Thanks Don, greatly appreciated. Hang on, your email has just arrived. I'll get back to you.'

He rang off and ran into the corridor and called Willi back.

'Cunningham and a man called Hunt entered Germany via Düsseldorf airport yesterday. Check out the hire car companies and get those fucking dunderheads in Research to trawl through the hotel databases. I want a quick response from them this time. Don Grant has emailed me Cunningham's photograph – I'll forward it to you. He hasn't a photo of Hunt yet.'

The Research team had clearly pulled their fingers out, because three hours later they reported that Cunningham and Hunt had checked in for one night at the Grunau Hotel in Bayreuth and had left early the following morning. They also confirmed that a man's body had been found in the basement of the hotel and that he had been shot in the head. The man had no identity documents or credit cards on him, absolutely nothing to identify him by. There were not even labels on his clothing.

Willi stuck his head around the door.

'We've got the details of their hire car, and I've passed them out with the photo of Cunningham.'

It was now just a matter of time before they picked the men up. Klaus gave orders that Cunningham and Hunt should be tracked down and arrested. He rang Don Grant and updated him before he went upstairs to speak with Junge.

He found Junge extremely cheerful and supportive of Klaus's actions. There wasn't even a mention of gangs. He was now the model of cooperation.

After Klaus had left his office Junge exited the building and made a call from a public telephone booth nearby.

Schwerzenfeld

Jack woke just after seven o'clock. Having washed and shaved, he went downstairs and rang Roly on a payphone. After a short delay he was patched through to Organov.

'General, we've found your package but we can't remove it without your help.' He explained as much as he could about their find.

'You are very resourceful men. Where are you?'

Jack told him.

'Stay there and call me at 1600 hours. I will get some of my people to you as quickly as possible; they will use the same codeword.' He rang off and Jack went upstairs to wake Martin.

Organov instructed the team at Waidhaus to get over to Schwarzenfeld and rendezvous with Jack as soon as they had been reinforced. He confirmed that the support team would be with Jack and Martin within the next three hours.

Jack was unaware that there were three Totenkopf teams in the village and that they had found the Range Rover. Following a brief search, they had located Martin and Jack's car in the market square car park although the teams did not yet know where they were. Deborah had joined the teams and had positioned blocking teams covering all exits from the car park as well as the entrances to the three hotels that abutted the square, including Jack and Martin's Gasthof. She went with one of her men to a nearby café and ordered coffee. It was now just a matter of waiting. She didn't want either Jack or Martin to see her until she was ready.

Meeting in the dining room, Martin and Jack enjoyed a leisurely breakfast. Finishing his last cup of coffee, Martin looked at his phone to see whether he had any messages. The battery was very low and he'd left the charger in his rucksack in the boot of the car. 'Give me the car keys as I need to go out and get my charger.' Jack gave them to him him as they left the dining room he said, 'I'll meet you back in my room.'

Getting to the car, Martin opened the boot and leaned in to access his rucksack. He suddenly felt something hard pressed against the small of his back.

'Do not move, Mr Hunt' said a voice. The man pushed the gun harder into Martin's back as another expertly searched him. 'He's clean.'

The man turned Martin around. 'Please come with us.' They escorted Martin into Brauhausgasse, where he was bundled into a white Mercedes van. He was searched more thoroughly and his hands were handcuffed behind his back. A short while later Deborah climbed into the van and sat opposite him. One of the men handed Martin's hotel room key to her.

'Hello Martin. Tell me which room Jack is in?'

'You bitch.' Martin spat the words out.

'Now, now Martin. We can make this very easy or very difficult for you. I can find out in due course, but it would inconvenience me and hurt you. You are currently irrelevant and I could have you killed right now; it would have no impact whatsoever on the bigger picture. Just call me sentimental for keeping you alive at the moment. Now, what's Jack's room number?'

Martin looked at her and knew it was hopeless. 'He's in room 24, just down the corridor from my room.'

Deborah nodded to one of the men and gave him Martin's room key. The man left the van and joined a woman and three other men who then proceeded to the hotel. Two of the men positioned themselves by the exits to the hotel, while the other three went up to the second floor.

Jack was lying on his bed when there was a knock at the door followed by a woman's voice. 'Herr Cunningham, it's housekeeping. I have some fresh towels for you.'

Jack got up and unlocked the door and was instantly bundled into the room by two men who pinned him to the bed. He was then searched, the woman pointing her pistol at his head.

'Do not struggle, Cunningham. We already have Hunt and any lack of cooperation will result in his death. Now come with us.'

Three of them escorted Jack to the van, where he joined Martin and was similarly handcuffed. They both had duck tape placed over their mouths to prevent them speaking to each other. Deborah had already left the van and was heading to the safe house.

The van drove out of the village and reached the safe house some 40 minutes later. Jack and Martin were placed in separate rooms, each with a guard.

The team at the hotel packed up Jack and Martin's rooms and the woman paid their bills. All their kit was placed in the boot of the hire car and was then driven the 50 kilometres to the safe house, entering a courtyard via large double gates. After unloading, Jack and Martin's possessions were taken to a room and searched thoroughly. Deborah joined the search team.

'Anything of the file?'

'Nothing yet Fraulein Balmer, but we've found these.' He handed her one of the two gold ingots. She smiled. Taking the ingot with her, she left the room and called Frederic.

'We have Cunningham and Hunt. As yet we have not fully completed our search of their possessions but we have discovered two gold ingots. Their markings indicate that they are part of the Chiemsee hoard. They have found Verglas'

It had long been thought that Nazi gold had been dumped in numerous lakes in Austria and Germany. The most famous was Lake Toplitz in Austria, where counterfeit British and American bank notes from Operation Bernhard had been found. Operation Bernhard had been Hitler's idea to trigger an economic crisis by flooding the American and British markets with counterfeit currency.

The Chiemsee hoard was named after a lake of the same name in Bavaria, where in 2003 a diver had discovered a solid gold cauldron at the bottom of the lake. The cauldron was decorated with Celtic and Indo-Germanic figures and was thought to have been commissioned by Himmler.

With their meticulous record-taking the Nazis had documented each batch of gold with an identifying mark. In the case of the Chiemsee hoard it was SS runes followed by three asterixes. Deborah had worked for Frederic in the recovery of many of these hoards and as a result she was familiar with the markings on the ingots.

Frederic instructed Deborah to obtain the whereabouts of the Verglas file by any means. Although pleased with progress, he was becoming increasingly impatient with the length of time it had all taken.

Deborah went upstairs to Jack's room and told the guard to leave.

'I wondered when you would turn up' said Jack, glaring at her.

She sat down in a chair. 'When did you know I was your enemy?'

'Your people at Wewelsburg expected Martin to be with

me. They're all dead, by the way. The only person who knew that Martin was with me was you, and I've since been told that you are Totenkopf.'

Deborah got up, walked over to the window and turned to face him.

'Jack, we know that you have found the Verglas hoard and the fact that you are still alive means we do not yet know where it is. How did you find the exact location? The file is not with you.'

'I have an excellent memory and I only needed to remember a map grid reference.'

'The people I report to have told me to use whatever means at my disposal to obtain the location of the Verglas file. Therefore so what I need from you is for you to tell me where it is. Now, you can cooperate in order that everyone wins or I can let some of my less savoury colleagues work on Martin and then on you. Martin is already expendable - I can have him killed this instant. You have an opportunity to save both of your lives and we may even be prepared to pay some money into your respective bank accounts to ensure your silence. But I would rather not go down the alternative; a much more difficult and painful route.'

She paused and looked directly into Jack's eyes. 'The time we have spent together has been rather special to me and I am in a position to protect both of your lives. However, you also need to understand that I have masters and they demand results. Once they have what they want, they will expect both of you to be eliminated. I am, in fact, putting myself at risk with this offer.'

Jack looked at her dispassionately.'

'If I give you the file, will you absolutely guarantee that at least Martin will be released with no retribution?

Deborah glanced up at Jack.

'Yes, I could do that but I must have the file first.'

'No, I must have your word. And I must know that Martin is safe. Then I will hand the file over.'

Jack paused. 'The file, or rather a copy on disc, is in Nuremberg, in a bank, you could have it pretty quickly.'

Deborah was taken aback. The file had been close to her all this time. 'Why is it in Nuremberg and not in London?'

'It's Kautenberg's bank. The disc is in his safe deposit box in the bank.'

'Where's the original?'

'I destroyed it after I'd scanned the file.' Jack looked at her. 'So, do we have a deal?'

'I'll have Martin placed on the first available aircraft to London, if possible today. You and I will go to the bank tomorrow after you have spoken to Martin and he's confirmed that he's safe. As for you, we can discuss your, our future perhaps, after I have the file. I'm now going to go and make the necessary arrangements for Martin.'

She leaned over to Jack and kissed him gently on the forehead. As she left the room, the guard re-entered.

Jack had very mixed emotions. On the one hand he was under no delusions as to how dangerous a position they were in. The Russians didn't know where they were - there was not going to be any rescue. They could also kill Martin after he had spoken to him in London. He did not trust Deborah at all and was astonished she had mentioned a possible future for them.

As Deborah and Jack had been speaking, the Russians had arrived at the hotel to learn that Martin and Jack had checked out. After talking to Organov and, after confirming that a woman had paid Jack and Martin's hotel bill, they were pretty certain that Totenkopf had taken the pair of them.

About an hour later, Deborah returned to Jack's room.

'All the arrangements have been made. Martin is booked on an Air Berlin flight departing Nuremberg at 18.50 this evening, arriving at London Stansted at 20.15. It is now time for your part of the deal.' She handed him a telephone directory. 'I'm sure your bank will be listed.'

A man entered the room and plugged in a telephone. Jack easily found the number and, while Deborah listened on an earpiece attached to the phone, he called the bank.

'May I speak with Dr Gutterman please, my name is Jack Cunningham.' Jack was asked to wait and after about five minutes Gutterman came on the line.

'Herr Cunningham, I'm sorry to have kept you waiting but I was with another client when you called. I hope you are well. How may I be of assistance?'

'I am very well, thank you. I will be in Nuremberg tomorrow and would like to have access to my box, preferably in the morning.'

'Yes, I can accommodate you at 10.30 am as I am tied up earlier on. Would that be acceptable? I would also be grateful if we could use the opportunity for you to settle the outstanding account. ' Jack didn't think to ask how much was owed.

'Yes, of course; that would be perfect, I look forward to it. Goodbye.' He hung up and the guard unplugged the phone and left the room. Deborah turned to Jack.

'Provided there are no flight delays we'll call Martin at 9.30 pm.' She turned and left the room.

A short while later Martin was given back his personal possessions, including his cell phone, and driven to the airport where he boarded the Air Berlin flight to London.

At 9.30 pm Deborah returned to Jack's room. She plugged

in the phone and passed the handset to him. He dialled Martin's cell phone.

'Martin Hunt?'

'Martin, it's Jack. How are you, where are you?'

'The sausage eaters put me on a flight to Stansted and it landed bang on time at 8.15, that's your 9.15. I'm waiting for the Stansted Express, which will get me into Liverpool Street in the next 30 minutes. It's all been plain sailing. How are you? I'm really concerned about you.'

Jack had enough time to say he was OK before Deborah disconnected the phone.

'See, Jack, I've kept my word. I'll see you in the morning.' She handed him his wallet and wristwatch. 'You'll need both of these. The key and pass numbers are all there where you had hidden them in the lining.' She paused and looked at him pityingly. 'Poor Jack, you really are out of your depth.' Jack smiled wanly back at her and said. 'I'll need some dollars. At least ten thousand as I'll have to pay Gutterman his fee when we see him.' Deborah said nothing and left the room.

Stansted Airport

Martin had not noticed a man and woman who had travelled with him on the same flight and who were now standing behind him on the railway station platform waiting for the Stansted Express which would take him to London. The train entered the station and a large number of passengers disembarked on to the already crowded platform. He felt someone bump into him, almost knocking him off balance.

'I'm terribly sorry, it's all these people' said the man, as he held Martin from falling.

Martin felt a sharp prick in his wrist. He turned to confront the man. There was a woman with him.

A powerful neurotoxin had entered Martin's system and was already causing paralysis. He felt leaden, unable to move, totally aware of his surroundings but incapable of action, unable to speak. The man and the woman held him up. The man called for help. 'Please clear a space, this man needs help. Call an ambulance.' He and the woman got Martin to a bench on the platform just as a train official arrived.

Martin felt helpless. As the toxin reached the muscles of his heart, he went into shock. He died silently and painlessly. He didn't hear the railwayman say that an ambulance was on the way. The subsequent autopsy would reveal that the cause of death was a heart attack.

The man made a brief international telephone call following which he and the woman went to the Hilton hotel at the airport and caught the first available flight to Munich the next morning.

Nuremberg

Jack and Deborah drove to Dellbach Bochman AG in Jack's hire car. Just before they got out of the car she gave him an envelope.

'There's ten thousand dollars in there.'

At exactly 10.30 am they entered the bank, where Dr Gutterman was waiting for them. Jack introduced Deborah, and Gutterman took them to the ground floor lobby by the elevator entrance.

Gutterman turned to Deborah. 'I'm sorry Fraulein Balmer, but I very much regret that you will have to wait here. It is bank policy that only the identified key holder may enter the vault.' Jack had hoped this would happen. 'Please take a seat and I will have some coffee brought to you.' He spoke briefly into a telephone.

Jack and Gutterman entered the lobby where Jack and Emma had originally gone to the vault only two weeks earlier.

'Mr Cunningham, please enter your code.' Jack opened his wallet and withdrew the piece of paper with the authorisation code. He entered the code into the console. They descended to the vault where they opened Helmut's safe deposit box and placed it on the table. Gutterman left the room leaving Jack alone.

Jack opened the box and retrieved a brown jiffy bag. He called Dr Gutterman to join him and pointed to the jiffy bag.

'Do you have any bags like this? I need two of them. And one more thing. You may think it strange, but do you have a CD or a DVD I can have? It doesn't matter what the subject is, but there must not be any labelling on the disc.'

Gutterman spoke into a phone and not long afterwards a CD and two bags, both plastic-padded, were delivered to him via a small service elevator similar to the ones used by restaurants. Gutterman left the room and Jack emptied the contents of the original bag into one of the new ones, sealed it and wrote an address on it. He then placed the CD in the other bag which he also sealed. Dumping the old bag in a nearby waste bin, he called Gutterman. When he appeared, Jack handed him the addressed jiffy bag.

'Would you please arrange to have this sent today?'

Gutterman looked at the address. 'That will be no problem; it would be a pleasure Mr Cunningham.' If he was surprised by the address, he showed no sign.

'I think that this is the end of our business, Dr Gutterman' said Jack. 'I will no longer require the box, so please close the account.' He opened the envelope Deborah had given him and handed it to Gutterman. 'Doctor Gutterman, here is ten thousand US dollars; I hope that this is sufficient to settle the outstanding bill'

'Absolutely, Mr Cunningham; that is exactly what is owed.'

I bet it is, thought Jack. Once a banker always a banker.

They returned to the lobby and rejoined Deborah. By the entrance to the bank they both shook hands with Dr Gutterman and left the building. It was all very Teutonic and businesslike.

Getting into the car, Jack said, 'Well here you are,' as he handed the jiffy bag to Deborah. 'This is the Verglas file. I've now kept my side of the bargain.' She opened the bag and removed the CD, checking that there was a disc in the case.

'I'll also keep my side of the bargain Jack but you must trust me. My masters are expecting me to kill you, not to leave any loose ends, and they will believe me if I tell them you are dead. I'm sorry but Martin is probably dead by now, the stakes have been too high to leave witnesses. I'm going to inject you with a drug that will place you in a temporary coma. To all intents and purposes, you will appear dead. You will have no easily detectable pulse or heart beat. It will also give our people a chance to confirm your death. You'll be out for about 24 hours and will probably have a really bad headache when you regain consciousness. I need your Russian friend's number so I can tell him where you are.'

He gave Deborah his cell phone. 'The number is under the name Roly. Why should you help me? There's nothing in it for you.'

'Call it love, Jack or whatever love is.'

Jack suddenly felt a sharp prick in his thigh.

'It will take a few seconds to work.' Deborah withdrew a tiny styrette which she had thrust into his thigh.

Jack was already starting to feel drowsy. He suddenly realised that by giving her the CD he had placed her in danger. 'Listen Deborah, we have to stop this.' He had to tell her that she didn't have the Verglas file, but he was unable to speak. His lips moved but no sound came. He tried to fight the drug but it was no use and he sank into unconsciousness.

Deborah placed the CD back into the bag and kissed him on the cheek.

'Goodbye Jack, goodbye.'

As she got out of the car, a silver Audi A8 pulled up alongside. She stepped aboard. The Audi pulled into the morning traffic and they drove to a helicopter which was waiting on the outskirts of the town. She would be in Münich in under an hour.

A short time later an Opel pulled up beside Jack's car and a man got in and checked Jack's pulse. He then got back into the Opel and called a Münich number. 'Cunningham's dead.'

Julia had rung Klaus to say she had some more forensic data from the Engels shooting but she didn't want to go to the headquarters in case she ran into Junge. Despite Junge's friendly behaviour, Klaus was still suspicious of his motives so they agreed to meet on the corner of Königshammer and Ketteler, a short walk away.

Klaus Schmidt left the headquarters building and walked north along Kornburger Strasse. He walked a further 20 metres before crossing the road. He suddenly heard the screech of tyres as a battered green Mercedes which had been parked nearby accelerated towards him. There was no escape. The car hit him, flinging his body across the bonnet and on to the road.

The car stopped 15 metres from Klaus's body and reversed

over his head, crushing it, before speeding away and turning into Germerscheimerstrasse. Passers-by ran to Klaus' assistance, but it was too late.

The Mercedes was later found in a car park to the east of the city. There were no fingerprints, the number plates were false and the engine number had been erased.

Frederic received a call from Junge telling him Klaus was dead. He called Henry.

'Please arrange for surveillance on Junge; he's a potentially weak link. Give it about two to three weeks and arrange for him to have a heart attack from which, sadly, he will not survive.'

Learning of Klaus' death, Julia decided that discretion was the better part of valour. She destroyed the new forensic evidence.

Münich

Frederic was seated at a large mahogany table in a windowless room. He was smoking a Bolivar Finos cigar and drinking armagnac. Henry opened the door and let Deborah into the room.

Frederic rose, kissed Deborah on both cheeks, and beckoned her to a seat.

'It would all seem to have gone very smoothly with both Hunt and Cunningham out of the way and, of course, all through natural causes. Terrible things, heart attacks.'

He smiled and went over to a side table, where there was a bottle of Krug champagne on ice. 'Some champagne my dear? You deserve it. I assume you have the file?'

He handed her a glass. She sipped the wine, smiled, and gave Frederic the CD. He placed the case on the table in front of him.

'You have done very well, but no less than I would have expected of you and, of course, the Russians go away empty handed. Have you seen the contents of the file?'

'No I haven't Frederic. I learned a long time ago that I only need to know what I need to know.'

'You are the consummate professional, my dear.'

They continued to make small talk while she finished her champagne. Frederic got up and said,' Now if you will excuse me, Wolf is waiting in the car to take you home.'

As the door closed behind Deborah, Frederic took out the CD and inserted the disc into his laptop. It was in German. It was a publicity recording featuring a Dr Gutterman and outlining the services of Dellbach Bochman AG.

Frederic picked up the phone and called Wolf.

The *Independent* Newspaper, London

The Facilities Manager walked over to Martin Hunt's desk. He had never met Martin but knew of him as a decent sort. Shame about the heart attack, and being so young. Well they needed his desk for another journalist. He emptied the contents of the desk that were of use and placed them in a cardboard archive box. The rest of the contents, including a folder labelled 'Chelsea Flower Show 2005' he placed in a black bin liner. He went into the corridor and gave the bin liner to one of the cleaners. 'Chuck this Steve, thanks.'

FSB, London

Roly received a telephone call from a woman who wouldn't identify herself. She told him where Jack was and gave a description of the car. She told Roly to move quickly and then hung up.

Roly rang Organov in Moscow. It was fortunate that they had kept one of the teams in the Nuremberg area and it was despatched immediately.

The team removed Jack's unconscious body and took him to a house on the outskirts of the town where he was examined by a doctor. The doctor confirmed that Jack was in a drug-induced coma. He would remain unconscious for nearly 36 hours.

FSB Headquarters, Moscow

Vladimir Organov entered his office, shrugged off his overcoat and shivered briefly. He had never really got used to the extreme cold of a Russian winter. An orderly followed him, placing a tray with hot tea and a plate of small pastries on his desk.

'Good morning Colonel, my wife thought you would like these. She baked them this morning.'

'Thank you Oleg; that is most kind. Please give her my thanks.'

Oleg was a long serving member of Organov's staff and his wife regularly made these wonderful sweet cakes. Organov was always delighted to receive them. He picked up his tea and stirred in his usual four teaspoons of sugar.

He noticed a package on his desk and picked it up, weighing it in his hand. There was nothing to indicate where it had come from, but it had his name written on it in black ink. Oleg spoke.

'It came from London station sir, it was addressed to you at the embassy. Uri forwarded it.'

'Thank you Oleg.' Organov sat down and waited until Oleg

had left the room before he opened the package. Ivan entered to deliver the morning situation report.

'Morning Vladimir, I see Oleg's wife is spoiling you again'. Organov chuckled as Ivan sat down. 'What with my love of beer and these cakes I am not really surprised that I am such a tubby bugger. How's Cunningham?'

'He's still unconscious but the doctor reckons he will fully recover. Our guys have analysed his blood. His coma was induced by a barbiturate but not one we have come across before. It really does create the symptoms of death. The doctor had a hell of a time actually confirming that Cunningham was alive. I'll let you know when he comes around. Do you want him brought here or to some other location?'

'Bring him to Moscow. Arrange for the analysis to be sent to our boffins. It could be quite a useful addition to our armoury.'

'A shame about Hunt; we were so close Ivan, I wish they'd trusted us earlier. I suppose it'll be a long time before we can finally shrug off our KGB legacy.' He paused and then said. 'Well, hopefully Cunningham will tell us something at last.'

Ivan pointed at the package, 'What have you got there Vladimir?'

'I don't know, but it came from Uri. It was addressed to me and sent from Nuremberg to the London Embassy. Let's see what it is.' He tore open the jiffy bag and pulled out a CD case. In it was a disc. He slipped it into his computer.

München

Frederic was having breakfast reading a copy of the Münich *Abendzeitung*. The front page carried the tragic story of a woman lawyer, Deborah Balmer, who had been found dead in an alleyway off Hansastrasse, the closest Münich has to a red light district. She had been raped and strangled with piano wire which had almost severed her head. What a shame, Frederic thought; such a beautiful woman.

He finished his coffee and called Wolf on his cell phone. 'I'm ready to go.'

Frederic caught the lift to the foyer, where Henry was waiting for him.

'Good morning Henry, I think this is going to be a wonderful day. I've just heard about Fraulein Balmer; a terrible tragedy.' Henry nodded and Frederic smiled. He climbed into the Bentley and Henry got into the front passenger seat.

'Good morning, Wolf.'

Wolf never had a chance to reply. The car exploded in a massive fireball, destroying the Bentley and blowing out the windows of the buildings for a radius of two blocks.

An elegantly-dressed young woman was standing some eight blocks away. When she saw the explosion she walked into a side street and joined a man in a waiting taxi. The car took them to the main railway station where they caught a train to Vienna. Arriving in Vienna, they took the City Airport Train to the airport and boarded a flight to Moscow.

London, New Scotland Yard

Richard White was sitting in his office when Don Grant rang.

'Hi Richard, I'm afraid I have some bad news for you. Your friend Klaus Schmidt has been killed in a hit and run incident. I spoke with his boss, Karl Junge, who reckons it was done by one of the gangs. It seems Klaus had been a little too effective with his operations against the them. Sorry, mate.'

Richard went ashen. 'Oh, my God, what a bloody shame; he was a great copper. That will have an effect on your investigation with that Cunningham fellow?'

'The file is still open, but Cunningham has disappeared off the face of the earth. The only other lead we had was with Cunningham's close friend Martin Hunt but he died of a heart attack at Stansted Airport. I'm afraid that, for the moment, it's a dry water hole. Fancy a drink before we go home tonight? Usual place?'

'Good idea. After that news, I'll need it. See you there around 6.30.'

Seventy-two hours later

In the strictest of secrecy, the replica Amber Room was dismantled and placed into twenty seven crates. Another set of crates were delivered and their contents assembled in the room where the replica had been. The Amber Room had returned home to St Petersburg.

At a crematorium on the northern outskirts of Moscow in the Zelenogradsky Administrative Okrug that had been used previously by the KGB, a black coffin with silver SS runes embossed on the lid was delivered and duly incinerated. No one at the crematorium knew or cared whose body was in the coffin. Himmler's body had finally been disposed of.

In vault number 4B, one of many underneath the old Kremlin building, Major Ivan Terpinski delivered a wooden box about two feet long to the duty archivist. The box was given a number and an entry was made in the duty log and a label attached to the outside. Ivan was escorted through a number of chambers to a small room where the box was placed among a number of other containers.

On the way back Ivan glanced into an anteroom where a number of paintings were hanging. He recognised Goya's painting of Wellington. He smiled to himself; it had been a good few days. The Spear of Longinus was secure.

Visiting the Hofburg Museum in Vienna the spearhead can be viewed, or rather a replica of it. Since its return to Vienna at the end of the war no one has been aware that it is a copy. Similarly, the German government still believe the Amber Room in St Petersburg is a replica.

Uri received a signal from Moscow instructing him to cease all payments to Coleridge. His services were no longer required. Uri had the phone number Coleridge called him to be erased. It didn't take long for Coleridge's boorish wife to notice their drop in income.

Virgin Gorda, British Virgin Islands

Mark Righton, real name Jack Cunningham, returned to his rented villa from his morning swim in the Caribbean. Jack had a perfectly good swimming pool at the villa but he always preferred to swim in the sea.

He made some coffee and logged on to his computer. There were perhaps a dozen e-mails, one of which was apparently from Roly, although he knew it was actually from Organov. The message said 'You probably missed this *Times* obituary that was printed shortly after we brought you to Moscow. He was Deborah's boss.'

Jack opened the attachment. There was a fairly long obituary of an eminent German industrialist who had been killed in a car bomb, a Frederic Kleinfurt; Jack had never heard of him, but he smiled to himself, knowing that this was Vladimir's present to him.

He sipped his coffee and logged on to his computer files. He was working on an article concerning offshore tax havens which he hoped one of the majors would accept. With his new name and no track record as a journalist, it was hard to establish himself again.

His phone rang; his bank manager. 'Good morning, Mr Righton. Are we still on for our meeting at eleven today?

'Yes, of course we are, John, and will you stop being so formal? You know I like being called Mark.' He rang off. John was always pestering him to do something with his money rather than just leave it on deposit. But even with low interest rates he still had a tidy income from $20million.

There had been considerably more of the Nazi gold than they had originally thought. It was Organov's idea to give Jack a new identity as he didn't want Totenkopf to find out that he had survived and start looking for him again. They had to believe he was dead. It was Organov who also arranged, as he said, for Jack to have 'a little petty cash' to help him get by.

He was enjoying his new-found wealth, though it all seemed pretty empty without Emma or Martin to share it with. There hadn't been a day when he had stopped reflecting that he had been the cause of the death of the only two people he had ever really cared for.

He looked at his wristwatch; time for his appointment with his banker. He walked out of the villa and climbed on to his motorbike, put on his sunglasses and looked up at the blue and cloudless sky.

It was a beautiful day.

THE END